"You're in danger."

Bella nodded. She was. In danger of falling for him...

"I need to stay focused," Tyce said. "I can't get distracted like I was earlier."

"You were distracted?"

"You know that I was. From dancing with you..." His voice lowered to a deep rumble in his chest. "I couldn't wait to get you back here, to get you back in bed."

Her pulse quickened and she struggled to breathe. She wanted that now—to be in bed with him. But then she remembered what had happened because he'd been distracted—he had been shot.

"I'm sorry."

"It's not your fault. I need to stay focused on my job."

He was her bodyguard. Only her bodyguard... She needed to remember that. Acting like her boyfriend was only his cover. Was only an act.

She lifted herself up on her feet again. Then she turned to walk away from him.

But he stood up and reached out. "Oh, hell," he murmured before he lowered his mouth to hers.

* * *

Be sure to check out the previous books in the exciting Bachelor Bodyguards miniseries.

* * *

If you're on Twitter, tell us what you think of Harlequin Romantic Suspense! #harlequinromsuspense

Dear Reader,

This month's Bachelor Bodyguards release, *Bodyguard Boyfriend*, brings us back to River City, Michigan, and the Payne Protection Agency. I love writing the Bachelor Bodyguards series because I love the dynamics of the Payne family. They are a close-knit family but also welcoming, as every bodyguard who joins the agency learns. When the Payne Protection Agency hires a bodyguard, he doesn't get just a job; he gets a family, as well.

And some of these guys can really use family, especially the team Parker Payne has hired that were all former vice cops with River City PD. As bodyguards, they wind up still working to take down the drug dealer who's been murderously ruling River City for years. Tyce Jackson is assigned to be the bodyguard for a judge's daughter, and sparks and bullets fly when he has to pose as her boyfriend in order to protect her. To fit into her high-society world, rough-around-the-edges Tyce needs a makeover, so he becomes a Cinderfella in this reverse Cinderella story. Bella Holmes is too busy trying to honor her late mother's legacy of charity work and nonprofit foundations to be Princess Charming to anyone. She also doesn't think she needs a bodyguard, but if she did, she wouldn't want Tyce. Or so she thinks...until she sees Tyce's transformation.

I hope you enjoy this latest installment of Bachelor Bodyguards!

Happy reading!

Lisa Childs

BODYGUARD BOYFRIEND

Lisa Childs

HARLEQUIN

ROMANTIC
SUSPENSE

HARLEQUIN®
ROMANTIC SUSPENSE™

Recycling programs
for this product may
not exist in your area.

ISBN-13: 978-1-335-62651-6

Bodyguard Boyfriend

Copyright © 2020 by Lisa Childs

This edition published by arrangement with Harlequin Books S.A.

For questions and comments about the quality of this book,
please contact us at CustomerService@Harlequin.com.

Harlequin Enterprises ULC
22 Adelaide St. West, 40th Floor
Toronto, Ontario M5H 4E3, Canada
www.Harlequin.com

Printed in U.S.A.

Ever since **Lisa Childs** read her first romance novel (a Harlequin story, of course) at age eleven, all she wanted was to be a romance writer. With over forty novels published with Harlequin, Lisa is living her dream. She is an award-winning, bestselling romance author. Lisa loves to hear from readers, who can contact her on Facebook, through her website, lisachilds.com, or her snail-mail address, PO Box 139, Marne, MI 49435.

Visit the Author Profile page at Harlequin.com for more titles.

For my late mother, Mary Lou Childs, who loved her family so selflessly and generously and for whom I will be forever grateful and forever try to emulate.

Chapter 1

Everything was perfect. The music was low enough and the lights high enough that everything and everyone could be heard and seen in the beautifully decorated ballroom. All the important people were in attendance. They were opening their wallets and checkbooks, making significant donations, which made all of Bella Holmes's hard work to pull off this event worthwhile. Since it was a black-tie affair, everyone was dressed so elegantly. They all looked beautiful—like movie stars.

Except for him...

She noticed *him* the moment he entered the ballroom of the River City Grand Plaza. How had he even gotten into the event? Of course, he was much bigger than the security guys she'd hired to watch the door. Their main duty was just to take tickets and invitations, though. There was no way this man had either of those.

She had not invited him and she doubted he could have afforded the price of a ticket. Unless he was one of those eccentric millionaires who enjoyed looking so unkempt and...

She shivered.

He looked like he didn't give a damn about anything or anyone. His black hair was long and thick and unruly, and a bushy black beard covered his square jaw and part of his neck. He wore a black jacket, but it wasn't part of a tuxedo. There was no white shirt or tie beneath the leather jacket, either. And he wore faded jeans with black boots like the ones motorcyclists wore. In fact, she suspected that was what he'd driven to the gala. He carried no helmet, though, so he'd either checked it at the door or chosen to ride without one.

Other people had noticed him—probably due to his size as well as his appearance. He had to be well over six feet tall, and his shoulders were so broad they strained against that leather jacket. The guests murmured and tittered among themselves.

He paid them no attention, though, as he looked around the expansive ballroom as if searching for someone. Was that why he was there? For someone in particular?

Then he turned his head and his gaze locked with hers. He didn't look away. He stared directly at her as he started walking toward her.

Bella's knees began to weaken and shake. He was here for *her*. Daddy had warned her. He'd told her that some criminal in an upcoming trial over which he was going to preside had threatened her.

Was this man that criminal?

Maybe she shouldn't have shrugged off her father's concern like she had. But as a criminal judge, Daddy was threatened all the time. Desperate claims by desperate people. This was the first time he'd seemed genuinely worried, though, so worried that he'd been insisting she have a bodyguard.

And now she understood why—if this was the man who'd made those threats. But that man had been denied bail; so he was in jail. That was why she'd told her father she didn't need a bodyguard and, more important, that she didn't want one. Had he sent one anyway?

This man was very focused on her. As he drew closer, she noticed that his eyes were brown but a very light, very golden brown, like topaz. And more alarming than that, she also noticed the bulge beneath his jacket. It wasn't from his muscles, though they strained the leather, as well. The bulge was from a gun.

With a gasp of outrage, she turned—breaking their visual connection. Then she began to move through the crowd, heading for the other end of the ballroom. Years of practice in social situations had her smiling brightly at the people who tried to stop her to speak. She just shook her head regretfully and promised she would be right back.

And she would be, once she handled this. Privately. She could feel him behind her, moving through the crowd, too, which parted for him as it compressed around her. She should probably head in the other direction, toward the entrance and the security guards positioned there. But they had let him pass—without an invitation or a ticket. Obviously they would not be able to stop him from doing whatever he intended to do to her. Did he intend to protect her? Was he her bodyguard?

She was about to find out. Because as she neared the end of the room, a strong hand wrapped around her arm.

A lot of other people had touched her as she'd passed them. But she instinctively knew the hand on her arm was *his*. It was so big and so strong—just like him. And even though other people had reached out to her, all of them had been too polite to just grab her.

No. She knew it was him. That he was the one who'd grabbed her. And he'd jerked her to a stop so abruptly that she teetered on her stiletto heels and began to fall.

Tyce caught her before she fell. As she stumbled and swayed, he wrapped an arm around her small waist and jerked her up against his body. He tensed as he felt a jolt as if she'd stabbed him.

But she only stared up at him, her green eyes wide with shock as if she'd felt that same jolt. She recovered quickly, though. Faster than he had. Pressing her palms against his chest, she pushed away from him. But with his arm locked around her waist, she couldn't put much distance between their bodies—not enough that he still didn't feel the heat of hers. Or the tension…

"What are you doing here?" she asked, her full red lips pursed in disapproval. She apparently didn't think he belonged at such a fancy event.

She wasn't wrong. Tyce was uncomfortable, the kind of uncomfortable he would be if he'd inadvertently volunteered to model naked for an art class and everybody was staring at him, studying his every pore. Like they were staring at him now, studying him. At least he had his clothes on, though, and they were his own damn clothes. He didn't care that he wasn't dressed like everybody else. They looked even more uncomfortable than he was, like they were wearing straitjackets instead of monkey suits. Even she had nearly tripped in her heels and long, golden-colored dress. But that was because she'd been trying to get away from him.

"I work for the Payne Protection Agency," he said, "which has been hired to guard you."

She shook her head. "I told him no."

Tyce had tried saying no, too. Why had *he*, of everybody on his team, been assigned to protect the princess? Tyce Jackson was nobody's idea of a prince.

She pushed harder against his chest. "You need to leave."

He'd been warned that she didn't want protection. She clearly didn't want him there. Probably didn't want to be seen with him. He'd dated women like her—in high school, college and after—ones who'd wanted to walk on the wild side with a bad boy. But they hadn't wanted anyone to see them taking that walk. "I'm not leaving without you."

Her green eyes narrowed as she stared up at him, as if doubting what he'd said. He'd heard she was an airhead who'd dropped out of college to spend her life going from party to party.

But then, with the trust fund she'd inherited from her dead mother and the one she would receive as her wealthy father's only heir, she didn't have to worry about her future. Financially at least.

Nevertheless, with notorious drug dealer Luther Mills making threats against everyone involved in his prosecution for murder of a police informant, her future wasn't secure physically. To get to her father—the judge for his trial—Luther Mills was threatening *her*.

"I told my father I didn't need a bodyguard," she said. "He's overreacting. If I feel like I'm in danger, I will call the police."

Her father had said he'd talked to her about Luther's threats, but apparently she hadn't listened. She didn't seem to be aware that there was a leak within the River City police department. With the exception of the chief, nobody within the department could really be trusted. Neither could anyone within the district attorney's office; there was a leak there, too.

"I'm here tonight to take you to a meeting," he said, glancing at the clock on the ballroom wall.

She shook her head again. Her blond hair, which had been piled high on top of her head, didn't move, the pins holding tightly.

Like he continued to hold her. But he had a feeling that if he released her, she would try to get away from him again. And he couldn't risk that. "We need to leave now," he said. "So we're not late."

She tensed even more than she'd been, drawing herself up as if trying to look down on him. She was tall, but still the top of her head just came to his chin, he was that much taller than she was. At six foot eight, he was taller than most people, though.

"I am not going anywhere with *you*," she said.

Of course not—if the situation was anything but what it was. "I'm not asking you out," he said. "I'm making sure you get to the meeting."

"Meeting?" she asked, arching a blond brow in skepticism. "I have no interest in any *meeting.*"

He was sure she didn't. "That's not my problem." It was her father's and, Tyce's boss, Parker Payne's problem. His job was just to get her there.

"And I can't possibly leave this event yet," she said, her voice full of condescension as if he was the airhead.

He snorted. "You can skip out early on a party," he said. "Especially when your life is at stake."

She sighed. "Now you're overreacting."

He shook his head. "Not me…" He knew Luther Mills too well to underestimate him. Everybody involved in the drug dealer's murder trial definitely needed protection. Tyce just wished he hadn't been assigned to protect this particular person. He didn't want to deal with a spoiled party girl who had no idea what the real world was like, that there were bad people out there who would have no problem hurting her.

Who *wanted* to hurt her.

The thought had his arm tightening around her a little more. He kept that arm around her waist as he turned her toward the entrance and he used that arm to nearly carry her along with him.

"Let me go," she said, the words emanating from between her gritted teeth. And her lips, painted a deep red, were curved into a superficial smile directed at all those people who watched them both now.

He shook his head.

"I'll scream," she threatened.

And he chuckled. "You obviously don't want to make a scene. I have no such problem. I'll swing you over my shoulder and carry you out of here if you make me."

"Try it," she said. "Security will stop you and then the police will come and arrest you."

He stared down at her, trying to gauge if she was bluffing or not. He couldn't take the chance that she might not be. If security stopped him until the police arrived, they wouldn't just be late for the meeting. They would risk tipping off Luther Mills's informant in the police department that his plan had gotten out. That was why they were meeting at the agency office, so Luther wouldn't find out about their new protection detail.

He uttered a ragged sigh. "Call your father," he said. "He's probably already at the Payne Protection Agency, which is where we're supposed to be." He reached beneath his jacket and pulled out his cell. Her father's number was the last one on his caller's list.

She must have noticed that because her lips parted as her eyes widened. "Daddy called you directly? He personally hired you?"

He grimaced at a grown woman calling her father "Daddy." He'd had no idea how spoiled she actually was, but he was beginning to understand, which only confirmed his belief that he'd gotten the worst of the damn assignments for this detail. He punched the contact number and handed her the cell.

She stared at it for a moment before pressing it to her ear, as if even his phone wasn't good enough for her. This was going to be a damn difficult assignment.

Across the ballroom another call was placed.

"Yes?" Luther Mills answered on the first ring.

The caller remembered that the drug dealer was sitting in jail; he had nothing else to do for now. He had sworn that he would be out soon, though. He was putting a plan in motion to get his charges thrown out, which was why he'd enlisted help to spy on Bella Holmes.

"Did you send someone after her here?" the caller asked, incredulous at Luther Mills's audacity. But then Luther was known for his boldness; it was also what had finally gotten him arrested, though, when he'd shot someone right in front of a witness.

"Where's 'here'?" Luther asked.

"The River City Grand Plaza."

Luther chuckled as if the idea amused him. He replied, "No. I just want her watched for now."

He was waiting to see if his case actually went to trial before deciding whether or not he needed to use Bella Holmes.

"That's what I'm paying you for," Luther said. "You are watching her."

Always, but not just because Luther had ordered it. "Yes. That's why I'm calling. This guy—" who looked more like one of Luther's crew than the caller did "—is obviously not a guest."

"Is he a cop?" Luther asked.

The dealer's spy chuckled at the thought of this ruffian being a police officer. "No."

"Hmm…boyfriend?"

The caller laughed harder. Luther did not know Bella Holmes at all. She was such a snob. She'd never even dated a man who wore jeans around the house let alone to a black-tie event. "Absolutely not."

"Then you better find out who the hell he is," Luther ordered. "And make sure he won't be a problem when we need to act on those threats we've been sending to the judge."

We?

Luther wouldn't be able to act—not from jail. That duty would fall to the caller. But hurting Bella Holmes would not be a problem; it would be a pleasure. In fact, the caller wasn't certain it would be possible to wait until Mills gave the order to kill her.

Bella Holmes deserved to die. Now.

Chapter 2

Bella Holmes clicked off the cell and held it out to him. Her forehead was creased and annoyance darkened her green eyes. "Daddy knows I have this event tonight," she murmured, glancing around the crowded ballroom. "I can't leave now…"

"But you have to," Tyce said. "The chief of police and—" he couldn't resist mocking her "—*Daddy* are waiting for us."

She glared at him. "Well, you can give me the address and I will meet you there."

He shook his head. "That's not how this works, Princess. You need to ride with me."

She looked him up and down like she had when he'd first walked into the ballroom. He hadn't missed her noticing him. Just like he hadn't missed noticing her.

With that kind of over-the-top, movie-star beauty, she was impossible to miss even in a ballroom full of similarly dressed-up women.

"I cannot jump on the back of your motorcycle," she said as she gestured toward her long gown and heels.

His brow creased with confusion. "Motorcycle?" He had one. He'd even ridden it to work earlier that evening, but she couldn't know that.

She ran her gaze down his body again and stared at his boots.

He tensed. The way she kept looking him up and down was beginning to affect him—not that she seemed to like much of what she was seeing. But for some reason, she kept looking...

Maybe she was just like all those other girls he'd known with their bad boy fantasies. Except that he wasn't really a bad guy. He'd just spent so much time undercover—even as a teenage informant—that the cover was too hard to shake even though he'd left vice nearly a year ago to work for Parker. Sometimes he didn't even know who he was.

He chuckled. "I'd love to see you on the back of my bike, Princess." He reached out and touched the artfully arranged pile of golden-blond hair on top of her head. "This wouldn't last long, though."

She jerked back as if she was afraid he might mess up her hairdo. Or maybe she just didn't want his hands on her because she considered him too far beneath her. "Stop calling me 'Princess,'" she protested.

He chuckled again. "But you are such a princess. Don't worry about your hair getting messed up," he assured her. "I didn't ride my bike here. I have a company SUV."

"Company?"

"The Payne Protection Agency," he reminded her. Man, she must have been the airhead he'd heard she was.

"So you're a professional bodyguard?" she asked, shaking her head as if she didn't believe it even before he answered her.

"Yes," he said. "*Your* professional bodyguard. That's why you're leaving with me." He wrapped his arm around her waist and began steering her toward the ballroom entrance.

She dragged her heels, though. "Can't you…can't you just get the car and meet me outside?" she asked. "I really need to say goodbye to some important people."

"And you don't want those important people to see you leaving with me," he deduced.

Her face flushed a bright crimson, confirming that he was right. "Nobody needs to know I have a bodyguard," she said.

"Nobody should know," he agreed.

"Then how do I explain who you are when people inquire?" she asked.

"You tell them it's none of their damn business," he replied.

Her green eyes widened with shock, as if the thought had never occurred to her. And maybe it hadn't. "I—I can't do that," she said.

"Why the hell not?" he asked.

She sniffed, but she didn't have a runny nose—just a stuck-up one. "It would be rude."

"So is keeping me, your father and the chief of police waiting," he said.

"But I can't just leave," she protested. "This is *my*
event."

He sighed. "I'm sure they're all *your* events." She
was known as the party girl of River City. "But for
once, you won't be the one shutting down the place."

"You don't understand—"

"No, *you* don't understand," he interrupted her. "And
that's why you need to get to this damn meeting." So
the chief and her father could explain the danger of the
situation to her.

Tyce already knew. A former vice cop, he'd spent
years undercover within Luther Mills's organization.
He knew very well just how dangerous and ruthless
the drug dealer was. Being behind bars hadn't made
him less so, either. If anything, it had only made Luther more dangerous because now he was desperate,
and he'd already been capable of anything.

Despite his leather jacket, a sudden chill passed
through Tyce, and he glanced around the ballroom.
Everybody was still staring at them—just as they had
been. But Tyce had a feeling that not everybody was
staring in curiosity. Somebody out there was more than
curious. He could almost feel the hatred in the stare and
that chill chased down his spine, making him shiver
with dread.

Nobody there knew him, so that look had to be
directed at Bella. He was done arguing with her. He
needed to get her the hell out.

"You have a choice," he told her. "You can either

walk out of here with me on your own two feet. Or I can swing you over my shoulder and carry you out."

He wasn't playing.

Bella instinctively knew that, so she agreed to leave with him—on her own two feet. Of course, those feet were clad in stilettos that made it difficult for her to keep up with his fast pace, so that he wound up nearly carrying her out of the ballroom.

Fortunately, he moved so quickly that only one person was able to intercept them as they left. Her good friend and assistant, Camille, ran up to them in the lobby.

"Where are you going?" the dark-haired girl asked. "You can't leave yet!"

The bodyguard opened his mouth but before he could say anything, Bella squeezed his arm to stop him from speaking. "He's taking me to see my father," she replied.

"Is everything all right?" Camille asked with concern. "Is the judge okay?"

Bella nodded, and the pins in her hair pulled at her scalp. "Yes."

Camille's dark-eyed gaze slid from Bella to the big man with his arm around her waist. "So *he's* a friend of your father's?" the woman doubtfully asked.

Before Bella could answer, the bodyguard tugged her toward the door. "We have to go."

"I'll explain later," Bella assured her friend. "Please, make sure everything continues to go smoothly." She ached at the thought of leaving everything in her assistant's hands. While Camille was quite capable, this was Bella's event. She'd spent months planning every detail and to not be able to see it through…

"What about Michael?" Camille asked.

Michael? Bella had completely forgotten about her date. Not that they were serious or anything…just old friends who served as each other's plus one for social obligations.

She was still being rude, though. And she hated being rude. "I'll text him when I get a chance, but if you see him, tell him I'm sorry I had to leave," Bella said, nearly shouting the words to Camille as the body-guard led her through the lobby.

A black SUV was parked just outside the lobby doors. She knew it was his even before he opened the passenger door for her. A valet stood nervously beside it. But he didn't have the keys. The bodyguard pulled those from the pocket of his black leather jacket as he slammed the door shut on her.

The vehicle smelled like him—like leather and… man. He pulled open the driver's door and slid in be-hind the wheel. He was so big that he filled the front seat, his shoulder nearly touching hers over the console between their seats.

She shivered.

"Are you cold?" he asked. After turning the key in the ignition, he reached for the heater controls.

"I'd like my jacket," she said.

"We don't have time to retrieve it from coat check." He started to move against the seat as he pulled at his sleeve. "I can give you mine."

She shook her head.

He chuckled as he moved both his hands to the steering wheel. He peeled away from the hotel.

Why did he find her so damn amusing?

But she didn't ask him. Maybe because she didn't want to know the answer. "What is your name?" she asked. That she did want to know.

"Tyce," he said.

"What?" He was driving so fast that the tires were squealing against the asphalt and she could barely hear him. "Is that your last name or your first?"

Or did he have only one name?

"Jackson," he said.

Her head began to pound. "Which is your first and which is your last?"

"Why?" he asked. "Are we on a first-name basis, Princess?"

"Bella," she replied. "That's my name." Through gritted teeth, she added, "Not Princess."

His beard moved, so she assumed he was grinning. Then he chuckled again. "Tyce is my first name," he told her.

"Tyce Jackson," she murmured.

"You've never heard it before," he said, as if he thought she was trying to place him. "Your path and mine have never crossed, Princess. And they wouldn't have crossed now if not for Luther Mills."

Her heart slammed against her ribs with fear. "He's the man threatening my father about—"

"Don't worry," he said. "*Daddy's* not in danger. You are. Luther is using you to threaten your father."

She knew that. Her father didn't care about himself. Threatening his life wouldn't affect him at all. But threatening hers...

"But he's in jail awaiting trial," she said. "Surely he can't hurt anyone from there. He's just some low-level drug dealer—"

"He's the biggest drug dealer in River City," Tyce interjected. "So not 'low level,' just lowlife. He might be the biggest drug dealer in the state, as well."

"You sound almost impressed."

He laughed but there was no amusement in his deep voice this time. "Nothing Luther Mills does impresses me," he assured her. "It doesn't even surprise me anymore."

Bella wished she could say the same, but everything about this situation had surprised her, though nothing and no one more than Tyce Jackson.

He looked across the console at her. "Luther Mills is capable of anything."

His topaz eyes were so filled with warning that she shivered.

He shifted against his seat belt and tried shrugging off his jacket again. "You're cold. Take my coat. You won't get my cooties from it."

"I'm not cold," she said. "I'm scared."

"If you're scared of Mills's crew hurting you, you don't need to be," Tyce continued. "It's my job to protect you from them."

Even though he was her bodyguard, Bella didn't feel particularly safe with him. Not that she doubted he could protect her but because nobody had ever unsettled her like he did.

She hated that he called her "Princess." And that he

was so big and formidable, which was probably good for scaring off the drug dealer's minions.

But what about her?

Who would protect her from Tyce Jackson?

Bradford Holmes had never regretted all the years he'd spent on the bench presiding over criminal trials—until now. His hand shook as he dropped the photograph onto the table in the conference room of the Payne Protection Agency.

Chief Lynch looked down at the picture and shook his head. "I'm sorry, Your Honor."

The judge didn't feel very damn honorable right now—not after having put his daughter in danger. While he knew it wasn't his fault she was being threatened—that was all Luther Mills—he wasn't proud of the way he'd handled it. Despite his efforts, he obviously hadn't made it clear to her how much danger she was in. When she'd called him moments ago, from Tyce Jackson's cell phone, she hadn't understood why she'd had to leave the fund-raising event she'd spent months planning.

Isabella was so much like her late mother—in appearance with her blond hair and green eyes and in personality with her sweetness and generosity—that his heart ached whenever he saw her. And it positively broke whenever he had to upset her. She'd already been through too much when she'd lost her mother five years ago.

He'd lost his wife then, too. But Elizabeth had been more than his wife. She'd been his best friend. His soulmate. If not for Bella, he might not have been able to go on without Elizabeth.

And if he lost Bella…

He wasn't sure that he could live in a world without her. But that was what the candid photograph of her appeared to be threatening.

"How did you get this?" the chief asked. "Did someone deliver it to you? To your house or to your office? Was there an envelope?"

The judge snorted. "You think I got it postmarked from jail? No such luck."

Luther Mills was smarter than that. But as the judge for his upcoming trial, Bradford had to remain impartial. He couldn't say that it was Mills behind the threat. He had no proof.

Even the chief had no proof—just suspicions that Luther Mills was behind the threats against everyone involved in his upcoming trial. The chief had also confided that he suspected someone within his department was helping Mills. And someone within the district attorney's office, too.

Maybe that was how Bradford had received the photograph. Maybe someone had slipped it onto his desk during a meeting in chambers. Or mixed it in with correspondence regarding another trial.

"It showed up at my office," Bradford told the chief. He couldn't look at it anymore.

Bella had probably looked beautiful—as she always did—even though she'd obviously been unaware that the picture was being taken. It was through the window of her apartment, so whoever was watching her knew where she lived. That was especially horrifying because of what had been done to the photo—of the slashes that cut across Bella's face and her throat and her body…

Nothing had been written on the picture. But Bradford had received the message loud and clear anyway. His daughter was in danger.

Chapter 3

Maybe the ballroom music had been louder than she'd realized—because Bella had this buzzing noise in her ears, making it impossible for her to hear what anyone was saying. She looked from face to face of the people gathered around the table. She could see their lips moving as they spoke, but she couldn't pick up any words. Not even when her father had rushed up to her when she and Tyce Jackson had first entered the conference room.

She'd seen the concern on his face, had returned his hug, but she hadn't heard his explanation, his apology. She'd just seen it in his eyes. "It's not your fault, Daddy," she'd whispered in his ear.

It was Luther Mills's fault. Tyce had told her that he might be the biggest drug dealer in Michigan. How powerful did that make him? Could he get to anyone?

Maybe that buzzing had started because of the photograph she'd seen when she and Tyce had taken their seats. The picture had been of her, but she'd had trouble even recognizing herself with the slashes across her face, across her body.

Somebody had sent that to her father. Somebody was threatening to hurt her. She really was in danger.

And so was everyone in the conference room. Nobody was happy about it. Arguments broke out around the table. While she couldn't hear the words, she saw the flushed faces. People jumped up from the table, left the room.

It was only when the chief returned, after leaving the room for a while with a few other people who hadn't returned, and the door closed behind him, that the buzzing stopped. He must have known about the arguments, even during his brief absence, because his voice was sharp and his words were obviously an order he was issuing when he said, "Everyone is going to have a bodyguard. No matter who they are, until this trial is over and Luther Mills is sentenced to life behind bars."

Beneath the table, her father squeezed her hand before he shook his head and said, "I can't be party to this conversation."

"You didn't need to be here," the chief told him. "Your daughter is the one being threatened."

Bella shivered as she glanced at the table. But the photograph was gone. The chief had slid it into an envelope earlier. For evidence?

"She wouldn't leave her damn party until her father told her she had to," Tyce grumbled through his bushy beard.

Heat rushed to Bella's face over how he made her sound like an idiot. She hadn't realized how dangerous this man was—this man her father was prosecuting. She could not lose her father, too.

"We are not going to stop living our lives just because of these threats," a red-haired woman told the chief.

Bella didn't know who she was. With that buzzing in her head, she'd missed all the introductions—if any had been made. Maybe everyone else knew everyone else. She was the outsider here—the one who had nothing directly to do with this trial or this case.

"So how do we explain having bodyguards?" the redhead asked. "How is the rest of the department going to feel that you didn't trust our fellow officers to protect me or Detective Dubridge or even Ms. Gerber?"

Bella shivered again. The chief of police didn't even trust the officers within his department. Luther Mills had gotten to some of them. She cast a sideways glance at Tyce Jackson. If Luther Mills could get to someone in the police department, couldn't he get to a bodyguard, as well?

"You told your father that I'm your boyfriend," the man next to the redhead shared. "Maybe we just tell everyone else the same damn thing."

Another man, farther down the table, chuckled. "That'll work for her. Everybody in the department knows she had a crush on Hart Fisher even back when he was married. But that won't work for everyone else."

Bella nodded in agreement and murmured, "I should say not…" Nobody would believe that she was dating a man like Tyce Jackson, especially when most people thought she and Michael were all but engaged because they'd known each other so long. She would be better off marrying someone like Michael, someone who cared about more than her money. Guys like Tyce Jackson only came after her for her inheritance—at least the ones she'd met in high school and college had.

"You're not my type, either," Tyce assured her, his voice so deep it was just a rumble.

"And chauvinist pig is certainly not mine," another blond woman remarked.

The chief groaned. Then, his voice rising with frustration, he yelled, "You're all supposed to be professionals here. Figure it out!"

"Professional partyer maybe," Tyce remarked with a disparaging glance at Bella.

She glared at him before jumping up from the table. She'd had enough. This was ridiculous. She obviously wasn't the only one who thought so as other people filed out of the conference room, too.

Her father caught her arm and stopped her just inside the door. "Bella—"

"I don't need a bodyguard," she told him. She especially did not need Tyce Jackson. "That man—that drug dealer—is just trying to scare you."

"That man doesn't make idle threats," her father said. "You saw that photograph…" Regret flashed in his blue eyes. He obviously hadn't wanted her to see it. "You know you're in danger. You have to have a bodyguard."

She shook her head. "No. I don't."

"So you're willing to go away, then?" he asked. "Into a safe house somewhere far from River City?"

She gasped. Her father was trying to send her away?

She'd dropped out of college five years ago because it had been too hard to be away from him—especially after losing her mother. She'd worried that something would happen to him without Mom and her looking over him. While she had her own apartment, she saw him every day—stopping by his house or his office.

"I can't," she said. "You know I can't." She'd also assumed her mother's responsibilities as chairperson for several committees and charities. She could not shirk those responsibilities.

"Then you'll have a bodyguard."

She opened her mouth but her father must have known what she was going to say because he continued. "You'll have Tyce Jackson. He's good."

He was big. She wasn't sure he was good. She glanced across the reception area to where he'd pulled aside the chief for a private and seemingly heated conversation. "I'm not going to pretend he's anything other than my bodyguard."

"You have to," he insisted. "The chief explained that it's best to not tip off the moles in his department and the district attorney's office. It'll make it harder for him to catch them and whoever is making these threats—"

"Whoever?"

"We have no hard evidence, just circumstantial," he said. "So, *whoever* is making these threats should not know that we're onto them. You need to pretend that Tyce is your boyfriend."

"But I have a boyfriend."

Her father shook his head. "You and Michael aren't serious, and you know why. Michael Leach will only ever be a boy. He will never grow up and become a man."

Michael was a couple of years older than her—in age. In maturity, her father was probably right. At least Michael had his own money, though, so he wasn't after hers. She and Michael had known each other so long that Bella owed him an explanation before she started parading around with a new man. She glanced at Tyce Jackson again.

Not that she wanted to parade him around. At the moment all she wanted to do was run.

"The chief is talking to Jackson now," the judge said. "He will make sure he acts accordingly to his new role."

"New role?" As a bodyguard? Or as her boyfriend? "What are you talking about?"

He shook his head and Bella noticed the paleness of his face. He was exhausted. So she didn't press him for more information. She squeezed his arm and said, "Go home, Daddy. Get some rest."

"You'll go along with having a bodyguard?" he asked. "I won't be able to rest unless I know you're protected."

She sighed and nodded. She would go along with it—once she settled a couple of things first. And she couldn't do that in front of Tyce Jackson. She had to get away from him—away from the Payne Protection Agency.

"There's my girl," her father said as he kissed her forehead.

Bella held tightly to his arm before he pulled away. "Did a car and driver bring you here?"

He shook his head. "No. I drove myself."

"Since I have to have a bodyguard," she said, "I want you to have one, too." She glanced at all the people in the reception area and just outside the doors of the building. "Have one of these extra bodyguards take you home."

"Bella, it's not necessary. I have a police car following me already."

"That isn't safe—if there truly is a leak in the River City PD. You need a bodyguard, too," she implored. "It's late. And you're tired. Please…"

"All right," he agreed with a sigh. "Parker Payne has bodyguards from his brothers' teams outside. I'll have one of them take me home and stay with me." He hugged her.

She kissed his cheek before releasing him. When she pulled away from him, she closed her fingers over the keys she'd lifted from his coat pocket. She was about to find out just how good a bodyguard Tyce Jackson was.

As her father headed toward the door, the chief broke away from his conversation with Tyce to talk to him. And Tyce turned to her.

"Daddy get through to you?" he asked.

She forced a smile and nodded. Then she asked, "Where is the powder room?"

He chuckled and gestured toward a hall. "Don't take long powdering your nose, Princess. We need to leave soon."

She needed to leave *now*. Before he noticed she'd slipped away from him. After seeing that photo, she knew she was in danger, so she would be extra careful. From what she had heard of the meeting, though, it seemed as though Luther Mills was focused on getting rid of the eyewitness, Rosie Mendez, first. So Bella would be safe for a little while, and if Tyce was any good, he'd find her easily enough. Just hopefully not before she handled something that she needed to handle privately.

"Where is she going?" Chief Woodrow Lynch asked as he watched the judge's daughter walk away from her bodyguard. "Why aren't you with her?"

"I'm not going to hold her purse while she uses the bathroom," Tyce Jackson replied.

Jackson had clearly never been in love, the chief realized, but then he didn't have to love Bella Holmes. He just had to protect her. "What did I just tell you?"

"That I can't get out of being her bodyguard and I need to treat her with respect," he replied with a sigh of frustrated resignation. "Did you tell Spencer to do the same with Keeli?"

During the meeting Detective Spencer Dubridge had disparaged another former vice cop, Keeli Abbott, by calling her Bodyguard Barbie. That was no better than Princess.

"Yeah, I need to talk to him, too," the chief admitted with a weary sigh. "Why the hell is everybody fighting having a bodyguard? Everyone associated with this trial has to know how damn dangerous Mills is."

Tyce's brow furrowed as he stared down the hallway. "Everybody but the princess. She doesn't know. She has no association with Luther Mills." She had no idea how dangerous he was—even in jail.

"She saw that photo," the chief reminded him as a twinge of regret struck his heart. He should have slid it into that evidence envelope sooner. She hadn't needed to see that; it had frightened her.

The chief had daughters of his own—ones he'd raised and ones he loved now that they had come into his life since his marriage to Penny Payne. He knew how upset Judge Holmes had to be—to know that his job had put his daughter in danger. Just before the judge had left, Woodrow had assured him that the Payne Protection Agency would keep his child safe.

"She saw the photo," Tyce said. "But I'm not sure she took it seriously. I'm not sure she takes anything seriously."

Officers often had to make snap judgments on the job to quickly assess a threat. But Bella Holmes was not a threat to Tyce. Why was he judging her so harshly?

Before the chief could ask him any questions, though, the bodyguard murmured, "I better check on her…" and headed down the hall in the direction she'd gone.

Woodrow was not about to stop him from doing his job. Tyce clearly wasn't excited that part of the job entailed him pretending to be her boyfriend. To sell that, the big, burly bodyguard might have to hold Bella Holmes's tiny, sequined clutch.

Woodrow chuckled at the image. He had wondered about the matchups Parker had made between his bodyguards and the persons, or principals, they were protecting. But from his wife, who was Parker Payne's mother, Woodrow had learned to trust the Payne family instincts. And nobody knew everyone involved better than Parker Payne did. Since he trusted Tyce to be able to protect the judge's daughter, Woodrow would, too.

* * *

A frisson of unease skittered along Tyce's spine as he started down the hallway. Or maybe that was just the chief's stare boring into him. He'd pissed off the chief when he'd made those comments about the princess. But he hadn't been able to stop himself. She was such a damn snob that he just had to tease her a little. Or maybe a lot…

He glanced back. The chief wasn't looking at him. So that frisson of unease had nothing to do with him. And everything to do with Bella Holmes.

Had she really had to *powder* her nose? It had looked ridiculously perfect, like everything else about her. But maybe "powder" to her meant what it had when Tyce was undercover. Maybe she wasn't the perfect little princess her father thought she was.

He knocked on the bathroom door and it popped open from the force of his blow. It was empty. Not even a drop of water in the sink. Nobody had used it recently.

Where the hell had she gone?

He looked around the hall and noticed the door at the end of it. The door opened onto the alley behind the building. And he groaned.

She'd taken off.

Damn it!

He pushed open the door and headed out into the night. He had to find her—before anyone realized he'd lost her. And before any of Luther Mills's crew found her.

He'd had that feeling back at the ballroom, and the

photograph of her at her apartment had proved it. Somebody was watching her.

Maybe just waiting for her to be alone so that she could be hurt, just like that photo had showed.

Chapter 4

"Did Camille explain why I had to leave?" Bella asked as Michael paced across the polished hardwood floor of her living room. She'd meant to text him, but she hadn't had time. And she'd forgotten because Tyce Jackson had distracted her.

Michael shook his head, but his blond hair was so short and gelled that not a single strand moved with the gesture. "No. I didn't see Camille. But I saw you leave with that guy," he said. "I didn't know you were into that…"

Her face flushed. "Into what?" What the hell did he think Tyce was?

"All I've ever seen you do is drink," he continued. "And that's usually just one glass of wine."

"Yes." While she wasn't sure where he was going

with this, it was true that wine was all she ever drank. Any more than one glass affected her, and tonight of all nights she'd needed all her faculties about her. She certainly hadn't wanted to be the center of a scene like the one Tyce had caused in the Grand Plaza ballroom.

"But there's only one reason why Jax would've been at the hotel." Michael stopped pacing to stare at her. Since she'd slipped off her heels, they were the same height. In her heels, she'd been taller.

She knew Michael hated it when she wore heels. But her gown had been too long for her to forego them. And she'd still nearly tripped over it—in her haste to get away from Tyce Jackson.

Tyce had to know by now that she wasn't in the Payne Protection Agency restroom. How furious was he? Her lips almost curved into a smile, but she forced herself to focus on Michael. What was he talking about?

"Jax?" she asked, repeating the strange name he'd uttered.

"The dealer," he said as if he expected her to know. "I've bought from him myself. It's been a while, though. I thought he got arrested and sent to prison. Or killed…" He shrugged as if it was of no consequence to him, as if a human life didn't matter.

She wasn't sure what really mattered to Michael, though. He was a trust fund baby—like she was. He lived off that money without doing anything to earn any of his own—which wasn't all that different from how she lived.

Maybe Tyce had been right to call her a princess. But she wasn't some pampered little girl who did nothing to take care of herself or others. She tried to contribute to society—like her mother had contributed. Her mother had done so much good, had raised money for so many causes, but there hadn't been enough money to save her from the brain aneurysm that had taken her life.

With a shaky sigh, Bella pushed aside those maudlin thoughts to focus on the man she thought she knew. She and Michael had practically grown up together. His father was a high-profile lawyer who'd attended law school with her father. Their mothers had been in the same sorority, and the couples had maintained a close friendship throughout the years. Despite that friendship, her father had never been a fan of his godson.

"What did you buy from him?" she asked.

"A little X, some Oxy," he said. "We could have been doing those things together, Bella." He wrapped an arm around her waist and pulled her up against him.

She tensed, and not like she had when Tyce Jackson had pulled her close to him. Michael suddenly felt more like a stranger to her than even Tyce had. Had she ever really known Michael Leach?

"How much do you owe him?" he asked. He was looking at her like he'd never seen her before, either. But for some reason, he seemed to like what he was seeing now more than he had before. "It must be a lot for him to drag you out of there like he did."

"Owe him?"

"I've gotten into him myself," Michael admitted ruefully. "Jax won't let you fall that far behind, though. 'Course, he has to answer to Luther Mills if he's short. That's why I figured he was dead, like his phone was when I tried calling him up."

Bella's head began to pound. She had no idea what

the hell Michael was talking about and, apparently, she'd had no idea who he really was.

"Jax?" Was he talking about Tyce? He had to be, since that was the guy with whom she'd left the hotel.

"Yeah, he works for Luther Mills. But then, pretty much everybody does."

That didn't make sense. Tyce Jackson was a bodyguard, not a drug dealer. But Michael seemed so certain…

She needed to talk to her father. Or the chief of police. Or the head of the Payne Protection Agency. She had to let them know what she'd learned. But first she had to get rid of Michael.

"I'm sorry," she said. "I don't know what you're talking about. I don't know any Jax."

"I could have sworn that was him," Michael mused, his brow furrowing.

She shook her head. "I wouldn't associate with a drug dealer. And I didn't realize that you would, either."

"Bella—"

"I asked you to meet me here because I thought it was time we ended this casual arrangement we've had," she said. "It never felt right to make it anything more. For either of us." And now she had the answer that had eluded her all the years they'd known each other—because she hadn't really known him. Nor had he known her.

"Bella, if this is about the drugs, they're just recreational for me," he assured her. "I'm not an addict or anything."

"I hope you're not," she said. "I wouldn't want anything to happen to you." That was one of the reasons she'd decided to break things off with him tonight. Not just so that her bodyguard could pretend to be her boyfriend but so that her childhood friend wasn't caught in the cross fire of someone trying to hurt her.

"So you care about me," Michael said. "I care about you. We are right for each other."

She shook her head. "I don't love you. And you don't love me."

"Bella—"

She pressed her palm against his chest to push him back like she had Tyce Jackson. She didn't feel the mass of muscles like she had with Tyce. Just the frantic beating of Michael's heart.

He really didn't want to end their relationship. She couldn't imagine why not. They'd never been in love. But maybe it was because he didn't want to disappoint his parents. Again. If they knew about his drug use…

She sighed. "Please go."

He cursed. But he finally turned around and walked out of the apartment.

Bella shivered as she realized how alone she was. She glanced at the windows. The glass was dark. She couldn't see anything outside. But someone had seen in—had been watching her, had photographed her. Usually she left the blinds open in the living room because she liked the light from the tall windows to brighten the room with its dark wood floor and trim. Even the coffered ceiling had dark beams. And the walls were a deep gray. She'd covered her couch with a white slipcover and a couple of chairs with a print on a white background to brighten the space.

She would have to add more lamps maybe—because she needed to close those blinds. She started across the room toward the windows when a knock rattled the door in the jamb. Michael had only been gone a few moments. He must have decided to return to try to change her mind.

His parents wouldn't be pleased if they broke up. Her father, though, would be relieved and happy.

"I'm not going to change my mind," she warned him before she even reached for the knob.

Michael wasn't used to not getting what he wanted. And for some reason, maybe because he thought she used drugs, too, he thought he wanted her now.

When she opened the door, it wasn't Michael returning to plead his case for staying together. It was Tyce staring down at her, his strange topaz eyes full of fury.

She tried to slam the door shut, but it bounced off his big boot as he forced his way into her apartment. She hoped he didn't really work for Luther Mills because he looked mad enough to kill her.

Tyce dropped his duffel bag inside the door and kicked it shut. "What the hell's wrong with you?" he asked. "You know you've got to have a bodyguard. Why'd you ditch me?"

Not that he couldn't guess. He'd arrived some time ago, but it hadn't been easy for him to get past the security at her door. He'd had to call her father and have him vouch for him. He hadn't dared have the front desk call Bella; he'd figured she wouldn't say anything good about him. After riding up in the fancy elevator to her floor and approaching her door, he'd heard the rumble of voices inside the apartment. So he'd waited…and from the shadows of the wide hallway, he'd watched the man leave.

The young guy had looked vaguely familiar to Tyce but probably just because he'd seen him in the ballroom earlier. Was this the Michael she'd asked her assistant to apologize to for her?

Instead of answering, Bella just glared at him. She was beautiful, but beauty alone didn't impress him after he'd learned—painfully—how shallow that beauty could be. Older and wiser now, he liked women like his former vice cop coworker and current fellow bodyguard, Keeli Abbott. Strong, smart, independent women…

But he hadn't dated anyone for a while. Working undercover had made it impossible for him to form attachments or have relationships, so he'd shut down his emotions. For so long that he'd forgotten how to feel…

Maybe that was why he reacted to Bella's face and figure and even the snobby way she looked at him.

He preferred that to the way she'd looked at him when she'd opened that door, though. "What's wrong with you?" he asked.

"You," she replied.

"Didn't you listen to a word anyone said in that meeting?"

Her face, which had been pale moments ago, flushed nearly as dark a red as her lipstick, and he realized she hadn't been listening. She'd probably been thinking about that damn party or meeting up with the boy who had just left.

He sighed and picked up his duffel from where he'd dropped it just inside the door.

"What's that for?" she asked.

"I'm staying the night and every damn night until the

trial's over." He glanced at the couch. It was all slipcovered and fancy but at least it was long. His legs would only hang off it a little.

"Why do you want to stay here?" she asked.

"I don't want to," he corrected her. "I have to because my boss ordered me to."

"Which boss?" she asked.

Apparently she hadn't been paying any attention at all during that meeting. Or she was just too much of an airhead to realize how protection duty worked. "Parker Payne."

She shook her head. "Not that boss."

Was she talking about the chief? Tyce had never worked under Woodrow Lynch before. He had already left River City PD before the former FBI Bureau chief had accepted the top cop position.

"Parker is my only boss," he assured her. "I don't work for anyone else."

"You used to," she said.

Somehow he didn't think she was talking about River City PD. What was wrong with her? He hadn't noticed a glass in her hand when he'd showed up at the Grand Plaza ballroom. But she might have had a few drinks before he'd arrived.

"I don't know what you're talking about," he said with a sigh, "so you might as well tell me."

"I was told you worked for Luther Mills."

He sucked in a breath like she'd sucker punched him. "What the hell are you…?" Then he realized from where he'd recognized the little friend he'd seen leaving her apartment. And he groaned.

"You didn't think I would find out that you used to deal drugs?"

He shook his head. "I guess I should have realized a party girl like you would know what I'd done."

"So you have dealt drugs for Luther Mills," she said. "Did he send you after me? Are you the one who took that photo my father received?"

"Princess, I wouldn't waste my time taking pictures." He stepped closer.

She quickly jumped back, but the foyer wall was behind her. And he was against her front. "Wh-what would you do?" she stammered, her green eyes wide again—with fear.

He wanted to do something to her, but it wasn't to hurt her. He didn't want to scare her, either, so he forced himself to step back. "I am your bodyguard," he said. "It's my job to protect you."

"B-but what about—"

"The dealing?" That tight knot in his gut came back— the one he had whenever he thought of his years with the vice unit. "I was undercover. Before I became a body-guard, I was a vice cop. I wasn't working for Luther Mills. I was trying to bring him down." Even before he'd become a cop, he'd worked as an informant for River City PD.

"Couldn't you testify against him—that he was your boss?" she asked.

Tyce shook his head. "He's too smart. He ran his organization with a lot of middlemen. That's who I 'worked for' and I did bring down a few of them. They wouldn't give up Mills, though. So your father sen-tenced them."

"That's how you know my father."

He nodded. Tyce had always liked the judge. He appreciated that the old man was a hard-ass when it came to drugs and especially to murder. That was, no doubt, why Luther had threatened his daughter. Bella was the killer's only hope for getting to the judge.

Tyce just had to make sure that Bella didn't get to him. He was her bodyguard.

Just her bodyguard...

Luther couldn't sleep and it wasn't just because of the jailhouse mattress being too thin and uncomfortable. He had an odd feeling.

First, Clint Quarters had showed up just as he was about to have the eyewitness taken out. And Wendy Thompson, the evidence tech, seemed to have disappeared from her place, as well. And then the spy he had close to the judge's daughter had reported some guy crashing her latest party...

A guy who hadn't looked like he belonged at some fancy ball, obviously. He hadn't looked like a cop, either—according to the spy.

But cops didn't always look like cops. They didn't always act like them, either—which was good for Luther since he'd been able to buy quite a few of them.

Then again, there had been the cops he hadn't been able to buy or threaten. They were, or had been, vice cops with River City PD—like Clint Quarters. After Luther had murdered his little informant, Quarters had quit. He hadn't been the one who'd arrested him for Javier Mendez's murder, though. Spencer Dubridge had done that, and Luther intended to deal with him.

Hell, he intended to deal with all of them—eventually.

First, he had to get these damn charges tossed out. He'd intended to start with eliminating the eyewitness, then the evidence…

And if that didn't work, he had the spy who could help him get to the judge's daughter whenever he wanted. But who else had gotten to her at that ball?

Was it a cop who didn't look like a cop? Or somebody who'd once been a cop?

Luther didn't really care who it was. If the guy got in his way, he'd wind up dead.

Chapter 5

Some bodyguard he'd turned out to be...

He was so sound asleep that he looked dead to Bella. Maybe trying to fit on the too small couch had killed him. His legs dangled over the arm of it. She had a guest room with a queen bed, but she'd been so angry with him barging into her apartment that she hadn't offered it to him. She felt a twinge of regret now.

He couldn't have been comfortable last night. So how was he sleeping?

She stepped closer to the couch and stared down at him, checking to see if his massive chest rose and fell with any breaths. He'd taken off his jacket. And his shirt...

Only soft-looking black hair covered the sculpted muscles. Her breath stopped in her throat, where her pulse pounded madly. She hadn't even given him a blanket last night. Wasn't he cold? She had been; that was why she'd wrapped a warm robe around her. It suddenly felt too warm now as heat rushed over her.

Bella couldn't tell if his chest was moving, but hers was, as she had to almost pant for air after holding her breath for so long.

How could he sleep so soundly? Had he passed out from something? Alcohol? The drugs he used to sell?

She hadn't felt very safe the night before, hadn't been able to sleep very well even with her bedroom door locked. She hadn't been worried about Luther Mills. She'd been worried about Tyce Jackson.

He was so big—with such an aura of danger around him. Sure, he was supposed to protect her, but… She shivered again despite the heat suffusing her. He had not moved yet.

"So much for protecting me…" she murmured as she started around the couch toward the kitchen.

She didn't make it past him before a hand shot out and jerked her down—on top of him. A small scream of alarm slipped through her lips before his hand covered her mouth. To catch herself, she'd automatically reached out, so her hands were pressed against his chest. The hair dusting his muscles was as soft as it looked, tickling her palms, while the skin was warm and smooth. His heart pounded hard and fast beneath one palm. She straightened her arms, trying to push herself up, but as she moved, her hips shifted against him and she felt his reaction to her closeness.

A gasp slipped out against his hand. He moved it from her mouth—slowly, though, so that his palm brushed across her lips. Her heart began to pound even faster.

She'd been smart to lock her bedroom door. But now she didn't know if she'd done it to keep him out or herself inside. She couldn't actually be attracted to him, though. With his bushy beard and long hair, she could barely see his face—just his light gold, heavily lashed eyes staring up at her.

No. Tyce Jackson was not her type at all. He was too big. Too uncouth.

Too exciting.

Tyce was tempted to show Bella Holmes just how awake he was and how much he wanted her. But he had a feeling she already knew, especially when she squirmed against him again. His body couldn't help reacting to the closeness of hers. She was so soft, so warm...

She was also damn beautiful, even more so than she'd been the night before. Her red lipstick was gone, but her lips were full and a deep, natural pink. Her cheekbones needed no blush to highlight their sharpness. Her eyes...the green was so bright, the lashes so naturally thick and dark. And her hair hung down around her shoulders like a pale gold silk curtain. Strands of it brushed across his hand and his chest. It was even longer than he'd realized, and he'd never felt anything so soft against his skin.

"I—I thought you were sleeping," she murmured.

He shook his head. He hadn't been able to sleep, and not just because she was so damn close and so beautiful, but because of that photograph. It had been taken through her apartment window. Someone was watching her for Luther.

"Your eyes were closed."

He'd closed them when he'd heard her bedroom door creak open; he'd been playing with her, to see what she'd do.

She'd watched him for a while. Had she liked what she'd seen?

She squirmed against him again, pushing herself off his chest. She slid onto the floor before scrambling to her feet. Apparently she hadn't liked what she'd seen, or felt, enough to stay on top of him.

He swallowed a groan. Yeah, this assignment—and Bella Holmes—was going to be a pain in his ass.

"Well, you need to get up," she said.

He was—his body aching with the need for release. But he was damn well not going to find that with her. He wouldn't cross the line with a client, especially the judge's daughter. Even though he didn't have much respect for the princess, he respected Judge Holmes.

"I have a busy schedule today."

He closed his eyes again. "Isn't it a little early for parties?" he asked.

"I have a luncheon I need to attend as well as following up on last night's fund-raiser."

He groaned.

"Then there's another event tonight…"

He groaned louder.

"This isn't going to work," she said.

He couldn't agree more. "No. You need to skip all the parties for a while and go away somewhere."

"I can't," she said.

"Why not?" he asked. "It's not like you have a job like everybody else Luther Mills is threatening."

She flinched, her full lips drawing together in a tight line.

He'd offended her. But that was all he'd done since they met. Hell, his appearance alone seemed to offend her.

"I have obligations," she said. "I have events I must attend."

"Or the world will end?" he asked.

"My world," she said. "This is my world. And I'm not going to stop living because of some threats. The trial hasn't even started yet."

She was right. Luther would probably wait to act on his threats against her until it mattered most—during the trial. That was when he would need the judge to rule on the evidence and eyewitness's testimony.

"Aren't you up for the job?" she asked, obviously goading him now.

"As your bodyguard or your boyfriend?" he asked. Since he'd caught her staring at him, he was actually up to both jobs, the tension still gripping his body.

"You're only acting like my boyfriend," she said as if he needed the clarification. "But you're going to have to do something to make that believable."

He nodded in agreement and rose from the couch.

While he'd taken off his shirt, he'd left on his jeans. He'd just unbuttoned the button. They hung low on his hips and her gaze dropped there, to where his erection strained against the fly. Her eyes widened even more.

He chuckled.

And her face flushed. She met his gaze with her eyes narrowed into a glare now.

"Yeah," he said. "You need to stop looking at me like you hate my guts. You need to stop cringing when I touch you."

"You need to stop calling me 'Princess' and treating me like I'm the snob," she told him.

He grimaced, not certain he could stop himself from teasing her. He loved her reaction too much.

"And there's one other thing," she said.

He had an idea, too. She needed to get used to him touching her, maybe even kissing her…so that they actually acted like boyfriend and girlfriend.

Before he could offer to make such a sacrifice, she said, "You need to get a haircut and shave."

"What?" His hand went protectively to his beard. He didn't remember the last time he'd shaved. It had gotten quite long.

"I can't even see your face," she said.

That was why he liked it; after so many years undercover, he'd gotten used to hiding his face, his feelings, his…

"And nobody I know has a beard," she added.

He couldn't remember if he'd seen any on the men in that ballroom last night. The guy he'd seen leaving her apartment certainly hadn't had one—but then he probably wasn't even able to grow one.

"And that's not all we need to change for anyone to actually believe that you're my boyfriend," she continued.

He wasn't going to hold his breath hoping she'd suggest his idea of getting used to intimacy with each other. She obviously wasn't worried about anything deeper than the surface, just like those other women he'd known.

"You need new clothes," she continued, confirming his suspicion.

"You really are a princess," he said. "Too good to be seen with someone like me."

Totally unrepentant, she nodded. "You're right. I don't want to be seen with someone easily recognizable as a drug dealer."

"By your *boyfriend*," he reminded her.

She flinched. "Michael is not my boyfriend any longer. I broke up with him last night. That's why I left the Payne Protection Agency. I wanted to talk to him alone."

Was talking all they'd done? Tyce felt some strange tightening in his stomach muscles and he wasn't sure what it was. Jealousy?

He snorted. He wasn't jealous of the princess. Sure, he was physically attracted to her. She was gorgeous. He really would have to be dead not to notice her face or her body. But she was also high maintenance as hell, like those other women he'd dated, and he wanted no part of that again. Michael hadn't seemed particularly upset when he'd left, either. He was probably relieved. "He took it well."

She narrowed her eyes. "Were you listening outside the door?"

"I'm your bodyguard, Princess. I'm going to watch and listen to everything you do and say."

She shivered despite her bulky velour robe. But even through that robe, he'd felt the heat and softness of her body. She was tall with a fullness to her curves he appreciated. Too much.

He'd just reminded her that he was her bodyguard. Now he had to remind himself—that was all he was. She was just an assignment to him. Nothing more.

Her eyes widened as if she'd had a sudden shock. And, in apparent horror, she murmured, "Michael might not be the only one who recognized you last night."

He chuckled. "If anyone recognized me from my days in vice, then those fancy friends of yours are some upstanding citizens, Princess. Doesn't that prove you shouldn't judge a book by its cover?" Like she had apparently judged him of being unworthy of even pretending to be her boyfriend.

She glared at him. "You know I have a point. We can't risk anyone else realizing who you are or who you were pretending to be."

Unfortunately, she did have a point, and she wasn't the first one who'd suggested he needed to lose his undercover persona. His grandma hated it. Every Sunday when he went home for dinner, she implored him to shave and get a haircut. She'd even gone so far as to pull out his photo from boot camp graduation for the US Marine Corps. So not only would he be making the princess happy, he'd be making Grandma happy, too.

He sighed in resignation and begrudgingly agreed. "Okay."

Bella smiled—so brightly that he had to squint and not at the sunshine pouring through the tall living room windows. He even had to suck in a breath because he felt like he'd been punched in the gut again. Damn, she was beautiful.

She clapped her hands together. "I'll call Daddy's barber."

He sighed again but with disgust now. "I don't need your daddy's barber to work me in today. I'm sure I can get in somewhere else."

"There's no time for that," she said and glanced at the thin gold watch on her delicate wrist. "Not with my luncheon coming up. He'll come here. And after he's done with you, we'll go buy you some clothes."

Tyce groaned. He'd known he'd gotten the worst of all the assignments for this protection detail. He just hadn't realized how much it would change him—physically at least. Emotionally, he wasn't going to let Bella Holmes get to him. Like all his undercover assignments, he had a job to do. Just a job...

Parker picked up the cell phone that vibrated on his desktop. He'd not been this busy since he'd opened his own franchise of the Payne Protection Agency nearly a year ago. Then again, this was an extraordinary assignment. He didn't have just one person's safety to worry about but the safety of everyone associated with Luther Mills's trial.

And also every member of Parker's team...

Luther had every reason to want to take them out, as well. Not only were they going to stop him from carrying out his nefarious plans, they were going to make sure he was finally prosecuted and punished for his crimes. Crimes for which they had all, Parker included, tried to nail him over the years.

"Tyce," he greeted his caller.

The guy had slipped away last night before Parker

had had the chance to talk to him again. But the chief had assured Parker that he'd made it clear to Tyce how important his assignment—how important Bella Holmes—was.

"Is everything all right?" he asked. He hoped like hell that it was. Thanks to Luther and the enormous crew of people who worked for him, none of the bodyguards was having an easy time with this job. The assistant DA, Jocelyn Gerber, had even gone so far as to accuse him of having a leak within his agency. Because Luther's crew had found the safe house where Clint had brought the eyewitness, she figured someone on his team was working for the drug dealer. That wasn't possible, though.

"No," Tyce answered.

Parker tensed, rising from the chair behind his desk. "What's wrong?"

"Everything!" Tyce replied.

"Oh, no!" Parker should have had backup for Tyce. But he hadn't thought he would need it yet—not until after the trial began and the judge had to start ruling.

Clint needed reinforcements with the eyewitness because taking her out was Luther's top priority, which he'd already proved with the attempts made on Rosie Mendez's life. Hart also needed backup with the evidence technician because Luther was determined to get rid of all the proof of his guilt before the trial began.

Tyce was the biggest, most fearless bodyguard on Parker's team. He didn't sound fearless now, though.

"What do you need?" Parker asked. "How many? Have you called the police?"

"Police?" Tyce repeated.

"Yeah, we really can't do that," Parker said with a

heavy sigh. "Not until the chief figures out who's Luther's mole within the department." That was where the mole was, not within his agency.

"I don't need the police," Tyce said. "I need someone else to take over this damn assignment."

"What's wrong?" Parker asked.

"I'm done," Tyce said. "I agreed to the haircut and the shave. But I'm not playing dress up and tea party with the judge's little girl."

Parker dropped back into his chair. "What?" Hart's young daughter was the one with the tea parties and the dress-up clothes. Judge Holmes's daughter was somewhere in her twenties.

"She thinks I'm what Spencer calls Keeli—a bodyguard Barbie doll."

A deep laugh rumbled in Parker's chest. He needed this—with all the danger. He needed this break from the seriousness of the situation everyone found themselves in—apparently, everyone but Tyce.

Though he did sound scared.

Parker laughed harder.

"I'm glad you're so damn amused," Tyce said, his gruff voice even deeper with resentment.

"You're not a Barbie doll," Parker assured him. "Since you're male, you would be a Ken doll. Or maybe a G.I. Joe." He and his brothers had had those growing up. His mother had thought that was why his brother Cooper had decided to become a Marine. But their sister had played with the G.I. Joes more than they had.

Tyce cursed him. "This isn't funny!"

"Yeah, it really is," Parker said. "You're just going

to have to suck it up and deal with her. Everybody else is busy."

"Everything okay?" Tyce anxiously asked. "Is everybody okay?"

Tyce Jackson acted all tough and independent, but just like he was the biggest guy on Parker's team, he had the biggest heart, as well. He fought so hard to hide it to protect himself. But Parker had been there when Tyce had had his heart broken.

"Yeah," Parker said. "Everybody's fine." For now. But Clint and Rosie had already had too many close calls. How the hell had Luther known where the safe house was? While they'd survived the latest attack, Luther Mills wasn't about to give up. And because of that everybody was in danger.

And though it might not be as immediate as the eyewitness and the evidence tech, the judge's daughter was in danger, too. The photograph her father had received was proof of the threat. Luther had someone watching her, waiting until he needed her.

"You need to do whatever you have to in order to stick close to her," Parker advised his employee.

Tyce groaned. "I know. I'm trying, but there's already been bloodshed."

"What!" Parker jumped out of his chair again. "Whose? Who's hurt?"

"Damn barber of her father's nearly cut my throat," Tyce grumbled.

Parker heard a giggle in the background. Bella Holmes was as amused as he was. That was good. When she'd seen that photograph of herself the night before, she'd looked terrified. Maybe she'd realized that Tyce would keep her safe.

But now Parker wondered who would protect Tyce from Bella Holmes?

Chapter 6

"He did *not* almost cut your throat," Bella protested when Tyce clicked off the call he'd made to his boss. She had a special relationship with her father's barber. Vito had been taking care of Daddy for years.

It was because he was mostly retired that he'd been able to get to her apartment so quickly, which had left them time to shop before the luncheon. She glanced at her watch. They needed to leave the dressing room soon or they would be late. But she was having so much fun.

Tyce pointed a slightly shaking finger at the nick on his muscular neck. "What do you call this?"

She snorted. "Nothing. I don't even see anything." But there was a trail of dried blood from the wound. Once she got him to close the top button of his new dress shirt and put on a tie, it wouldn't even be noticeable, though.

"This isn't nothing," Tyce protested as he ran his fingertip over it. Then he turned to look into the mirror behind him. He tensed as if he didn't recognize the stranger staring back at him.

She half expected him to draw his gun from his holster and point it at the mirror. He looked that different from the man who'd showed up at the ball last night. Nobody who'd been at that event would realize he was the same man—not even Michael.

She had no idea what drug dealers looked like, but Tyce no longer bore any resemblance to the man Michael had recognized—but for his enormous size.

He looked great in his new dress pants, shirt and tie. Of course, the red tie hung loose around his neck as he inspected his wound in the mirror.

She hadn't realized how long and muscular his neck was until Vito had shaved it and all the hair off Tyce's face. What a face…

It looked as if it had been carved from teak with sharp cheekbones and a strong jaw. His lips were sculpted, too, and wide and sexy, especially when he grinned. Not that he'd grinned much since the shave and haircut.

The unruly mop of black hair had been cut back to just a bit longer than a brush cut. It was still thick and soft looking, like the hair on his chest. Not that Bella had touched it.

She'd been tempted, though, as she'd done up buttons on his shirt and wound the tie around the collar for him. No wonder he'd complained to his boss that she thought he was a doll. But she'd been very aware that he was a flesh-and-blood man. Too aware.

"That guy's barber license should be revoked," Tyce said, turning to face her again. "He's so damn old, he couldn't even hang on to the blade, he was shaking so bad."

"That's your fault," she said. "You made him nervous. You kept glaring at him and grumbling."

"I made him nervous?" Tyce repeated incredulously. "He was the one with the blade."

"You have a gun," she reminded him. Despite her requests for him to hide it, he'd kept it out. She didn't know if that was for her protection or because he just didn't trust anyone.

"I should have threatened to use it on him," Tyce grumbled again.

"You are such a baby," she teased. "It's just a boo-boo."

He arched a dark brow. "A boo-boo?"

"Yes, do you want me to kiss it better?" As soon as the words left her lips, she sucked in a breath. What the hell was she saying? And why was it that she wanted so badly to do it, to rise up on tiptoe and press her lips to that small cut on his neck before skimming them across his skin to where his pulse had seemed to leap in his throat?

He stared down at her, his topaz eyes more intense than she'd ever seen them. And he always looked intense.

But now he almost looked frightened.

She stepped back and held up her palms. "Don't worry," she assured him. Then remembering some of his snarky comments from the night before, she added, "I won't touch you and give you my princess cooties."

He chuckled at her joke, but it sounded a little uneasy. And he looked a little uneasy, as well.

Her pulse was racing and her skin was hot. She couldn't imagine having to walk into that luncheon looking all flushed and bothered…on Tyce Jackson's muscular arm. But she glanced at her watch and gasped.

"If you're done admiring your good looks, we need to go," she said. "Now."

Because she was in a hurry, she didn't think. She just rose up on tiptoe and reached for the top button of his shirt. As she slid it through the hole, though, her fingers trembled. His chest was so hard, so warm…

Her hands shook even more as she pulled the tie around the collar and knotted it at the base of his throat.

"Are you trying to kill me?" he asked.

She didn't know if he was talking about how tightly she tied the tie or her nearness. His closeness was killing her, or at least chipping away at her common sense. She had no business being attracted to her bodyguard.

He was only pretending to be her boyfriend. They had nothing in common besides Luther Mills. And nothing good could come of the commonality of a murderous drug dealer.

Tyce's head throbbed with a pounding ache. He'd never spent a day like the one he'd just had with Bella Holmes. Now he understood that she didn't just attend these parties—like the ball the night before or the luncheon today. She ran these things. She was responsible for getting the caterers and the speakers and the music and every damn minute detail—just as she had been with his new wardrobe.

He'd tried to pay for that, but Bella had insisted on putting it on *Daddy's* account since the judge was the one who wanted her to have protection. He suspected she'd paid for everything else, too—for the luncheon and the ball. But she'd also brought in money from both events—money for charities.

He glanced down at her where she stood next to him in the fancy elevator of her apartment building. She'd slipped off her heels already; they dangled from her fingertips as she leaned against the smoky mirrored wall of the elevator. Her eyes were closed, her thick lashes casting shadows onto her cheeks.

She hadn't worn a ball gown for the luncheon. But her dress was sexy without trying to be. The red cashmere clung to her curves and ended just above the dimpled knees of her long, slender legs. His tie matched that dress. It hung loose around the collar he'd unbuttoned the minute they'd gotten into the SUV.

She had nearly killed him when she'd tied it—but it wasn't because it had been too tight. It was because she'd been too close.

His head wasn't the only part of his body that was throbbing. Another part had been throbbing since he'd caught her watching him on the couch.

He groaned in frustration.

Without opening her eyes, she wearily remarked, "Stop being a baby. It wasn't that bad."

He bristled at her condescending tone and that there might be some truth to it, as well. "I'm not a baby," he said.

"I'm not a princess."

He snorted. "Yeah, you are." Everybody today—no

matter where they'd been—had treated her like royalty. Maybe because they'd all seemed to respect her, they hadn't asked too many questions about him. She'd introduced him as a friend and nobody had pried for more information.

There was something about her—that haughty thing that drove him crazy—that kept everyone else from getting too close to her. Was she a snob? Or did she act that way to protect herself? To keep people from getting too close or asking too many questions?

It was his job to protect her now. So he'd had to stick close to her the entire day. Even though she hadn't introduced him as her boyfriend, he'd acted like he was. He'd kept his hand on the small of her back or on her forearm when they'd moved through the crowd at the luncheon. Once, at the table, he'd even slipped his hand over hers.

But he'd just been playing the part because it was his job. He'd checked out everyone in attendance at the event, watching all of them to see which one of them might be watching her for Luther Mills. He snorted at the thought of any of those blue bloods working for Luther, though.

Then again, her boyfriend had been associated with him—had bought drugs from Tyce back when he'd been dealing undercover. He cringed as he thought of that time, of going against everything he'd believed in, but it had been for the greater good. They hadn't been after the users then, so he hadn't busted any of them. But now he wished he had.

He really wished he'd busted her boyfriend. Exboyfriend.

She'd dumped him.

For Tyce…

A grin tugged at his mouth over the thought of someone like her choosing someone like him over a trust-fund frat boy. But it wasn't real. It was just another undercover assignment for him. He'd thought he'd left those days behind when he'd left the vice unit, though.

The elevator stopped and the doors began to open. She straightened away from the wall. But he stepped forward, using his body to block hers from whoever might be waiting out in the hall.

She sighed—probably because he'd been doing that the entire day. Checking out the situation before he let her proceed.

He didn't see anyone lurking in the shadows where he had been lurking the night before. Still he stepped out of the elevator first and guided her down the hall, keeping his body between hers and every open door.

"Luther Mills does not live in my building," she remarked.

"No. He's in jail. And that's where we want to keep him." For the rest of his miserable life.

"So you don't need to sleep here," she said. "I'm safe when I'm home."

"Did you forget about that photograph?" he asked as he held his hand out for her keys.

"That was taken through the window," she said, reaching into her small purse. "Not inside. I'll pull my blinds." She held on to her keys.

He covered her hand with his big one. "Hand them over. You know my job is to stick close to you—twenty-four-seven."

She shivered and stared up at him with that look again—that look she'd had when he'd showed up at her apartment last night. Her green eyes were wide and full of fear.

He slid his free hand over his face, which felt so strange without the beard he'd worn for years. But there was already some stubble growing back. "You still don't like what you see when you look at me, huh?"

She shook her head. And then she lifted her free hand to his face and slid it along his jaw. "No. That's the problem…"

His body tensed, the throbbing intensifying as he considered what she was saying. She liked what she saw? Was that what scared her?

That she was attracted to him, too?

Because he was so damn attracted to her…

She was so beautiful. Her hair was up again, not in as complicated a style as she'd worn to the event the night before. This was more casual with some tendrils hanging down around her neck and along her face.

She was so damn sexy.

He found himself leaning down, as if more than their hands were touching, as if she was somehow pulling him toward her with just that intense, fearful gaze of hers. She wasn't talking, but he found himself murmuring, "Shh…"

He wanted to calm her fears even as he felt them, too—that sudden rush of uneasiness. This was wrong. He had a job to do. She was just an assignment to him.

But he'd never wanted to kiss an assignment like he wanted to kiss her. The attraction was just too intense for even him to keep fighting. He brushed his mouth across hers.

She gasped. Maybe she was appalled.

Instead of pulling back and slapping him, she dropped her keys to the floor, where they clattered, and wrapped both hands around his nape, holding his head to hers. And she kissed him back.

Her lips were like the shirt she'd bought him, as smooth as silk. But there was heat, too. It moved through him from his mouth, throughout his tense body. She kissed with a passion he wouldn't have thought she possessed.

Where was the haughtiness now?

Where was the princess?

She moaned in her throat. Or was it in his? He parted her lips and deepened the kiss, sliding his tongue into the sweetness of her mouth. She tasted rich. Maybe it was the fancy chocolate cake they'd had for dessert. Or the champagne.

Whatever it was, he was getting drunk on the flavor of Bella. So drunk that he'd forgotten where they were. In the hallway.

When he tried to pull back, she clenched the back of his neck and kissed him deeper—sliding her tongue into his mouth, tasting him like he'd tasted her.

And he groaned.

He wanted her so damn badly that it felt like his body was about to explode from the tension gripping it—that had been gripping it for so long. His hands shook as he lifted them to hers, as he gently tugged her wrists down to her sides.

She murmured a protest as he stepped back, and she was trembling, just like he was.

What the hell was this?

He'd never felt an attraction like this before. Was this feeling why people did drugs—this out-of-control feeling? He wasn't sure if he liked it or not. Hell, he wasn't sure if he liked her or not.

He was pretty damn sure she felt the same way about him. Hell, he was pretty damn sure she didn't like him at all.

But that didn't stop them from wanting each other.

Badly.

They panted for breath. And he knew if they stepped through that door together, he wouldn't be sleeping on the couch. He'd be sleeping in her bed—if they slept at all.

As he bent to pick up the keys, though, he heard something. And it wasn't just his blood rushing through his veins or the pounding of his heart anymore. It was a crash inside the apartment as something toppled over.

He cursed and moved her aside, away from the door. "Somebody's in there," he said. As he slid the key into the lock, he drew his gun from his holster.

Bella gripped his arm, as if trying to stop him from entering. But this was his job—not kissing her. He was supposed to be protecting her.

"Stay here," he whispered. Then he pushed open the door. As he stepped over the threshold, he heard the tinkle of glass breaking from within the apartment.

Bella gasped and pushed against his back, as if trying to get inside with him.

"Stay here," he told her again. Then he gently shoved

her into the hall and shut the door behind him. He turned the lock, locking her outside and him inside— with the intruder.

The guy who'd been shadowing her all day was big. But even as big as he was, he moved fast—his heavy footfalls warning of his approach.

The intruder didn't want to get caught. Not yet.

Hell, not ever.

But the sudden arrival of this guy—this guy that nobody knew anything about—had warranted an intrusion. Bella made notes about everything in her calendar. But there had been no notes about the guy—whoever the hell he was. A peek at the calendar wasn't the only thing taken, though.

Not wanting to get caught, the intruder hurried out through the broken bedroom window onto the narrow balcony outside. It stretched across Bella's entire apartment—ending at the corner of the building where the wrought-iron fire escape led to the street five stories below.

The intruder didn't take every flight to the street, though—only to the fourth floor where a window had been strategically left open. Once the intruder scurried through it, the window slid shut.

The door to the stairwell was just steps away. But instead of going down to the lobby, the spy headed up.

While the man was inside the apartment, Bella was alone in the hallway and completely unprotected.

This might be the only opportunity to get to her— with the big guy sticking so close to her now. This might be the only chance to give Bella Holmes what she deserved.

Pain.

And death…

As the intruder pushed open the door to Bella's floor, a blade flashed in the light from the hall. That blade would soon be buried in Bella's back.

Chapter 7

Damn him!

He'd locked her out of her own apartment. But he wasn't the only one in there. Someone else had broken in—had invaded her space and her privacy.

Why?

To carry out the threat of that photograph? To slash her face, her neck…to kill her?

Bella shivered, feeling a sudden draft as if a door had opened onto the hall. The hair lifted on the nape of her neck as a feeling of fear rushed over her.

More fear.

She'd already been frightened—even before they'd heard that noise inside her place. She was frightened of her overwhelming attraction to Tyce Jackson. He was so damn good-looking—now that she could see every chiseled feature in his handsome face.

And his lips… They were just as sculpted and full and soft and hot as she'd imagined they'd be. That kiss…

Heat rushed through her now.

But it wasn't just attraction. It was anger.

He couldn't lock her out of her own place. Fortunately, she'd stashed a key in the hall for just such an instance. She rose on tiptoe and slid her fingers over the door casing until she found it. Once the key was in her hand, she quickly pushed it into the lock and opened the door. As she stepped inside, she glanced back into the hall and noticed a shadow had fallen across the wool carpet where she'd been standing.

She hadn't heard the elevator. Had someone used the stairs? The last thing she wanted was to talk to a neighbor now, though, so she slammed the door shut. But before she could turn around, a strong arm wrapped around her—nearly lifting her from her feet. She thrashed her legs and cried out, and was so abruptly released she nearly dropped to the floor. But a strong hand caught and steadied her.

"What the hell are you doing?" Tyce asked her. "I told you to stay in the hall until I cleared the place."

She couldn't remember anything he'd said after he'd disappeared inside with his gun drawn and an intruder apparently in her home.

"I didn't know how long to wait for you."

He groaned. "Well, you should have known—"

"I've never had a bodyguard before, and this is my place," she reminded him. "I wanted to see what was going on." And she'd wanted to make sure he wasn't hurt. He didn't look hurt. But he still had his gun drawn in the hand that wasn't on her elbow, steadying her.

She was shaking. And it wasn't just for fear of someone being inside her apartment; it was for fear of Tyce rushing inside to confront that someone.

"Did you clear it?" she asked, and now she lowered her voice to a whisper.

Tyce nodded. "They're gone."

"They?" she asked, her voice cracking. Had he confronted more than one intruder on his own?

He shrugged his broad shoulders. "I didn't see anyone. Could have just been one. But Luther usually sends a big crew when he comes after someone."

Even knowing that, Tyce had not hesitated to rush inside, to take on that big crew all by himself. She gasped as she considered the dangers he faced regularly as a bodyguard, and the dangers he must have faced as a vice cop. She shuddered in horror.

Maybe she was the princess he accused her of being—because she could not fathom living like he did, constantly in danger. The thought of a life like that terrified her. *He* terrified her—because of what he made her feel, the passion she'd felt from his kiss and the fear she'd felt for his safety. It was good that they'd been interrupted before things had gotten any more out of hand between them—because she had to remind herself that he was her bodyguard.

Not her boyfriend. She could never get involved with a man like him, one who constantly put himself in danger. She couldn't wind up like her father—alone and heartbroken. So it was better to never risk her heart at all.

* * *

Anger coursed through Tyce. But he wasn't angry at the bastard who'd broken into her place. He was angry at himself for being distracted. If he hadn't been kissing the woman he was supposed to be protecting, he might have heard the intruder sooner. He might have caught him.

Instead all he'd seen was a shadow moving across the balcony. He'd followed the shadow across that balcony to the fire escape. He hadn't chased it down the stairs, though. Instead he'd rushed back into the apartment to make sure that Bella was safe—that the intruder hadn't circled around to attack her when he'd been distracted.

Because maybe that was all the break-in had been… a diversion. He'd been so on edge that when she'd let herself inside, he'd nearly hurt her before he'd recognized that it was her.

Ironically, he could hurt her, and he was the one who was supposed to protect her. That was what he needed to focus on—not on how beautiful she was, how sweet she tasted…

He had to focus on keeping her safe. "You need to pack up a few things and we need to get out of here," he said. "I'm going to take you to a safe house."

"Safe house?"

"A place that's secure," he said. "This place is not." Especially not now with her bedroom window broken. "You're not safe here."

She shivered but shook her head. "I didn't pull the blinds," she said. "The person who broke in would have seen that I wasn't home. They didn't break in to attack me." She glanced around. "Where did they break in?"

"Your bedroom window's broken," he said. "Your blinds were closed there. They didn't know you weren't in bed—alone…"

Luther could have ordered a member of his crew to rough her up. Seeing his daughter wounded would certainly affect the judge.

She shivered again but headed toward her bedroom. She pushed open the door and stepped inside, and within seconds, a cry slipped from her throat. He was right behind her, but he should have been in front of her—in case the intruder had come back through that broken window.

He drew his gun and pointed it around the room. But she was alone, standing in front of her dresser. The mirror was broken. Maybe that was the message the intruder had sent—that he was going to slash her up, so her reflection in that broken mirror looked like that picture the judge had received of her. But she wasn't looking at herself, she was looking at the jewelry box that had been upended on the dresser. Her hands shook as she searched through the shiny pieces atop the mahogany surface.

"No, no, no," she murmured, her voice thick with sobs.

"What?" he asked.

"My mother's earrings—" her voice cracked "—and her broach." Tears rolled down her face and her breath came in gasps, like she was beginning to hyperventilate. "Even her necklace…"

She was shaking so badly that she dropped the pieces of jewelry she'd picked up. So he didn't think those were the ones she was talking about.

"What about them?" he asked.

"They're gone!" she cried. "They're gone!"

"Oh, damn." A lot of other necklaces and earrings were strewed across the dresser from the upended box. "Only the stuff that was your mother's?"

She nodded. "I—I usually have them in a safe-deposit box. But I wanted to wear them last night. And there wasn't time today to put them back."

"I'm sorry, Bella," he said. He'd already known that her mother was dead because it was common knowledge that Bella had inherited a lot of money then. If he hadn't known, he would have learned it today—with everyone commenting how much Bella was like her late mother.

Every time she'd heard that comment, tears had glistened in her beautiful eyes. Her mother had meant a lot to her.

"We need to call the police," she said. "We need to report the break-in."

He hesitated. If they called, it was possible that Luther's informant would show up to take the report. And then he would learn that Tyce worked for the Payne Protection Agency. He shook his head. "We can't."

"We have to!" she insisted.

He wondered what she was worried about. "Do you need a report in order to collect the insurance money?"

She gasped. "What? What insurance money?"

"I don't know," he admitted. "Didn't you have the jewelry insured?"

She shook her head. "I don't want the money," she said. "I want the jewelry back. And the police won't look for it unless there's a report."

He sighed. "They probably wouldn't look for it with

a report," he said. "Not with them being as busy as they are." Though they might make an exception for the daughter of a prominent judge.

Her teeth nipped into her bottom lip. "You're saying I won't ever get my mother's jewelry back?"

He didn't want to say it. He wanted to say that he would find the jewelry himself, but he didn't make promises he couldn't keep. And he didn't have the time to check with every pawn shop in River City to find her jewelry. There were just too many of them.

His priority was to make sure she stayed safe. He only wished he could make her happy, too. But that wasn't his responsibility. He wasn't really her boyfriend. He was just her bodyguard. Still he found himself saying, "I'll call Parker and see what he can do—if he can spare some guys to try to track down the jewelry."

She launched herself in his arms, clinging to him as her tear-streaked face dampened his shirt. "Thank you. Thank you."

He wanted to hold on to her and not just while she cried but for the entire night. He forced himself to grasp her shoulders and ease her away from him. "Now pack up some clothes. We can't stay here."

"Why not?" she asked. "This break-in was just a theft. Nothing else. Just someone stealing."

He wasn't as convinced. He gestured at the dresser. "Why leave all the other stuff then?"

"It's not as valuable as my mother's pieces," she said.

Anyone working for Luther wouldn't have noticed the difference. If they'd wanted to steal jewelry to scare her, they would have taken it all.

"I shouldn't have worn it last night," she said. "Someone must have seen me wearing it and decided to steal it."

How had anyone noticed the jewelry with as beautiful as she was? He certainly hadn't.

"Anybody could find out where I live," she continued. "If they asked around."

"That's why we need to leave here," he said. "We need to get you into a safe house."

"But why? It was just a theft."

He pointed to the broken window. "That's why. It's not safe here."

"I want to call the police. And someone to fix the window."

"We can't call the police," he said. "We can't give anyone in the department a heads-up that you have protection."

She sighed. "But we can fix the window."

"Probably not tonight," he said.

"We can go somewhere else tonight," she said. "And come back tomorrow—once the window's fixed."

He wasn't convinced. "You need more than new glass. You need a security system. Even if Luther wasn't threatening you, you should have an alarm. It's not safe for you to live here by yourself."

"I'm not by myself right now," she pointed out. "Not until after the trial."

After what had nearly happened earlier, Tyce wasn't certain he would survive until after the trial.

Bradford Holmes did not receive visitors anymore. His wife had been the social one of the two of them—like Bella. But Bella wasn't a visitor. This was her home.

After her mother had died, she'd only stop in from time to time. She seemed to prefer to visit him in his chambers at the courthouse rather than at the home where she'd grown up. So he was surprised when Bella had called to tell him that she was coming over to spend the night.

He was even more surprised when he opened the door. She'd brought a guest with her. A tall, handsome guest. Bradford stared up at the man. Had he met him before? Who the hell was he? And where was her bodyguard?

Then he realized that the guy was Tyce Jackson—without the bushy beard and the long hair. For years, prosecutors had tried to get Tyce Jackson to cut his hair and shave his beard before testifying in court against the drug dealers he'd brought down. He had always refused—even when Bradford had made the same suggestion. But Tyce had never met anyone like Bella before. She had her inimitable way—her mother's way—of getting everyone around her to do what she wanted.

A loud chuckle slipped through Bradford's lips. "I didn't even recognize you."

"Glad you think it's funny," Tyce remarked as he ran a hand over his strong jaw.

With his height and muscle, the guy was a giant. But even he didn't stand a chance against Bella. Nobody did.

Bradford closed his arms around his daughter and pulled her close. She was trembling. "What happened?" he asked as all the humor left him.

"Someone broke into her place," Tyce answered for her.

Bella couldn't talk. She just clung to him, and he felt her tears soaking his sweater.

"Was she hurt?"

Tyce shook his head. "Didn't even get close to her."

Bella pulled back and met his gaze. She looked guilty and miserable. But why? She'd done nothing wrong. "They didn't break in to get to me," she said, her voice trembling like her long body. "They broke in to steal Mom's jewelry." Her beautiful face crumpled as she began to cry again.

Bradford reached for her. But he wasn't the only one. He noticed Tyce's hand extend toward her—as if he was about to pull her into his arms, as well.

Tyce Jackson?

He'd never gotten personally involved—even as an undercover cop or maybe especially as an undercover cop. Some officers, who'd gone too deep, hadn't made it out; they'd become addicted to the drugs they'd tried taking off the streets. But not Tyce. Nothing ever rattled him. That was why Bradford had been happy that Parker had assigned him to protect Bella.

But now he wasn't so certain—especially after the photograph he'd received today.

Bradford focused on his daughter, though. She was all that mattered to him anymore. But how had Luther Mills figured that out?

Who had told Luther that Bradford's weakness was his child? Was there a leak in his office, as well? Like the assistant DA suspected there was one now within the Payne Protection Agency? Or had the drug dealer just instinctively figured it out?

He eased her back and cupped her beautiful, tear-stained face in his hands. "My darling girl," he said. "None of this is your fault."

She shook her head. "It is, Daddy. I should have put her jewelry back in the safe-deposit box, or I shouldn't have even worn it at all."

"Your mother wanted you to wear it," he reminded her. "She wanted you to enjoy it." Elizabeth had passed it on to her daughter even before her sudden death— as if she'd somehow known she wouldn't need it much longer. But doctors had said that no one could have predicted the aneurysm.

"Enjoy it," Bella agreed. "Not lose it."

"You didn't lose it." Tyce spoke now in her defense, even though the frustration in his deep voice made it sound as though he was irritated with her. "Someone broke in and stole it. You couldn't have known that would happen."

She drew in a deep, shaky breath and nodded. But she didn't look as if she agreed with either of them. Her eyes were still wet with tears, but she blinked furiously. "I'm going to clean up," she said and reached for the bag dangling from Tyce's hand.

He carried two of them in one hand. Her designer bag and a beat-up duffel.

"You're going to stay here?" Bradford asked. He'd known about her staying tonight but now it sounded more open-ended, and the tension he'd felt since he'd begun to receive those photographs eased slightly. His estate had the top security system on the market, which the Payne Protection Agency had installed a few years ago.

"Just for tonight, Daddy," Bella reminded him. "Until the window can be fixed."

"And a security system installed," Tyce said.

Bradford had been trying for years to buy an alarm for her apartment. She'd declined, saying that she would be the only one setting it off.

She knew that wasn't true now, though. She didn't argue; she just tugged on the bag in Tyce's big hand.

"I'll bring it up for you," he said.

"I'm not a princess," she said. "I can carry my own damn bag."

Tyce released it so abruptly that she nearly stumbled back under the weight of it.

Apparently the animosity between them had not changed much. Bradford wasn't sure if that was a good thing or a bad thing, though.

When Tyce started to head after her, Bradford grasped his arm and held him back. "I want to talk to you."

Tyce tensed and his face flushed a little.

"Let's go into my den," Bradford suggested. He didn't want Bella to see the photograph he'd received that day. She'd already been through a lot with having her mother's jewelry stolen. He knew how much that meant to her—how anything of her mother's meant so much to her—because it was all they had left of the wonderful woman.

"I wanted to talk to you, too, sir," Tyce said as he followed him through the French doors off the foyer into Bradford's darkly paneled den. "We need to get Bella to agree to go into protection until the trial is over."

"You're her protection," Bradford said. Despite the assistant district attorney's doubts, he trusted Tyce Jackson and the Payne Protection Agency more than he trusted anyone but the chief within the police department.

Tyce nodded. "I am, and that's my recommendation—that she go to a safe house."

Did Tyce want her to go with other bodyguards? Or did he still intend to protect her? Just how much had his daughter already gotten to the tough, cynical, former vice cop?

"She says the break-in was just about the jewelry," Bradford said. But he could tell that Tyce wasn't convinced. "Do you think Luther was behind it? That it was some kind of message?"

The big man shrugged. "If he was, I think he would have had everything taken, or at least destroyed, to send his message. Why just her mother's jewelry?"

"They're the more valuable pieces," Bradford said. He'd liked spoiling his bride. But he liked spoiling his daughter, too. She had some expensive items of her own.

"That's what she said…" Tyce murmured. But his brow was furrowed as if something about the robbery bothered him.

And he hadn't even seen the photograph yet.

Bradford walked around his desk and lifted it from the leather blotter. At the chief's recommendation, he'd dropped it into a clear plastic bag when it had showed up in his chambers earlier that day. Woodrow was going to send over someone he knew from the FBI to pick it up and process it. He didn't trust his own crime lab anymore.

Neither did Bradford.

He wasn't sure he should trust Tyce Jackson, either,

though. In his photograph the bodyguard's eyes were closed. Was he sleeping?

That didn't mean that he wouldn't have woken up quickly had there been a threat against Bella. But this threat wasn't against her. It was against him.

He held it out to Tyce, who lifted the bag and stared through the plastic at the image of himself lying across Bella's living room sofa, his feet dangling from the edge.

Tyce cursed and murmured, "The son of a bitch was out there last night…" He shook his head. "This must have been taken from that balcony. This proves her apartment is not safe."

"Not for either of you," Bradford agreed.

Tyce didn't say anything, but he must have noticed that the photograph had been desecrated—just as the one of Bella had been. Instead of slashing it, like her image had been, this one had a hole in it—right in Tyce's forehead, as if the person sending the picture was saying there was going to be a bullet sent through Tyce's brain.

Chapter 8

Luther Mills was pissed. Nothing was going right for him. The damn eyewitness wouldn't die. Neither would Clint Quarters. And the evidence tech refused to be intimidated.

He chucked his pillow at the wall, wishing it was something heavier. But he couldn't hurl his cell phone. The guards were getting skittish about smuggling them into him. They were worried about the assistant district attorney. Jocelyn Gerber had gotten court orders to check out bank accounts for the jail employees to find out who might be taking bribes to help Luther.

Jocelyn was beautiful, but she was also a pain in the ass. So was the spy he had watching the judge's daughter. What part of *just watching* didn't the damn idiot understand?

And why hadn't Bella Holmes reported what had happened that night? Why had a neighbor called in about the broken window and someone lurking on the balcony? Had she been taken away, like Clint Quarters had taken Rosie Mendez from her apartment?

Luther's guts tightened with frustration. He hated this—hated being stuck inside this damn jail, hated that he had to rely on others to carry out his orders. He'd learned long ago he couldn't trust anyone.

But anyone who'd betrayed his trust had paid for that crime with his life, like Javier Mendez. This particular informant just might, too—once Luther got out.

Until he got out, though, he wanted to keep the damn spy in line. He pressed a number on that untraceable cell. The minute the call was answered, he bellowed, "What the hell are you doing?"

His reply was a dead silence. Shock, no doubt. Luther was in jail but that didn't keep him from being aware of what was happening on the outside.

"Don't you understand yet that I know *everything*?" he asked.

There was a gasp and a stammered, "Wh-what are you talking about?"

"You're supposed to just keep an eye on her until I need her." Luther reiterated the order he'd given once he'd learned who the presiding judge for his trial would be. A trial he hoped like hell would not take place. "Not break into her place."

"I—I didn't break in," his spy protested. "I didn't have to. I have a key."

Luther cursed. He hated liars. "Then how the hell did the window get broken?"

"I did that when I heard them coming in," the liar

explained. "I think she was with that guy from the night before—the one I took the picture of and sent to the judge."

Luther wanted a copy of that picture, but he couldn't risk someone finding it in his cell. He wanted to know who the hell had been sleeping on Bella Holmes's couch, though.

"When I heard them, I broke the window so it would look like a break-in. So they wouldn't realize it was someone with a key—someone who can get to her any-time I want."

And clearly this idiot wanted to get to her now.

Luther swallowed a curse. This spy was close to Bella Holmes, so close there would likely never be sus-picion of an association with him. So he needed this damn idiot—enough that he couldn't threaten. Yet. He could only remind. "You'll do it when I tell you to do it."

He clicked off the cell. But he still had that sick feeling—that out-of-control feeling he hated so damn much. He didn't trust this spy to wait until he gave the order.

What the hell kind of enemy had the judge's daugh-ter made in this person?

And who was the guy who'd slept on her couch? It had to be a bodyguard. The eyewitness had Clint Quar-ters. The evidence tech had Hart Fisher. So it had to be someone Luther knew. All of Parker Payne's team were ex-vice cops.

Which one of Luther's old frenemies could it be? The next time he spoke to his little spy, he would make damn certain he got a good description. Maybe he'd even risk getting a copy of one of those pictures the judge had been receiving…

Bella wanted to go home now. Not home here—in the Tudor mansion where she'd grown up. She wanted to go home to her apartment even though the window wouldn't be fixed until morning. There were too many pictures of her mother in this house; her father kept it like a shrine to her.

Bella didn't need the photos to remind her of what her mother looked like; all she needed was a mirror. But seeing those photos reminded her of all the happier times that could never happen again. And looking at them now caused her such guilt. She'd let her mother down when she'd lost her jewelry.

But she'd been having so much fun making over Tyce Jackson that she hadn't had time to take the jewelry back to the safe-deposit box at the bank. She should have made time.

It was too late now, though. And unfortunately Tyce was probably right. She would undoubtedly never see that jewelry again.

"You're not eating," her father said as he gestured at her untouched plate.

He sat at one end of the long dining room table while she and Tyce sat across from each other in the middle. The chair at the other end sat empty, like it had since Mom had died. She couldn't even glance that way.

"We had a big lunch," Bella said.

But Tyce was having no trouble polishing off his plate. Daddy's cook was good, though—Bella had made certain of that when she'd hired her. She'd wanted to make sure that her father ate. He'd lost so much weight after Mom had died.

Bella had thought for a while that she might lose him, too, of a broken heart. That was why she didn't want to fall for anyone the way he had—so deeply that losing that person could destroy her.

She pushed her plate aside, feeling sick and broken-hearted herself.

Her father reached out, covered her hand with his and reassuringly squeezed it. "Stop beating yourself up about your mother's jewelry, sweetheart. She would understand."

She would—because she was Mom. Because she was loving and generous and forgiving and amazing...

Bella glanced at her empty chair and pain gripped her heart.

And gone.

Mom was gone.

Her father squeezed her hand a little more tightly. "I can't lose you, too," he said as if he'd read her mind. "Tyce is right. You need to go into a safe house until the trial is over."

Her father said it, but Tyce was the one she glared at—because he'd worked on her father, frightening him even more than he'd already been.

"It was a robbery," Bella said. "That was all it was."

Her father shook his head and murmured, "But the photographs..."

"Photographs?" she repeated. She'd only seen the one. "Are there more?"

The men exchanged a glance but neither answered

her. She glared at them both. "Stop trying to protect me. I want to see them."

"Just one new one," her father replied.

"You don't need to see it," Tyce replied. "It's not of you."

She jumped up from her chair. "Daddy? Is it threatening you, Daddy?"

"No," he assured her. "Luther Mills is too smart to threaten me."

Because he would know it wouldn't frighten her father. Ever since her mother's death, he'd cared nothing about his own life. She was all he cared about now.

"If not you, then who?" she asked. Then she followed his glance at Tyce. "You?"

He shrugged his broad shoulders. "It was nothing."

"I want to see it," she insisted.

"It's evidence," Tyce replied.

"But you saw it, so it must be here," she said. He had not left her side at all that day except for when she'd gone upstairs to her old bedroom. So she knew where the photograph had to be. She whirled on her heel to head out of the dining room.

As she rushed out, she heard Tyce say to her father, "Finish eating, sir. I'll make sure she doesn't tamper with it." Her father wouldn't worry about her tampering with it. But he obviously didn't want her to see it. She headed for his den anyway, her heels clicking against the hardwood floors as she nearly ran to stay ahead of Tyce.

She didn't want him to stop her from seeing it. She had to know.

She pushed open the French doors to the den and hurried over to her father's desk. When she glanced down at the photograph, clearly visible beneath the transparent plastic, she gasped.

"It's not that bad," a deep voice said.

Through the plastic, she touched the hole that was pierced through his forehead. "Yes, it is," she murmured.

She didn't want Tyce Jackson dead. Just a short time ago, before they'd heard the intruder, she'd wanted him. She'd wanted to keep kissing him and touching him. And she'd wanted him to keep kissing and touching her.

But something had changed since the break-in. He wasn't looking at her like he had then—with desire. Even though he was still sticking close to her, he'd distanced himself.

Why? Was he trying to protect her or himself?

She pointed at the picture. "Is this why you want to go to a safe house?" she asked. "Are you scared?"

Tyce was terrified—that something might happen to her. He didn't want her getting hurt any worse than she'd already been when she'd noticed her mother's jewelry missing. She'd been devastated then. And he hadn't been able to help her.

If Luther carried out the threat in that photo, Tyce wouldn't be able to help her, either. She would be unprotected when Luther really came after her. And he would.

Despite all of Luther's efforts to take out the eyewitness and the evidence tech, Parker's team was too good. They would keep everyone safe. And because Tyce was part of that team, he would keep Bella safe.

Or just like that photograph portrayed, he would die trying.

"Are you scared?" She repeated her question.

Tyce chuckled. "Oh, Princess, I've been in far more dangerous situations than this."

He'd been so deep undercover that the other members of the vice unit hadn't been able to find him let alone back him up if he'd needed it. He'd needed it. A few times he'd been jumped—by other members of Luther's crew trying to make sure he didn't take their place.

He hadn't wanted to take anyone's place; he'd just wanted to get close to Luther to bring him down. But he hadn't ever gotten close enough despite their—

He drew in a shaky breath and shook his head. He didn't think about that. Ever.

"What?" Bella asked as she stepped closer to him. "What were you thinking about?"

He couldn't tell her about any of that; he didn't tell anyone about that. So he exaggerated a shudder and replied, "I was thinking about that shave this morning. You sure Daddy's barber didn't take that picture?"

"If he knew how you kept whining over that little cut, he might have," she said. But her green eyes were narrowed; she hadn't completely bought his claim.

She wasn't at all the airhead he'd thought she was. Those rumors must have been spread due to jealousy over her wealth and beauty.

Was that what the break-in had been about? Why only the pieces most special to her had been stolen?

Luther wouldn't have ordered a robbery. He wouldn't have wasted his time. And he wouldn't have known enough about Bella to know that stealing her mother's jewelry would upset her.

So had the robbery been random? Just a thief who

knew his jewelry and knew what pieces had been most valuable? Or had it been someone else? Someone close enough to Bella that he or she knew how stealing her mother's jewelry would hurt her?

Tyce hoped it wasn't the latter. Because then there was more than one person—more than Luther Mills—who wanted to hurt Bella.

"Cut?" the judge asked. "What cut?"

Tyce hadn't heard him join them in the den. He was already too distracted where Bella was concerned.

"It was nothing," Bella said. "Vito nicked Tyce when he shaved that bushy beard from his face."

Tyce felt his jaw. The stubble was a little more pronounced now. If he wanted to keep the beard off, he'd have to shave twice a day. But he'd rather do it himself than risk the elderly barber doing it again. "I won't need to shave where we're going," he said.

"Where are you going?" the judge asked.

"Safe house," Tyce replied. In the middle of nowhere so nobody could sneak up on him again—or take pictures of him without his realizing it.

Bella shook her head. "I am much too busy to leave town now."

"Too busy doing what?" he asked. He'd spent the day following her around from that luncheon to the ballroom at the hotel to add up everything she'd collected the night before. "Going to parties?"

He knew it was more than that, but he wanted to goad her.

Predictably, she glared at him. But unpredictably, she agreed with him. "Yes, parties. And if you want to keep being my bodyguard, you will need to keep that beard shaved off. Or—" she held up the plastic bag with the photograph "—if you're too scared, you can have someone else take over for you."

She didn't wait for an answer—just flounced out of the room.

Tyce curled his fingers into his hand so he wouldn't reach for her as she passed him in the doorway. She was so damn infuriating and beautiful and…frightening.

He was scared. And the judge must have seen it, too, because he remarked, "Do you want to be replaced?"

Did the judge not think Tyce could protect his daughter? Or was he worried about a broke bodyguard getting too close to his little heiress?

"Do you want to replace me?" Tyce asked.

The judge glanced at the plastic bag on his desk.

"You'll just get a picture of whoever replaces me," Tyce said. "With that bullet through his brain…"

But he wasn't so sure about that.

Luther Mills had another reason for wanting him dead that had nothing to do with his protecting Bella Holmes. In fact, Tyce was surprised he hadn't gotten a bullet through his brain long before now.

Chapter 9

Bella had won. They'd returned to her apartment. They'd attended all the events she had already planned. But she didn't feel victorious. She felt frustrated as hell.

Her apartment wasn't small, but it felt that way with Tyce living with her. He'd moved from the couch to the guest bedroom. And he'd installed that security system he'd insisted she should have. Bella had set it off a few times—just opening her bedroom window for some air.

And Tyce had run in—wearing only his boxers, with his gun drawn. He hadn't even looked at her, though. It was as if that night hadn't happened—as if he had never kissed her. Never touched her...

Maybe she'd only imagined it.

And maybe her father had only imagined that Luther Mills was threatening her because nothing had happened these past couple of weeks. No break-ins. No threats. But Bella had seen the photos, too. The photograph of her and the one of Tyce…with that hole in his forehead.

"What?" Tyce asked, rising from the couch he'd been sitting on in the living room of her apartment.

Bella realized she was staring at him now, at his forehead. He touched it. "Do I have something on my face?"

She shook her head. He looked so damn handsome. She knew he hated dressing up, but the man was made for expensive clothes. Her breath caught as she ran her gaze over him in his tuxedo. He jerked at the bow tie, fighting to loosen it.

She laughed and shook her head. "Leave it alone. You had it tied."

Which was a shock. But they'd gone to so many events in the past couple of weeks that he must have gotten used to tying it. He seemed to prefer doing it himself to having her mess with it. Every time she'd tried, he'd jerked away from her as if he thought she was going to strangle him with the tie.

She'd thought about it a few times. Maybe more than a few…

But that was only because he was so damn infuriating, still calling her "Princess." He'd been the most infuriating when that alarm had gone off the night before. How had he walked into her bedroom and not looked at her?

Wasn't he her bodyguard? Wasn't he supposed to make sure she was okay?

While she'd studied him—his naked chest, the knit boxers molded to his impressive ass—he hadn't even glanced at her. Or maybe she hadn't noticed because she'd been so focused on his body.

He wasn't looking at her now, either, and she was wearing one of her prettiest gowns. The strapless dress was a deep emerald that brought out the green of her eyes and the gold of her hair. But he didn't compliment her at all.

And she wasn't about to fish for one. It wasn't as if he was really her boyfriend. He was just her bodyguard.

"Do you want me to fix that for you?" she asked as he fumbled with the tie again.

"I've got it," he insisted. But he wasn't looking in a mirror and he couldn't see to fix it as he stared down at the ends.

Bella glanced at her watch. It was her mother's delicate gold band with the mother-of-pearl face. At least that hadn't been stolen, but she rarely took it off. "We're going to be late," she said.

"Isn't that fashionable?" he asked.

"Not when you're the hostess."

"You're hosting this shindig, too?"

She knew she took on too much—too many events. But there were few other volunteers and so many worthy charities. That was why she found herself chairing so many of the events.

She nodded.

"You love throwing a party, huh?"

It was more than a party, and she'd hoped he would have figured that out by now. Apparently he'd only been paying attention to whoever might threaten her life—not to what she was actually doing with her life.

They hadn't just gone to events, though. He had

taken her around to some pawn shops, as well, to try to find her mother's jewelry.

"I prefer parties to pawn shops," she admitted.

He chuckled.

He'd admitted that he'd taken her to the ones he'd known from his years in vice where users brought stolen property to get money for drugs. She hoped that wasn't why someone had taken her mother's jewelry. But if they had, they hadn't tried to get money out of those pawn shops.

"I'm sorry," he murmured, his voice gruff.

She furrowed her brow as she stared up at him. "Sorry for what? I appreciate that you took me to look for the jewelry."

"I'm sorry we didn't find it," he replied.

A wistful sigh slipped through her lips. She wished they had, but Tyce had warned her that they might never recover it.

"You didn't think we would," she reminded him. "Why not?"

"Because I'm not sure that someone took it to make money off it."

"Then why else would they have stolen it?"

"To hurt you."

Thinking of that, of someone wanting to hurt her, had a twinge of pain hitting her heart. But she shook her head. "Nobody wants to hurt me."

"Luther Mills."

"From what you and Daddy have said about him, stealing jewelry doesn't sound like something he would have someone do for him."

"No, it doesn't," he agreed.

"So you think someone else wants to hurt me?" She shivered at the horrific thought. She was careful to always be nice to everyone. Even Michael had not been that upset when she'd ended their arrangement.

Could someone want to hurt her, though?

Tyce stepped closer to her and touched her chin, tipping her face up to his. "I won't let anything happen to you," he said. "Don't worry."

She was worried about him hurting her—because she'd never been as attracted to anyone as she was to Tyce. She felt so incredibly drawn to him that she found herself rising up on tiptoe and leaning toward him.

When her breasts bumped into his massive chest, a jolt of heat and desire rushed through her. She wanted him so badly.

He tensed and stared down at her. His startling topaz eyes turned dark. With desire?

Did he feel it, too?

If he did, he was better at fighting it than she was because he stepped back and murmured, "You don't want to be late."

No. She didn't want to be late. But she didn't want to be hurt, either—and the way he kept ignoring her attraction to him was hurting her.

He must have seen it because he cursed. Then he reached for her, dragging her up against his body again. She felt his erection straining the fly of his tuxedo pants.

The attraction was not one-sided. He wanted her, too. But he wasn't happy about it because he cursed right before he lowered his head to hers. His mouth took hers—passionately, hungrily. He kissed her deeply, sliding his tongue between lips she parted with a gasp.

She hadn't imagined how he tasted, how he'd touched her. Just his fingertips slid along her jaw, but she shivered with the sensations racing through her. She had never wanted anyone the way she wanted him.

She wanted those hands all over her. She wanted hers all over him. She reached for his tie. But instead of tying it, she pulled it free of his collar and moved to the buttons on his shirt—releasing them.

He tensed even as his magnificently muscled chest rose and fell with heavy pants for breath. "We're going to be late," he warned her.

She didn't care.

He must have sensed that because he swung her up into his arms and carried her to her bedroom. As he set her on her feet, she wobbled slightly in her heels before stepping out of them. His hand was at the tab of the zipper in the back of the dress, pulling it down. The strapless gown dropped to the floor.

He cursed again as he stared down at her, his topaz eyes molten with desire. "You are so damn beautiful…" He shook his head. "It just isn't fair."

"I didn't think you noticed," she said, gesturing at the bed.

"I notice everything."

Because he was a bodyguard? Or because he was interested in her? Attracted to her?

She pushed his shirt from his broad shoulders. Then she reached for his belt.

He caught her hands as he caught his breath. "Bella…"

Was he going to stop her? Was he going to pull away again? It would kill her to stop now.

But instead of pulling her dress back up, he lifted her

out of the pool of fabric at her feet and carried her to the bed. Then he moved down her body, kissing and caressing every inch of her ultrasensitive skin. She squirmed against the blankets beneath her and cried out as his lips closed over a tight nipple. She arched up, clutching his head to her breast. He tugged on it gently as he moved his fingers beneath her panties. He stroked them over her mound and then inside her. She cried out again and clutched at his shoulders.

She needed him. Now.

"Tyce!"

Instead of joining her, joining their bodies where she ached for him, he moved off the bed.

"Please!" she implored him. She couldn't remember the last time she had begged for anything. But she didn't want him to push her away again or to act like he didn't see her.

He was looking at her now, though, his topaz gaze moving over her like his hands and mouth had. As he stared at her, he fumbled with his belt. After unclasping it and unbuttoning his pants, he pushed them down and stepped out of them and his dress shoes. Then he rolled his socks off, as well. He wore only his boxers, which were molded to his impressive erection.

She reached out, wanting to tug them off his lean hips. But he was bending over, pulling his wallet from his pants and a condom from his wallet.

And finally he pushed down the boxers.

She gasped at the size of him. He was so big. So thick and strong-looking. Needing to touch him, she reached for him.

But he stepped back, like he had so many other times

before. His hand shook as he tore open the packet and rolled on the condom. Then he moved toward her—joining her on the bed and removing her panties. Even though he held his weight on his arms, his body was heavy and warm against hers.

Bella wrapped her legs around his hips and arched against him, needing to have him inside her—as part of her. He touched her again, as if making sure she was ready for him.

She was so ready, so needy, that she cried out.

"Wow," he murmured. "You're so hot." Then he eased inside her and a low groan rumbled in his throat. "So hot and so…"

He moved slowly, probably so he wouldn't hurt her, given how big he was, and sweat beaded on his forehead as a vein twitched on his temple.

She arched her hips and he slid deeper. The groan that had rumbled in his throat broke free. Then his mouth covered hers, like his body covered hers.

He moved inside her, like he kissed her—deeply, passionately.

Then he rolled onto his back and held her astride him. And he slid deeper yet.

A cry slipped through her lips. And he stilled, clutching her hips. "Are you all right?"

She nodded and her hair tumbled around her bare shoulders. "So right…"

It felt that way, like they were meant to be together like this. But he tensed, as if he disagreed.

She would have to prove it to him. So she traced her hands across his chest as she moved her hips against his—riding him. His hands traveled from her hips up her rib cage to her breasts. As he cupped them in his big hands, he rubbed his thumbs over the nipples.

She'd already ached with her need for release, now the tension threatened to break her in two. But then he thrust up from the mattress and she cried out at the pleasure that overwhelmed her. She'd never had as intense an experience before.

His hands moved back to her hips and he guided her to match his rhythm. But he didn't immediately take his release—instead he built that tension inside her again before releasing it.

She screamed his name. But he kept moving. Then finally his body tensed and a groan tore through his gritted teeth as he came. She collapsed onto his chest, panting for breath—boneless with pleasure.

But his body was still tense. "I'll clean up," he said, using his hands on her hips to lift her off him. "Then we need to go."

"Go where?" she asked.

"The party you're throwing."

Bella gasped. She'd forgotten all about it. She'd forgotten everything but her desire for him.

She scrambled out of bed to clean up, too, and repair her hair and makeup. If he'd reached for her again, she would have forgotten about the party. But he was already distancing himself.

She felt a sharp twinge in her heart as she realized he probably regretted what they'd done. Her only regret was that he might not want to do it again.

Tyce ignored the burning sensation in his chest. It wasn't heartburn—not from the delicious meal the ca-

terers had just served in the ballroom of the River City
Grand Plaza. He wasn't even sure if it was regret.

But it should have been.

Despite how deeply he'd gone undercover with the
vice unit, Tyce had never forgotten who and what he
really was. He'd always known he was a cop and his
job had been to bring down the bad guys. He'd never
let himself go so deep undercover that he'd ever forgotten who he was—until now. This time he'd begun to
believe his cover—that he was Bella's boyfriend, she
his girlfriend. And that just wasn't possible given their
backgrounds.

They had nothing in common. Their worlds were far
too different for either to fit into the other's.

Her world was entirely too social, revolving solely
around parties, luncheons and black-tie events. But she
didn't just attend them. She planned them, spending end-
less hours on the phone with caterers and bartenders
and her assistant as well as everyone who was anyone
in River City.

Tyce Jackson was a nobody and he preferred it that
way. He preferred a solitary lifestyle. He hated parties,
hated having to make small talk. And because he'd gone
to so many of these events with Bella, people were be-
coming curious about him—curious enough to try to
quiz him about who and what he was.

Bella usually saved him from the inquisitions, though.
If someone was grilling him, she always noticed and in-
tervened, even as busy as she was at the events, moving from patron to patron like a butterfly flitting from
flower to flower. She was so damn beautiful—especially
in that strapless green gown.

He wanted her even more now than he had before they'd had sex—because he knew how amazing it could be between them, how hot and tight she felt.

The way she'd moved…

It hadn't been like she was moving now, but it made him think about that, seeing her in the strapless dress had him thinking about how her hair had fallen around her bare shoulders. He forced his mind back to the present and focused on her flitting around the ballroom, smiling and charming everyone she encountered.

"You never take your eyes off her," an elderly woman remarked. But she'd had to grab Tyce's arm to get his attention. "You've really fallen for our girl."

Mine! That was the thought that had reverberated in his mind and his heart when he'd eased inside her. *Mine!* But he had nothing to offer a woman like Bella, so he had no right to claim her.

How did this woman?

"Our girl?" he asked.

"That's how we all feel about dear Bella," the woman replied. "Like she belongs to us. When her mother died, she left her trust to Bella, and Bella to us." She smiled up at Tyce. "It looks like we have to share her with you now." Her smile widened and a little twinkle sparkled in one of her blue eyes. "You must be the reason she was late for the party she's hosting."

That damn tie felt way too tight again and he tugged at it.

The older lady chuckled at his reaction. Then she asked, "How did you and Bella happen to meet?"

"Through her father," Tyce replied. He'd been answering this question the past couple of weeks with as much of the truth as he could safely share.

"You know the judge?" the woman asked, a trace of skepticism in her voice.

He'd been keeping his hair trimmed and his face shaved, but he still didn't look like he fit into Bella's world. And they all knew it. So what did the lady think, that he was some escort Bella had hired to service her?

His face heated as he tensed, and he nearly jumped when a bare arm slid through the crook of his. Pressing against his side, Bella answered for him. "Tyce and my father go way back and know each other quite well."

That was true—to an extent. They knew each other professionally. But until the night of the break-in, Tyce had never been to the judge's home.

"Mrs. Kreiser, do you mind if I steal my date from you? This band is so wonderful that I have the sudden urge to dance." She didn't wait for the older lady or for Tyce to agree. Using her arm linked through his, she tugged him toward the dance floor.

"I don't dance," Tyce reminded her. He'd told her that at previous evening events. And while she'd had time to sic Daddy's barber on him and buy him some clothes, she hadn't tried to give him any dance lessons.

But they had moved together well earlier that evening— as if they'd been dancing to a routine they had choreographed together.

"It's a slow song," she pointed out, stopping in the middle of the dance floor and turning to face him. "Just put your arms around me." She stared up at him and, while she wore a smile as beautiful as her dress, it didn't quite reach her eyes. She was tense and nervous and…

Maybe she was nervous that he was going to leave her standing alone in the middle of the dance floor. But he couldn't embarrass her like that—even if he embarrassed himself with his physical reaction to her. He'd never had a release as powerful as the one he'd had inside her, but that felt like it had happened days ago, not hours. He ached with wanting her again.

The willpower he'd used to resist her before was gone. He wasn't sure how he'd managed even then to resist her those nights she'd set off the alarm and he'd rushed into her bedroom. He'd had to force himself to look away from her—from how beautiful she'd looked in her thin silk nightgown.

He slid his arm around her small waist and pulled her against his body. He was tense and nervous, too. He had never been as attracted to anyone as he was to Bella Holmes.

After having sex with her, he'd hoped that attraction would have abated but, if anything, it was only more intense. Because now he knew how amazing it would be between them.

Tyce had had some dangerous undercover assignments during his years with the River City PD vice unit. But this one, acting as Bella Holmes's boyfriend, was his most dangerous assignment yet.

Not to his life.

But to his heart.

The big guy had to die. That was the only way Bella Holmes was finally going to get what she had coming. Because he was always around her, always glued to her side.

He had to go…

Luther Mills hadn't given the order to do anything to him or to Bella. Yet. But waiting wasn't an option.

Bella Holmes had been the belle of the ball of life for far too long. Everything she wanted came so effortlessly to her. The money. The jewelry. The men.

She had the respect and adoration of River City. But she'd done nothing to earn it.

Nothing but been born to money and privilege. It wasn't fair. But that was about to change…

Once the man was out of the way, Bella Holmes's charmed life would come to an end.

Chapter 10

Bella did not arrive late and leave early at the events she hosted. Except for tonight. Tonight she'd arrived late—because she'd been making love with her body-guard. And now she wanted to leave early to do that all over again.

She'd thought he might distance himself from her—like he had right after they'd made love. But when they'd danced, she'd felt the tension in his body, which had been pressed so tightly against hers that she'd had no doubt he wanted her, too. She ached for him and that ache yawned inside her as Camille caught her at the entrance to the ballroom.

"Bella, where are you going?"

She was meeting Tyce in the lobby. He was just a couple of steps in front of her. Usually he would have been at her side or within sight of her. But she'd convinced him she would be fine in the busy ballroom while he retrieved the SUV from the parking garage.

But then Camille had chased her into the lobby.

"I'm leaving," she told her assistant—although Camille had been her friend much longer than she'd worked for her.

The dark-haired woman gasped in shock. "But what about the guests and the caterer?"

"I've told everyone to enjoy the rest of the evening," Bella reminded her. After her last dance with Tyce, she'd borrowed the singer's microphone to thank everyone for coming, for their generosity, and had encouraged them to stay and party. She, on the other hand, wanted a private party—with just her and Tyce Jackson.

Her lips curved into a smile as she remembered the pleasure he'd given her. Her smile widened with anticipation of feeling that pleasure again. "And the caterer and bartenders? Everyone has been paid." And generously tipped, as well. She was in an extremely generous mood right now. "I'm including a big bonus in your next check, too," Bella assured Camille. "I know you've been working extra hard lately, picking up my slack."

Camille laughed. "Your slack? You work harder than anyone I know. That's why I'm worried about you."

"Worried?" Bella asked. Despite the threats, she was better than she could ever remember being since her mother's untimely death. And she suspected she knew whom she had to thank for that—the man protecting her because of those threats.

Camille nodded. "Yes. Maybe all these years of working so hard have affected you."

"Affected me?" Bella asked. She was curious now. She'd known Camille for a long time. They'd attended the same private school and had gone to the same college—until Bella had dropped out after her mother's death.

"You've not been yourself these past couple of weeks." Camille glanced around as if looking for someone. Then she lowered her voice to a whisper and added, "Ever since *he* showed up."

Bella had been on edge—because of the threats, because of her attraction to Tyce. But he'd reciprocated that attraction…at least enough to make love to her.

Had anything really changed, though? He was still just her bodyguard. Not her boyfriend. She was still just an assignment, not his girlfriend.

"I'm sorry," Bella said. "I didn't mean to worry you." But telling her about the threats and the bodyguard would only worry her more.

"I am worried," Camille said. "You just broke up with Michael and then the next day this guy shows up and never leaves your side." She stepped closer to Bella and studied her face intently. "Is he threatening you?"

Bella laughed, yet there was a hollow sound to it. "No. He's not." But she was in danger of falling for him.

"Who is he?" Camille asked. "And where the hell did he come from?"

"I told you." What they'd been telling everyone else. "He's a friend of my father's."

"Michael is a friend of your father's," Camille said.

"No," Bella corrected her. "His parents are friends of my father's." Her father certainly didn't consider Michael a friend.

Camille shrugged as if it was of no consequence to

her. "You've known him your whole life. You've never mentioned this guy before."

"I haven't met every friend of my father's," Bella said.

Camille narrowed her eyes speculatively. She knew how often Bella visited her father in chambers.

Now Tyce knew, too, because he'd made several trips with her to bring her father lunch.

"Well, I hadn't met Tyce until recently," Bella said, which was all truthful.

Camille must have seen that because she stepped back. But there was still skepticism in her voice when she asked, "So when you did meet him, it was love at first sight?"

Bella remembered her first sight of Tyce—walking into the ballroom with his bushy beard, long hair and those motorcycle boots.

She had to force the smile. "Yes. It was."

He had certainly made an impression on her—scaring the hell out of her.

Now Camille's eyes widened in shock. "You're in love with him?"

Not wanting to backtrack now, Bella nodded. "Yes. That's why I'm acting differently. I've never felt this way before." That much was true.

But love?

She couldn't be in love with Tyce Jackson. She barely knew him. Lust, yes. But love…

That took time. That took true intimacy. And she doubted Tyce would ever give her that. She hadn't been able to give it, either, when she devoted so much time to her mother's charities and she was so afraid of falling for someone and losing him like her father had lost her mother. Devastatingly…

"Are you sure it's love?" Camille asked.

Bella forced herself to nod.

"I was never a huge fan of Michael's," Camille admitted. She'd made it clear that she'd thought Michael acted spoiled and entitled. Camille had only been able to attend the same private school they had because her mother had worked as a teacher there. "But at least you'd known him a long time."

But Bella hadn't really known him. She hadn't known that he used drugs.

"You just met this guy," Camille said. "You don't really know much about him. So, please, be careful. I don't want you to get hurt."

Bella didn't want to get hurt, either. But she had a feeling it was inevitable. Once the trial was over and she no longer needed a bodyguard, she doubted that Tyce would want to continue acting like her boyfriend.

He would move on to his next assignment and she would…be just fine without him. It wasn't as if she was really in love with him.

Parker had that damn feeling he'd inherited from his mother—that weird sixth sense, sickening certainty that something *bad* was about to happen. But to whom?

The eyewitness, Rosie Mendez, and Clint Quarters were safe. Only the chief, and probably Parker's mother, Penny, who knew everything, knew where they were hiding until the trial. Even Wendy Thompson, the evidence tech, had been convinced to finally take a break from work to await the trial in a safe house. A safe house very few knew about, just in case Jocelyn Gerber was right and there was a leak somewhere within the agency. Luther could not get to them now. But it was his many, many attempts to have them taken out that had finally convinced Rosie and Wendy to go into hiding.

Maybe Parker needed to thank him for that. Maybe he needed to talk to Luther again—to see what he was up to next—because there was no way that the drug dealer was giving up. He had to have something more planned, which was probably why Parker had that bad feeling.

He knew that until Luther Mills was convicted and locked away for life, he was still a threat.

That sickening feeling intensified. So he reached for the cell phone on his desk. It had to be…

He punched in the number, and his pulse quickened as he waited for the person to pick up.

"What?" Tyce asked when he finally answered. "Everything all right?"

He knew about all the attacks on the others. Parker had been keeping the entire team apprised of the situation.

"That's what I'm calling to ask you," Parker said. "Everything all right?"

"Why?" Tyce's tone was sharp. "Did the judge get another photograph threat?"

"No."

"Then why do you sound so worried?"

Parker had tried to keep it from his voice, but Tyce was good at reading people. If he wasn't, he wouldn't have survived his deep undercover assignments. "I don't know," he admitted. "I just got one of those feelings…"

"Oh," Tyce said.

He must have heard about the legendary Payne sixth sense. His mother, Penny, had started it. Parker's half brother, Nick, who wasn't even Penny's son, had always had it. And now, since opening their own franchises of the Payne Protection Agency, he and his brother Cooper had been getting it.

"It's not about me," Tyce told him. "Nothing's been happening. I think she was right about the break-in—it was just to steal her mother's jewelry."

"Did you find it yet?" Parker asked. He knew they'd searched some pawn shops.

"Not where I looked," Tyce said. "But the thieves knew to take the most valuable pieces, so they know no pawn shop will offer them what they're worth."

"I'll have the Kozminskis check with some fences they know," Parker offered.

The Kozminskis were his twin brother Logan's brothers-in-law. Their late father had been a jewel thief and had trained them to follow in his footsteps to become thieves. But after their sister had married Logan, they'd become bodyguards.

"Thanks," Tyce said. "It's really bothering her."

"Anyone else bothering her?" Parker asked. He knew how Tyce teased her, so he added, "Besides you?"

Tyce chuckled, but it sounded a little uneasy.

"Are you still giving her a hard time?" Parker asked with a sigh.

There was no reply—just dead silence.

"Are you there?" Parker asked.

"Yeah, yeah, but I have to go," Tyce said. "I left her alone to get the SUV from the parking garage."

"What!" Parker said. "You can't leave her alone." Even though there hadn't been any recent threats, she was still in danger.

"She's in a ballroom with about a billion people," Tyce replied. "She's fine."

Maybe she was. But what about Tyce?

Something was going on with him. Parker could hear it in his voice. And that damn sixth sense of his intensified. Something bad was about to happen...

And Parker was pretty damn sure it was about to happen to Tyce.

Tyce knew better than to discount Parker's sixth sense. That Payne predictor of something bad about to go down was legendary. And it was legendary because it was rarely, if ever, wrong.

He ended his conversation with his boss and clicked off his cell. And he wondered...

Had that something bad already happened to him? Was he getting too involved with Bella Holmes?

He'd gone to the parking garage to get the SUV because he hadn't wanted to wait for the valet to bring it around. He was in a hurry to get Bella back to her apartment and back to bed.

His body ached with wanting her, with needing to be buried deep inside her.

That was the something bad—needing someone like this. He'd learned long ago that it was better to be independent, self-sufficient. Then you never got hurt.

Not that Bella could hurt him. He knew better than to fall for her. What had happened earlier only both-

ered him because it was unprofessional. He needed to
focus on protecting her, not on…

Leaving her alone in the Plaza was not protecting
her. Tyce clicked the key fob and the lights flashed on
his SUV. He jumped inside and quickly started it. He
needed to get back to her and not to take her to bed.

He had to make sure nothing had happened to her.

Damn Parker for calling him about his *bad* feeling.
But maybe it was a good thing that he had—because
Tyce had become complacent.

With no more threats against her, he'd started letting down his guard—so much so that he'd given in to
his desire for her. He couldn't let that happen again.

He couldn't be distracted—not with her life at stake.
And his…

But he wasn't worried about himself. He'd survived
far more physically dangerous undercover assignments
than this one. But unlike when he'd been undercover,
he'd let himself start feeling, so this job and she were
getting to him emotionally—like those old girlfriends
had. But none of them had wanted a true relationship
with him, and he doubted Bella would, either. She was
even richer and higher classed than any of them had
been.

Hopefully she had stayed in the ballroom with all
those guests. She would be safe there. But as he pulled
up to the front of the hotel lobby, he saw her standing
just on the other side of the glass doors.

A twinge of fear struck his heart, and not just because of how vulnerable she was—anyone could shoot
her. Or grab her…

The valets would be no protection against Luther's

crew. Because one might actually be one of Luther's crew, Tyce preferred to either leave his vehicle at the curb or park it himself.

Someone had planted a bomb on another bodyguard's SUV, and Tyce hadn't wanted to risk that happening to his. But a bomb was just one of his many concerns. She'd gotten to him—way too much, way more than anyone else ever had.

She stepped into the turnstile to join him and he jumped out of the SUV. He needed to focus on his job again—on keeping her safe. But as he rushed around the SUV to meet her at the door, shots rang out.

And he knew he was too late to protect her. "Get down!" he shouted at her and at the valets, as well.

Parker had been right. Something bad was about to happen. Tyce dropped to the ground—not because he'd ordered the others to do that, but because of the bullet that ripped through his shoulder.

Pain gripped him, but he forced himself to his feet—forced himself to run toward Bella and knock her to the ground. But was he too late? Had she already been struck, too?

Chapter 11

Bella struck the ground hard, knocking all the air from her lungs. She could only gasp as she lay sprawled on the cement sidewalk. Other people screamed and ran. A scream burned in the back of her throat, but she couldn't run.

Tyce was hit. She'd seen it happen—had seen the bullet strike his shoulder and spin him to the ground. But he'd jumped back up. He'd run—toward her.

He'd knocked her down, so she wouldn't be shot. And she didn't think she had been...

At the moment she couldn't feel anything but fear for him. Was it just his shoulder that had been hit? Or had he taken another bullet?

She gulped in a deep breath and called out, "Tyce! Tyce!" Shaking uncontrollably, she rolled to her side and found him sprawled next to her on the ground, blood pooling beneath his body. "Tyce!"

She bent over him. His lashes were dark against his cheeks, hiding his topaz eyes. His lids didn't so much as flicker. She reached for his wrist, to check for a pulse, but blood ran down his arm, over his hand, and trailed onto the concrete beneath them.

She knew he'd been hit. But how many times?

"Call an ambulance!" she shouted.

But she wasn't certain anyone was around to hear her. Once the shooting had started, everyone had run— the patrons who'd been waiting for their vehicles and the valets who'd been bringing them. So she fumbled around on the sidewalk, trying to find her purse. It must have flown from her hands when Tyce had knocked her down.

He'd probably saved her life. But had protecting her cost him his?

Tyce could not believe he'd lost consciousness. Some damn bodyguard he'd proved to be…

Sure, it had been for just a few minutes—from the impact of his wounded shoulder hitting the concrete when he'd knocked down Bella. But his intention had been to protect her. Knocking himself out wasn't going to help her.

Instead she'd wound up helping him. She was the one who'd called the police and the ambulance.

If he'd been conscious, he wouldn't have allowed her to do either. He would have loaded her into the SUV and gotten the hell out of there. Sure, someone would have called the police. But he wouldn't have had to talk to them. He wouldn't have had to risk someone recognizing him or asking too many questions.

The ambulance had saved him from that, though, as it had carried him away from the scene with Bella at his side. He'd kept telling her that he was fine.

But until the ER doctor told her the same thing, she didn't relax. She didn't release the breath she must have been holding until the doctor pulled aside the ER curtain and walked away.

"I told you it was nothing," Tyce reminded her.

"You needed stitches and a tetanus shot," she reminded him.

He flinched as he remembered the shot. He hated needles, which had made going undercover as a drug dealer excruciatingly uncomfortable. Not that he had ever used. He'd hadn't gone that deep—as deep as some other vice cops had done. He hadn't wanted to wind up like they had, addicted to the very drugs they'd been trying to get off the streets.

But he didn't even like being around needles. He shuddered as he glanced at the receptacle on the wall that held the used needles.

"You really are a baby," Bella teased him. "I can't believe how pale you got over those needles."

The tetanus shot would have been bad enough if he hadn't needed stitches, as well. He reached for his tuxedo shirt, which was torn and stained with blood. "We need to get the hell out of here."

"Not so fast," a deep voice murmured as the curtain around his stretcher moved again.

Tyce wasn't a cop anymore, so he was surprised to see the chief. Of course, in a way Tyce did work for him since Chief Lynch had hired the Payne Protection Agency for this assignment. He was not alone, either.

The Payne he'd hired, Tyce's real boss, stood on one side of him while Judge Holmes stood on the other side. The judge wasn't worried about him, though, as he rushed toward his daughter.

"Are you all right?" he asked as he studied her. He reached out a trembling hand to the blood smeared across her cheek. That wasn't her blood, though. It was Tyce's.

"Yes," she assured her father. "I'm fine. Not even a scratch."

That was true but only because she'd had her coat on when he'd knocked her down. She was certain to have some bruises beneath that long coat, though.

"Tyce protected me from the gunfire," she said. "He saved my life."

She was being too generous. She shouldn't have been put in that position at all. She never should have been that close to an active shooter.

"Did they find him?" Tyce asked the chief. When he and Bella had left in the ambulance, the police had been searching for the shooter.

The chief shook his head. "Did you see him?"

Tyce shook his head. He'd only seen the flash as the shots had come out of the dark, from the shadow of the building across the street from the hotel. "I couldn't see anything."

And he'd been too worried about Bella to look. Protecting her had been his priority. Fortunately, with the SUV between her and the shooter, she'd been shielded from a bullet.

"Shell casings were recovered across the street from the hotel," the chief said, confirming Tyce's suspicion.

"Across the street?" Parker repeated, his brow furrowing with confusion. "But the SUV was parked with the passenger's side next to the lobby."

Tyce nodded. "So Bella could get right inside."

"So how did the shooter think he was going to get *her*?" Parker asked, his blue eyes narrowing in suspicion.

"Nobody in Luther's crew is a marksman," Tyce reminded his boss, which was good for Parker's team or one of them would have been killed before now. The only losses had been on Luther's side.

"But they're not all idiots, either," Parker said. "How did they hope to hit her from that distance with the SUV between them?"

Tyce shrugged then grimaced as the movement irritated his wounded shoulder.

"Are you okay?" Bella asked.

He nodded. "Yeah. I'm just a baby, remember?" he teased her.

Her lips curved into a smile that didn't reach her beautiful green eyes. She was worried about him.

She wasn't the only one. Tyce looked away from her to see that the three men were staring at him now, their faces intense. He shuddered and grimaced again as the movement pulled at the stitches beneath the bandage.

"I'm fine," he assured them all. "The gunshot wound was a through-and-through. A few stitches are all I got out of this." And the much needed reminder that he was a bodyguard, not Bella's boyfriend. He needed to be focused on his assignment to protect her and not focused on her…assets.

And that overwhelming attraction between them.

The men continued to stare at him.

"What?" he asked.

"How many shooters were there?" Parker asked.

"Just one," Tyce replied—which was damn fortunate since he'd been distracted. He hadn't even had a chance to draw his weapon to return fire.

Parker shook his head.

"I'm sure of it," Tyce insisted.

The chief nodded. "Evidence techs confirmed one shooter."

"Since when does Luther send one shooter?" Parker asked.

"The police officer who nearly shot the eyewitness worked alone," the chief reminded his stepson.

"Because he was a cop," Parker said. "Because he could get close to her without drawing suspicion."

Her bodyguard, Tyce's friend, Clint Quarters, had been suspicious. He'd saved Rosie Mendez.

"Do you think this was one of my people again?" the chief asked.

The judge had turned his focus from his daughter to Parker. His eyes were narrowed as he mused, "You don't think this has anything to do with Luther Mills."

"I didn't say that," Parker replied.

"Well, you don't think this has anything to do with my daughter."

"I didn't say that, either," Parker pointed out. "I'm just considering all possible explanations for there just being one shooter."

"That the shooter wasn't after my daughter," the judge said. Now he turned back to Tyce. "The shooter was just after you."

Tyce looked at his boss. "Is that what you think?"

Parker shrugged and Tyce envied him the easy gesture.

"I'm sure you made your share of enemies from your years on the police force," the judge continued. "One of them must have come after you."

Tyce figured the guy preferred to think that than that his job had put his daughter in danger. But he didn't want anyone to lose sight of what really mattered. Keeping Bella safe.

Tyce pointed to his still cleanly shaved face. He'd shaved before getting dressed that evening, before he'd made love with Bella. "After what your daughter did to me," he said, "nobody from my past would recognize me." And he wasn't sure that was just because of the haircut and the shave.

He'd changed beyond his appearance. He didn't even feel like himself anymore—and maybe that was because he was feeling again. When he'd worked undercover vice, he'd had to shut off his emotions, or they would have destroyed him. And even after he'd quit the force, he hadn't been able to turn them back on, but somehow Bella had found the switch.

The chief chuckled. "He's right," he told the judge. "Not even his own mother would recognize him now."

It was true. But Tyce flinched. His change in appearance wasn't why his mother wouldn't recognize him. The reason she wouldn't recognize him was that she hadn't seen him since she'd abandoned him.

But she'd done him a favor because his grandparents had raised him. Sure, they'd raised her, too. But he'd made certain to never disappoint them like she had. Like the women he'd once dated, she'd always gone for the bad boys as well as other bad things. Hell, he wasn't sure she was even still alive. None of his family had seen her in years.

Tyce sighed and shook off the past. It—and his mother—didn't matter to him anymore. What mattered was keeping Bella safe.

"It's more likely," he said, "that Luther figured out I'm Bella's bodyguard and ordered me taken out of the way." He'd tried having the other bodyguards killed and probably not just to get them out of his way.

He had a reason for wanting all the former vice cops dead: revenge. But he had even more reason for wanting Tyce dead. When Tyce had taken him on, Luther hadn't accepted that he was just doing his job. He'd taken it personally and he'd considered it a betrayal.

"You should have known I'd hear about this!" Luther yelled into the cell phone. "What the hell were you thinking?"

The last thing he needed was his idiot spy blowing his plan. The shooting was going to scare the judge—maybe enough to put his daughter into protective custody or one of those damn safe houses that the eyewitness and evidence tech must have gone to. Luther hadn't been able to find them yet, which was why he had to make damn sure he always knew where Bella Holmes was. He had a feeling he was going to need to use her soon.

The trial wasn't far off now. The thought sent a shiver of apprehension chasing down his spine. It shouldn't have gotten this close. He should have had the charges tossed out before now. He'd hired the best damn lawyer money could buy.

And the lawyer wasn't the only person he'd bought.

He had sources within the police department and the district attorney's office. And this idiot…

"You are not supposed to kill her." Not yet. Not when Luther still needed her.

"I wasn't trying to kill her," his spy replied. "I was trying to kill *him*."

"The guy you say is always around?"

"Yes. He's in the way. He needs to go. Or your plan will never work."

Luther didn't entirely disagree, but he knew that if this guy was one of Parker Payne's bodyguards, Payne would just replace him with another one. Or he would put her in one of those damn safe houses…

"I didn't tell you to get rid of him yet," Luther said. "We're not even sure what he is…"

"Her *boyfriend*."

Luther recognized the jealousy in his spy's voice and grimaced. That explained the unpredictability. Jealous people seldom acted rationally.

"What does he look like again?" Could he risk getting a photo on one of these cell phones?

"Tall. Really tall, with black hair and these weird light-colored eyes…"

Luther's blood chilled. "Have you heard what she calls him?" The spy must have heard it by now given how close they were.

With all that jealousy and bitterness, the idiot replied, "Tyce."

Tyce Jackson.

Luther chuckled now.

Hadn't the vice cop learned the last time he'd taken on Luther? He wasn't going to win. But Luther should have punished him with more than failure. He'd gone easy on him, and Luther rarely went easy on anyone. But if Tyce kept coming after him, he was going to wind up dead.

Hell, he should have been dead long ago—for his betrayal.

"Did you hit him?" Luther asked.

"Yes."

Luther felt a strange twinge. It must have been satisfaction. And maybe a little regret that he hadn't been able to personally pull that trigger.

"How badly?"

"Bad enough that he had to leave in an ambulance."

That wasn't good enough. Tyce Jackson needed to leave in a hearse next time.

Chapter 12

The look on Tyce's face haunted Bella. Not the look when he'd been shot or when he'd slipped into unconsciousness after protecting her.

No. The look that haunted her was the one on his face in the hospital, when the chief had chuckled that even Tyce's own mother would not recognize him.

Such a strange expression had crossed his handsome face. Later, in the SUV one of his fellow bodyguards had brought to the hospital for him, she'd tried asking him about it on the way back to her apartment, but he'd ignored her question. She wasn't sure why. Maybe he'd just been too focused on watching the rearview mirror to make sure they weren't being followed—at least not by anyone other than the additional Payne Protection Agency bodyguards that Parker had assigned to her.

Agreeing to have the extra people following her around was the only way she'd been allowed to go to her apartment. Otherwise she would have either had to hole up at her father's estate or in a safe house.

Well, she wouldn't have had to. She could refuse to have any of them protecting her. But she was already concerned about her father. He was too worried about her. In the weeks since she'd learned of the threats against her, he had aged. There were more lines on his face. More gray in his hair. And he looked thinner, as if he wasn't eating again.

She couldn't go into a safe house because then she wouldn't be able to see him. And she was all he had.

Who did Tyce have?

They'd made love just hours ago, but she knew very little about him. No. They hadn't made love. They'd had sex. He didn't love her. He didn't even seem to like her very much.

And she didn't...

She couldn't love him. She didn't even know him.

So once they stepped inside the apartment, she asked him again, "Why did you look like that when the chief mentioned your mother?"

"Look like what?" he asked, but he wouldn't meet her gaze.

"Like you got shot again," she said. "You flinched."

"I'm in pain," he grumbled as he dropped onto the couch.

She could believe that he was. He'd refused any medication beyond the tetanus shot for his wound. She'd thought he'd just wanted to keep his head clear to drive. And to protect her...

"Are you in pain over your mother?" she asked. Maybe they had something in common, after all. "Is she gone?"

He nodded. "A long time ago."

She crossed the room and knelt before him where he sat on the couch. She put her hands on his knees and squeezed. "I'm sorry."

She was sorry she'd touched him, too, as heat streaked through her body. She'd been so concerned about him during the shooting and after that she'd nearly forgotten what would have happened had those shots not be fired.

They would probably be in her bed, giving each other that intense pleasure they'd experienced earlier that evening. It was late now, though, the apartment dark but for a few can lights in the coffered ceiling.

"Why are you sorry?" Tyce asked.

Maybe he knew how she felt—about the heat rushing through her along with desire. Maybe he felt it, too.

But that wasn't the only common emotion they shared. "About your mom dying."

"She's not dead," he replied. "At least, I don't think she is. I've never met her. She took off right after she had me—leaving me in the neonatal ICU."

Bella gasped. "She abandoned you?"

He shrugged then grimaced again. "She probably didn't think I'd make it. Nobody did." Despite his grim words, his lips curved into a slight smile. "Except my grandma, I guess. She stayed with me. She prayed for me."

"Were you born premature?" Bella asked.

He nodded. "My mom never told her parents that

she was pregnant, so she didn't have any prenatal care. They weren't able to handle her. She was hanging out with the wrong people. With bad people…"

Had his father been one of those bad people? Bella wanted to ask, but bringing up his mother had already upset him. "Is that why you worked vice?" she asked instead.

He shrugged. "I grew up working vice," he said. "Back in high school, I volunteered to be an informant."

She sucked in a breath. Luther Mills had murdered a police informant. "You're lucky you survived," she murmured.

"I went into the Marines after high school, so I've survived a lot," he said. "That's why I entered the police academy and became a vice cop, too. I thought I could change the world back then. But after a few years as a vice cop, you know that the problem is too big."

She sighed. "Stopping Luther Mills won't solve that then."

"No," he agreed. "But it'll make it less of a problem here in River City. That's why it's so important he finally goes down for his crimes."

There was such passion in his voice now—more than she'd even felt when they'd made love. Luther Mills was personal to him. Maybe because of the years he'd spent trying to take him down.

"He will," she assured him. "He will. Daddy will do the right thing."

"Not if you're threatened."

"Then he'll recuse himself."

"That's what Luther wants," Tyce said. "He probably has another judge or two in his pocket. But not your daddy."

She glared at his teasing her even while her pulse quickened. As much as it irritated her, it also excited her. If they were kids, it was like he was pulling her pigtails, letting her know he liked her.

Or maybe that was what she preferred to think.

He looked down at her hands on his knees and his body tensed while his topaz eyes darkened with desire. Even if he didn't like her, at least he wanted her.

Like she wanted him…

"You're in danger," he said.

She nodded. She was.

In danger of falling for him…

"I need to stay focused," he said. "I can't get distracted like I was earlier."

"You were distracted?"

"You know that I was," he said. "From dancing with you…" His voice lowered to a deep rumble in his chest. "I couldn't wait to get you back here, to get you back in bed."

Her pulse quickened even more and her lips parted as she struggled to breathe. She wanted that now—to be in bed with him. But then she remembered what had happened because he'd been distracted; he had been shot.

"I'm sorry," she murmured again.

"It's not your fault," he said. "I need to stay focused on my job."

He was her bodyguard. *Only* her bodyguard.

She needed to remember that. Acting like her boyfriend was only his cover, was only an act.

She used her hands on his knees to lever herself to her feet. Then she turned to walk away from him.

But he stood and reached out. Catching her wrist, he whirled her around to face him. "Oh, hell," he muttered before he lowered his mouth to hers.

He kissed her hungrily—like he had earlier. His lips nipped and nibbled at hers, tugging until she parted them. Then he slid his tongue inside where it tangled with hers.

She gasped and panted for breath as passion overwhelmed her. Her legs trembled and she might have stumbled had he not lifted her then.

She swung an arm around his shoulders before remembering his gunshot wound. "Put me down," she said. "You're hurt."

"I'm hurting," he agreed. "But it has nothing to do with my shoulder and everything to do with you." He carried her from the living room down the short hall to her bedroom. He pushed open the door with that wounded shoulder but didn't so much as flinch. "It is your fault that I can't focus," he said as he carried her to the bed.

She didn't apologize again. She just pulled him down onto the bed with her. The sheets were still tangled from their earlier tryst. They still smelled like their passion.

That passion was even hotter now, more overwhelming. Bella wanted him even more at this moment than she had before. Maybe because she'd thought she'd lost him. For those few horrifying minutes on the sidewalk, she'd thought he was dead.

She clutched at him now, kissing him deeply. And as she kissed him, she pushed his tuxedo jacket from his shoulders and moved her fingers to the buttons of his blood-stained shirt. She needed that off him. She needed everything off him.

But before she could undress him, he pulled away from her. And he finished the job himself—until he wore nothing but the bandage on his shoulder. She stared at it as that horrific thought rushed through her mind again—that he might have died—that he still could die while protecting her.

"Bella," he murmured. He used his fingers on her chin to tip her face up to his. "It's not really your fault."

No. It was the shooter's fault for pulling that trigger. Still, he'd been protecting her. And he was trying to do that now, trying to assuage her guilt to protect her feelings.

But it was too late. She'd already fallen for him.

She quickly stripped off her clothes, needing her skin against his. Needing nothing between them…

He kissed her and touched her like he had earlier, driving her out of her mind with desire. Building that tension inside her to the breaking point. She'd never felt passion like this—not even the first time with him.

Because now she knew that she loved him.

She couldn't tell him. He would be as horrified at that fact as she was that he'd been shot. But she showed him. She pushed him onto his back and she kissed and touched him everywhere.

He pulled her down, though. And he focused on her. On the tip of each breast before moving his mouth lower. Then he made love to her with his lips and his tongue.

She wriggled against the mattress and cried out as

pleasure rushed through her. He was such an amazing lover.

If only he loved her, too…

At least he wanted her. He rolled on a condom and joined their bodies, sliding inside her—filling her. She'd never felt as complete as she did with him. Then he began to move. And that tension built inside her again, winding tightly with each stroke of his body.

He lowered his head and kissed her, staring into her eyes as he did. The topaz was just about gone, swallowed by his black pupils and his desire. He watched her as she came, screaming his name.

He closed his eyes as his body tensed then shuddered as he joined her. A deep, guttural groan broke from his lips.

He didn't say her name. He didn't say anything, just separated from her and left the room.

She didn't expect him to come back. She figured he was going to the guest room. But, just moments later, strong arms wrapped around her as Tyce pulled her close.

She sighed and relaxed. But she didn't feel completely safe. Not even in his arms.

She didn't feel completely safe because of him, though—because she knew he could hurt her—now that she'd fallen for him.

What the hell was wrong with him? Why hadn't he been able to walk away from her? He never should have touched her again. But even after he had, he should have left her room. Instead he'd crawled back into her bed and pulled her close.

She slept in Tyce's arms, curled against his chest. She was so warm. So soft.

So damn beautiful.

And he wasn't strong enough to resist her—to resist the pull of the attraction between them. But attraction was all it was.

They could never have anything else. They had nothing in common. Even though they'd both lost their moms, she'd lost a loving mother. From all accounts, an almost virtual saint.

And his mother?

She had been no saint. And no great loss to him. He hadn't suffered any for not having her in his life. In fact, he'd probably had a better life because she'd left him.

But that life was a far cry from Bella Holmes's privileged upbringing. Maybe he needed to show her that— needed to show her how different their lives were, so that she knew he would never fit into hers as anything other than her bodyguard.

"Thank you for coming to my chambers," Judge Holmes told the man sitting across from him.

Parker Payne nodded. "No problem, Your Honor. I'm sure you're concerned about your daughter. I put an extra detail on her."

"They should have come back to my estate," the judge said. Maybe he would have been able to sleep then—with Bella under his roof. He hadn't slept soundly since receiving that first threat, since knowing someone was watching her, waiting to hurt her. He always awoke from a nightmare of losing her, like he'd lost her mother.

"Your daughter refused," Parker reminded him.

Bradford suspected it was because she hadn't wanted to put him in danger. But he wasn't the only man she'd been concerned about last night. She'd obviously been shaken over her bodyguard getting shot.

And that worried Bradford nearly as much as her physical safety worried him.

"I'm not sure that Tyce Jackson is the right man to protect her," he said.

"Why not?" Parker asked. "Nothing's happened to her. She's safe."

Maybe physically but emotionally... He was worried she was beginning to fall for her bodyguard. Maybe she'd gotten all mixed-up with his pretending to be her boyfriend to protect her and now she was looking at him like he was her hero.

Hell, maybe Bradford was just jealous. He'd been her hero all her life. Now he was the one putting her in danger, though, and Tyce Jackson was protecting her.

"Tyce is one of the best bodyguards on my team," Parker assured him. "He already took a bullet for her to protect her. He won't hesitate to do that again."

"The trial's starting soon," Bradford said. "He may be put to the test."

"Tyce wouldn't hesitate to give up his life for hers," Parker assured him.

But it was no assurance to Bradford.

He'd seen how upset his daughter had been over her bodyguard getting shot. What would it do to her if he died? Would she be as devastated as she'd been when she'd lost her mother? As Bradford had been when he'd lost his wife?

He was beginning to worry that she would be. He

was beginning to worry that his daughter had fallen for her bodyguard, and with Tyce's dangerous career, that was nearly as big a threat as Luther Mills was.

Chapter 13

Bella shuddered as she stared out the passenger window of the SUV. Graphic graffiti covered the storefronts, most of which were boarded up.

"Are we checking another pawn shop?" she asked. She doubted even her robber would have risked coming to this neighborhood, though.

Tyce shook his head.

"Then where are we going?" After the shooting the night before, she wouldn't put it past him to try to put her into one of those safe houses even though she'd told them all that she would not hide.

But she doubted there was anything safe about this neighborhood. No. Tyce was not bringing her here to protect her.

"You seemed curious about me last night," he said.

She had been curious—to know what excited him. And all through the night, as they'd made love, she had discovered what turned him on. Blowing in his ear, kissing the side of his neck and that dimple at the base of his spine...

He'd shuddered then as passion had overwhelmed him. But he'd done the same to her; he had discovered her every erotic secret. So what was left?

But reality.

She figured that was what this was. He was trying to show her that last night had just been a fantasy—that there was a real world out there.

She knew that. But she couldn't have imagined the world would look like this.

"This is where I grew up," he said. "I worked there after school."

He pointed toward a corner store with kids gathered around it. They didn't look as old as teenagers, yet it was apparent they were carrying guns. A couple even raised their weapons as the SUV passed, as if they were going to fire at them just because they were bored. She suspected they might not make it to their teenage years.

"Was it like this when you worked there?" she asked.

"Worse," he said. "The chief has police stationed down here now. Back in my day, the police didn't even dare come down here."

She shivered. How had he survived?

He drove a little farther and turned a corner. This street wasn't as bad as the ones they'd passed. A few houses showed pride in ownership with fresh paint, sparkling windows and neatly trimmed lawns. He stopped in front of one of the houses.

"This is where I grew up," he said. "Grandma and Pops still live here."

Bella narrowed her eyes as she studied his handsome face. She knew he hadn't brought her home to meet his family because he wanted to show her off to them. This was about something else.

He stopped the SUV, shut it off and came around to her side of the vehicle. As she stepped out, she heard the blast of gunfire not very far away. Dogs barked and snarled from behind nearby fences. And closer yet, a baby cried—not a cry of discomfort but something harder, something more poignant.

Hunger. Despair. Was that how he had been when his grandmother had brought him home? Without his mother, had he cried that desperately?

"Are...are they expecting us?" she asked.

He shook his head. "I never know when I have time to visit, so I don't call ahead." He led her through a small gate and up the steps to the front porch of the house. As he knocked on the door, he called out, "It's me, Pops." He glanced down at Bella. "He has a gun, and I want to make sure he doesn't use it on us. He doesn't see as well as he used to."

The knob rattled and the door swung open. "Smartass," a tall black man admonished. "I see just fine!" Then he blinked and rubbed his eyes. "At least I thought I did. But my eyes must be failing me now. I can't believe you finally got a haircut." The older man stepped forward and pulled Tyce into a bear hug. He might have been taller than Tyce had his spine not had a slight stoop to it. His hands patted Tyce's back. They were big like Tyce's, but the knuckles were swollen—probably with arthritis.

This was a man who'd worked hard his entire life. And from the looks of his house and yard, he continued to work hard maintaining it. He pushed Tyce back and focused on her. "Now I can't believe my eyes at all—that my grandson would manage to find someone this beautiful…" He shook his head. "Not possible. Has he kidnapped you? Do you need to use my phone to call for help, miss?"

"Who's the smart-ass now?" Tyce grumbled.

Bella laughed. "Thank you for realizing that," she said. "I didn't know how I was going to slip you the note."

Pops threw back his head and roared with laughter. "She's a quick one! You're going to have to work to keep up with her, Tyson." Then he reached out and pulled her into a hug.

He smelled like tobacco and cinnamon.

The scent of cinnamon wafted from inside the house, too.

"Come in," he said as he half pulled her into the home with him. "Grandma's just about got dinner done." He slid his arm around her to lead her toward the kitchen.

The house was old but spotless. Every surface shone with polish and fresh paint. And it smelled…delicious. Bella's stomach rumbled softly.

"Ma's cooking will do that to you," he said. "You don't know you're hungry until you smell it." He led her into the kitchen, which had painted metal cabinets and old appliances. And, like everything else, they sparkled.

A woman looked up from the stove, her blue eyes widening with wonder. Her pale skin wrinkled as a smile creased her face. Then she saw Tyce walk in behind them and she cried out with surprise and pleasure. "You shaved!" She clasped her hands to his face and held it tightly. "You finally shaved. Isn't he handsome?"

The woman had looked at Bella, who could only nod in agreement. He was…far too handsome for her own good.

"And who is this?" the woman asked her grandson. "Who have you brought for dinner?"

"A client," Tyce said.

His grandmother snorted. "Yeah, right."

Tyce's face flushed. "She is."

"I'm Bella," she introduced herself. "Bella Holmes. It's an honor to meet you."

"I'm assuming you're the reason he finally shaved," the older woman replied, "so the honor's all mine."

"No," Bella said. This was the woman who'd raised Tyce to be the man he was—who'd helped him navigate and survive in what was probably the most dangerous part of River City. "It's mine."

And the woman, whom Bella had just met, pulled her into a tight embrace—as if she somehow knew that Bella needed it. As if she knew how badly she missed her mother and that she needed a maternal presence in her life again.

Bella understood why Tyce had brought her here— to scare her away from his life. But she was going to get far more out of this experience, out of these people, than he'd realized. And not just information about him.

* * *

Tyce had made one hell of a mistake. He'd thought bringing her here—to where he'd grown up—would show Bella that they came from two, and much too different, worlds. But while Bella had noticed the bad neighborhood, she didn't seem at all aware of the worn linoleum, old appliances, and the hardwood floors that had been sanded so many times that they were thin and cracking beneath their feet. Or if she was aware, she didn't give a damn.

That made him like her even more, and he already liked her too much. She was not the princess he'd told her she was.

But now that term had become an endearment to him in its irony. When he'd started calling her "Princess," he'd thought she was spoiled and entitled. But now that he'd gotten to know her, he knew how hardworking she was and how much she cared about everybody, but most especially her father.

"Do you look at all your clients like that?" Grandma asked as she slipped her hand beneath his chin. She acted like she was closing his mouth for him.

Maybe it had been hanging open. Maybe he had been panting after Bella. She'd certainly had him panting last night. He'd forgotten all about his shoulder wound. He'd forgotten his own damn name a few times. And he had nearly blacked out again, but not from pain. From ecstasy.

She had made him feel so much pleasure.

And also so much fear.

He couldn't get used to nights like last night. He

couldn't get used to something that wasn't going to last. And there was no way that they would.

He dragged his gaze away from her and focused on his grandmother, taking a heavy platter of steaming pot roast from her hands to carry to the table. He didn't see his grandparents as much as he should. When he'd been deep undercover, he hadn't been home for weeks—even months—at a time, so he'd gotten out of the habit.

Bella hadn't. No matter how busy she was with all her charities and events, she always made time for her father, as well. Tyce needed to do that with his folks. They were getting older. He'd felt it in his grandfather's hug. Pops hadn't lifted him off the ground like he used to. And he saw it in the lines in Grandma's pale skin.

But even though they'd aged, they looked happy.

Grandma patted his cheek. "I love this smooth skin," she murmured. "I love seeing your handsome face. Reminds me of your boot camp photo."

"Boot camp?" Bella asked.

"Tyson is a Marine," Pops said proudly. He had been one, too.

"Was a Marine," Tyce said. Unlike Pops, Tyce had only done one tour. He'd seen more action as a vice cop than he had overseas.

"Once a Marine always a Marine," Pops said. He drew himself away from the cabinets where he'd been leaning. His stooped back straightened with pride and he saluted. "Semper Fi."

Tyce saluted him right back. "Semper Fi."

Grandma chuckled. "These two soldiers…"

"Says the drill sergeant," Pops teased with a big grin

at the woman he still called his bride nearly fifty years after their marriage.

Bella gazed at them with fondness already, and something almost wistful and envious. "My parents were a lot like you two," she murmured.

"Were?" Grandma asked, glancing up from the potatoes she'd just mashed at the stove. "Not anymore? Did they get divorced?"

"No," Bella said and sadness darkened her beautiful green eyes. "My mother passed away suddenly from a brain aneurysm."

Grandma reached for her hand and squeezed it tightly in her own. "I'm sorry, sweet girl."

Bella nodded. "It was nearly five years ago now."

"But it still hurts," Grandma said knowingly.

Did his grandmother still miss his mother? Tyce wondered. They never talked about her. Tyce never mentioned her because he didn't want to hurt them. He knew they blamed themselves for her going wild in her teens, but they'd done their best. And for Tyce, their best had been damn good.

If not for them, he might have wound up like someone else…someone with whom he also shared some blood.

He suppressed a shudder and reached for the bowl of potatoes, but Bella already had it. Pops took his seat at one end of the table while Grandma took hers at the other. He and Bella sat across from each other. The table was old and the metal was worn.

He had tried, when he'd been in the Marines, to give his grandparents money. But they'd been offended and had refused. So just as he didn't mention his mother for fear of hurting them, he didn't mention money, either—no matter how badly he wanted to help them.

Bella squeezed his grandmother's hand, offering her comfort now. "I'm sorry," she said. "I can't imagine having a child and not knowing where she is…"

Tyce flinched as his grandmother turned to him in surprise.

"You told her?" But she didn't sound upset. Instead, she seemed happy about it.

"I'm sorry," Bella said again. "I shouldn't have brought her up."

"Too many people tiptoeing around stuff like that," Pops said, "for too damn many years."

Tyce gasped. He hadn't known that was how they felt.

Bella reached for his grandfather's arthritic hand and gently patted it. "People tiptoe around each other because they care too much to risk hurting them."

Grandma sniffled. "You are a special one, aren't you? I knew that's what it would take…" She glanced at Tyce.

He tensed. What the hell did his grandmother think? That he had brought Bella here for his family's approval? Of course she would think that, though, since he hadn't brought a woman home with him before. He'd tried, but none of his old girlfriends had wanted to go past the neighborhood to get to the house.

"She's a client," Tyce said again. "I'm her bodyguard. Just her bodyguard."

Bella flinched now.

And he regretted hurting her feelings. But it was better that she accept the truth now before she started having feelings for him. Not that that would actually happen…

Sure, she was taking the time to be sweet to his grandparents, but she wasn't really comfortable here. And since bringing her, neither was he.

"Why do you need a bodyguard?" his grandmother asked Bella. "I can't imagine anyone wanting to hurt you." She shot Tyce a look full of recrimination. His grandmother never missed anything.

"My father is a judge—"

"Judge Holmes," Tyce interjected.

Pops nodded in approval. "He's a good man."

"Yes," Bella agreed with a smile. "He's the judge for the upcoming trial of a drug dealer. And that drug dealer is threatening him."

"Luther Mills," Grandma murmured. It wasn't a question. She knew.

Tyce nodded anyway.

"Ask *him* where your mama is," she said. "He'd probably know."

"Do you want me to?" Tyce asked.

"Do you want to find her?" Grandma asked.

He opened his mouth to say no, but then he stopped. "I never thought about it before."

Yet knowing how much Bella missed her mother had him wondering if he'd missed anything…

But if his mother had gotten cleaned up, wouldn't she have come home?

"Think about it," Grandma urged him. "And then figure out what you need to do for you."

He glanced at Bella then. *She* was what he needed to do for him. She was what he wanted. Too much.

"I will," he promised his grandmother.

She gave him a knowing smile. She never missed a thing.

"We'd better go now," he told Bella. He wanted her out of this neighborhood before dark, especially since he'd temporarily ditched his bodyguard backups. They would have drawn more attention than offering any protection. He'd left a message for Parker letting him know that they were fine without reinforcements.

"After I help with the dishes," Bella said. And even when he and his grandparents protested, she helped anyway—plunging her perfectly manicured hands into the sink full of hot, soapy water. She didn't agree to leave until every plate was rinsed and dried.

And even then she hesitated, hugging both his grandparents twice before heading for the door. His grandmother caught him in a tight hug. And his grandfather patted his back and said, "She's special, Tyson. Like your grandmother. The first time I saw her, I knew to never let her get away."

Tyce just shook his head and turned toward the door where Bella waited for him. He hurried out to check outside before guiding her to the SUV. As he opened the passenger door for her, she assured him, "Don't worry about what I overheard. I know your grandfather misunderstood your reason for bringing me here. You're not making sure I don't get away," she said. "You're trying to scare me into running away."

Scare her?

He hadn't wanted to scare her. He'd only wanted to make it clear to her that they had no future. Nothing in common. But as he pulled away from the curb, he saw his grandparents standing in the doorway. And he realized that those two people, who loved each other so fiercely, had also had absolutely nothing in common when they'd met. They'd told him often how hard it had been for them when they'd started out together. The world had been very different then.

And their worlds had been very different. But then they'd built one together. His grandparents loved each other, though. They'd loved each other from the first moment they'd met.

He would not be building a life with Bella Holmes. He just had to do his job, so that she had a life to live.

They had to die. Now. Both of them.

Luther Mills hadn't given the order, but the spy didn't care. Luther Mills was in jail. He wouldn't be able to do something about it.

Nobody would.

That was why Tyce Jackson had to die. Now. Before he figured out who had fired those shots the night before. The gun had been too risky. What if someone had seen the shooter?

What if Tyce Jackson had? But he hadn't been looking across the street. He'd been rushing toward Bella, desperate to save the damsel in distress.

This time he wouldn't just get a bullet in his shoulder for his efforts to save her. This time he would die. They both would. This plan was so much better than a gun. There was no way either of them would survive the trap that had been set for them.

Chapter 14

The sun had set a while ago, so Bella couldn't see much beyond the darkened glass of the passenger's window. But she knew that Tyce was not heading back to her place. There would have been more lights given her apartment was close to downtown and all the venues she used for the charities she chaired.

"Where are you taking me now?" she asked. "Jail? Going to show me where we might wind up if we're together?"

"Jail isn't out here," he said. "I wouldn't take you anywhere near that and Luther Mills."

"Will you talk to him?" She wondered. "Will you ask him about your mother?"

Tyce snorted. "I doubt he knows, either. Luther isn't much older than I am."

She whistled. "And he's already the biggest drug dealer in the state?"

"Impressed?" Tyce asked.

Afraid. But she wasn't about to admit to her fear when Tyce had been working so hard to scare her. She wasn't going to give him the satisfaction of knowing he'd succeeded.

"Bored," she said, trying to act like the princess he accused her of being.

"My grandparents bored you?"

"Not at all," she said. "You're boring me. You're a broken record trying to keep me away from you." Maybe he was afraid, too. But she was too angry to feel any sympathy for him right now. He'd ruined what would have been a lovely dinner with the amazing couple who'd raised him.

"That's not why I brought you here," he said.

She just realized he'd stopped the SUV and had put it in Park.

"Where are we?"

He didn't answer her. Instead he opened his door and stepped out. The headlights had already gone out and it was dark outside. She couldn't see anything. Not where they were or where he'd gone.

She reached for her door with a trembling hand. She hadn't decided whether to open it or lock it when it opened and Tyce held out a hand to her.

She ignored it. But she was too curious to stay inside the SUV. She wanted to see where he'd taken her now. But it was so hard to see anything. She stumbled on an uneven surface and he caught her arm, steadying her. Then he guided her toward a darker structure.

Once they got closer, he moved her around it and she could see water shimmering behind it.

"You brought me to a lake?"

It couldn't have been more removed from where they'd been—from the neighborhood with all its graffiti-covered buildings and gangs loitering outside them.

"This is where I live," Tyce remarked.

"You have a lake house?"

"Didn't think I could afford one, Princess?" he asked.

There was a bitterness to his tone that made her think she'd offended him. "I didn't say that. You're the one who keeps trying to convince me that we have nothing in common. So why would you bring me here?"

"The house is not much," he said. Keys jangled in the darkness and a door creaked open.

She sighed. "That's why. Are there rats and bats inside?"

He chuckled. "No. At least, I don't think so." A light flipped on that illuminated both the deck on which they stood and the interior of the tiny cabin.

It wasn't much in that it wasn't very big. She could see most of it through the windows that looked onto the deck. There was a tiny kitchen and sitting area, and a bed in one corner. Like his grandparents' place, it looked neat and clean.

"Do you live here?" she asked.

He nodded. "Yeah. I think pretty much all of us who worked vice have some kind of getaway place from the city."

"It's your vice?" she teased.

He chuckled again. "Yeah, but I live in mine year-round."

He held open the door for her to step inside and she saw the fireplace with its wide stone hearth. That would easily heat the entire place in the winter.

"Is there a bathroom?" she asked as she looked around the small area with its knotty pine walls.

He pointed to a door near the entrance, one she had assumed was for a closet. When he opened it, she saw that the bathroom was much smaller than her closets and still included a pedestal sink and narrow stand-up shower.

"Do you fit in there?" she asked.

He shrugged. "I manage. But it's not at all like your spa bathroom."

"I'm not going to apologize for having nice things," she said. But she heard the defensiveness in her voice. Sometimes she did feel guilty because she'd done nothing to earn her incredible good fortune. That was why she worked so hard to give back to her community, to the people and causes that needed help the most.

"I'm not asking you to apologize," he said. "I'm just showing you how different our lives are."

"You don't have to keep pounding it into my head that we don't belong together," she told him. "I get it. You are not interested in me."

"I wished that were true," he said. His hands closed over her shoulders and he spun her around to face him. Then he lowered his head and kissed her. His lips slid over hers—back and forth—before he deepened the kiss. A groan rumbled in his throat.

Bella lifted her hands, intending to push him away. But passion ignited and she found herself clasping him to her instead. Heat rushed through her and she pulled at his clothes, stripping them off him.

He undressed her just as quickly before he lifted her in his arms. He didn't carry her to the bed, though. He made love to her standing there, in the middle of the cabin. He slid her up to guide his latex-covered erection inside her.

She clung to him as ripples of pleasure ebbed through her. She came so quickly. But he took his time, building the tension inside her again and again.

She didn't know how he kept standing when her legs were trembling—her entire body shaking as another orgasm overwhelmed her. She screamed his name.

He thrust, and his body tensed before shuddering as he found his release, too. Then he carried her into the bathroom and pulled aside the shower door. "Let's see if we can both fit."

It was tight, but they managed—because they stayed skin-to-skin—as close as if they were still making love. And then they made love again.

At least Bella did. She loved him. Even though she understood what he meant about how different they were, she loved him. Maybe because they were so different, she loved him. But she knew he didn't feel the same way. While he desired her, he didn't return her love.

Tyce had brought Bella home with him to show her how minimally he lived—how small and basic his place was. Few people even knew where the cabin was; that was why he hadn't called his backup into service again. If Jocelyn Gerber's claim about a leak in the Payne Protection Agency proved true, it would be on one of the backup teams from Parker's brothers. It wouldn't be on Parker's team, which was where those few people who knew about this place worked. Now that Tyce had Bella here, he didn't want her to leave. She looked good lying in his bed, the morning sunshine casting a golden glow on her bare skin.

She stretched and reached out, patting the bed beside her as if she was looking for him. But he stood at the stove, flipping over the bacon he'd taken from the freezer. "Hungry?" he asked.

She nodded.

He was hungry, too, but not for food. How could he want her again? Still?

They'd made love several times the night before—unable to get enough of each other. When she pulled back the sheets to crawl out of bed, he shut off the stove. Then he jerked off his shirt and dropped his jeans and joined her again.

She giggled and laughed. But she seemed just as hungry as he was—for more of the pleasure they gave each other. She was the one who pushed him onto his back and took over, riding him until she screamed his name. He clutched her hips in his hands and thrust again and again until her name slipped through his lips with a shout of ecstasy.

When he returned from cleaning up in the bathroom, she was at the stove. His lips twitched with a smile. "Can you cook?"

"Yes," she said. "Mom taught me." Her smile dimmed slightly.

When he'd first met her, Tyce had thought she had

everything she wanted—the money, the apartment, the clothes and jewelry. But now he knew that she would never have the one thing she wanted most: her mother.

"You miss her."

It wasn't a question, but she nodded.

"You can't bring her back, you know…"

Her brow furrowed as she looked at him. "What do you mean? I'm not trying to bring her back."

"You're trying to be her," he said. "With all her causes and charities."

Her face flushed and he didn't think it was from the heat of the stove. "That's not what I'm trying to do."

He had his doubts about that. "If that's true, put the parties on hold until after the trial. Stay here."

"What?"

"You would be safe here," he said. But he wasn't sure how safe he would be with her living in his home. He would get too used to it—to having her with him all the time.

She shook her head.

"Why not?" he asked. "Is it not nice enough for you?"

"That's not it, and you know it," she said with a weary sigh. "I have work to do."

"Parties," he said disparagingly as he felt a rush of resentment. He was already so into her, he was jealous that she'd rather attend her parties than spend time alone with him. He needed to end this assignment before he got in any deeper than he already was.

"You know that's not what it's about for me."

"You don't like dressing up and being the center of attention?"

Her face flushed some more and she glared at him.

"That's not…" Then she blinked as if fighting to clear her eyes. She lifted her chin, looking as regal as a real princess, and stared down her nose at him. "That's not any of your damn business. You're supposed to protect me. If you can only do that here, then I'll have to have another bodyguard."

He felt that sickening rush of jealousy again. And he hated it. He hated how stupid she made him feel. "That would probably be for the best," he agreed.

She flinched. But she nodded in agreement.

Even though he'd been trying to prove to her how little they had in common, he wanted her to protest, to tell him she needed him—unlike those other women who'd wanted nothing more than sex from him. But she said nothing. She just shut off the stove and walked toward the door.

She moved slowly, though, as if waiting for him to stop her, but he didn't. This really was for the best…

Before either of them got hurt.

"What the hell do you mean?" Luther bellowed into the cell phone. "You've got one damn job—to keep eyes on her. Where the hell is she?"

"I don't know," his spy replied.

"No!" he shouted, and a guard glanced into his cell. He'd been paying the man, so he just kept walking past, like he hadn't seen or heard anything.

Apparently neither had his damn informant.

"She can't have just disappeared!" Luther shouted.

But he was afraid that she could have. The eyewitness and the evidence tech had both disappeared—into some safe house none of his sources knew about.

That could not have happened this time. He needed the judge's daughter, especially since those other two had disappeared.

"Bella Holmes is too social to stay hidden for long," the spy assured him. "She has too much of a need to be the center of attention."

She was the center of Luther's damn attention right now. And she must have been the center of Tyce's, too.

Where had he taken her?

"She has an event this evening," the spy said. "She'll need to go back to her apartment for her dress."

Luther heard something in the voice that he'd not heard before—something that sounded like excitement or anticipation.

"What did you do?" he asked warily.

"What do you mean?"

"You can hardly wait for her to go back to her place," he said. Then his stomach dropped. "Oh, you did something stupid…" Something that was going to get the damn idiot killed for certain. Luther never should have trusted someone so unhinged.

"Not stupid at all," the spy maintained. "Something long overdue."

"I don't want her dead," Luther said. Bella Holmes would be of no use to him then. He wouldn't be able to use her to manipulate her father if she was already gone. And he couldn't count on the judge recusing himself to deal with his grief. After his wife died, he'd thrown himself even more into his work.

"Maybe it'll just get the bodyguard," the spy said, but the excitement was bubbling over now, as if it was too great to even be contained.

"It?"

"My trap." The reply was followed with a self-satisfied chuckle.

"You have to get rid of it," Luther ordered. "Now. Before anyone gets hurt." He wasn't a big fan of Tyce Jackson's, but if someone took out Tyce, Luther wanted that someone to be him—not some nutjob.

"Too late." The nutjob nearly chirped with anticipation. "They're here."

Luther cursed. "Stop them! Stop it from happening!" he demanded.

The spy chuckled. "I hope you have access to the news. You're going to want to see this big blast!"

The cell clicked dead in Luther's ear. That damn spy was going to be dead, too, if Luther's plan was ruined. If the judge's daughter died...

Chapter 15

At first she'd been hurt, but now Bella was furious with Tyce. How the hell did he not know her at all? He'd been following her around for a couple of weeks. Didn't he understand that what she did wasn't for attention? Or to bring her mother back? But to honor her memory…

How could he think so little of her but yet want her as much as he'd seemed to want her the past couple of nights? He must have just been using her for sex, or worse, maybe he wanted money from her. She hated him.

"I want to call Parker," she demanded like the princess he accused her of being. "Let me use your phone."

She hadn't known they weren't coming back to her place last night, so she hadn't brought her charger with her. Her cell was dead.

"We're almost to your apartment," he pointed out. He'd pulled into the parking lot across the street from the tall Chicago brick building.

But she didn't want to wait another second to make that call. To get rid of Tyce Jackson…

"Is your phone dead, too?" she asked.

He shut off the ignition. "You can wait two seconds to make your damn call."

"I thought you agreed this was for the best," she said. And she felt a flicker of hope. Maybe he'd changed his mind. Maybe he didn't want to be relieved of his bodyguard duties.

"It is," he said, dashing her hope. "But until Parker sends someone else over, it's my job to protect you. So we're going up to your apartment before you make your call."

She winced. He just didn't want to be a sitting duck in a parked vehicle. "Fine," she said and reached for her door handle.

But he moved quickly, getting out and coming around to the passenger's side before she fully opened the door. He kept his body between hers and the street, in case anyone tried shooting at them again.

But no one was around.

Or were they?

A strange chill chased down her spine. Maybe that person, the one who'd taken those photographs her father had received, was out there, taking more. Or maybe she was just apprehensive over losing Tyce as her bodyguard.

She didn't really want anyone else protecting her. And she'd never wanted anyone else the way she wanted

Tyce. But he was right. They were too different. He was never going to understand and respect her life like she did his.

She was impressed that he'd been a Marine, that he'd served his country, and that as a vice cop, he'd risked his life to get drugs off the street. And, that as a bodyguard, he'd risked his life for her, as well. He'd taken a bullet for her.

Because of his dangerous life, she should want nothing to do with him; she shouldn't have fallen for him at all. But she didn't really want to call Parker Payne. She really didn't want a new bodyguard.

She had no choice, though. Tyce no longer wanted this assignment. And she wasn't going to beg him— to keep protecting her or to keep making love to her.

She had more pride than that. So she lifted her chin and blinked back the tears threatening to pool in her eyes. She would not cry, either.

Not over a man who had so little respect or regard for her. She hastened her pace across the street and rushed into the lobby of her building. It looked more like the lobby of an elegant hotel with all its marble and smoked glass. She forced a bright smile for the security guard and doorman sitting behind the desk near the door before she headed for the elevators. Of course Tyce, playing the bodyguard, dogged her every step.

Fortunately, no one else had been waiting for the elevator, so they didn't have to share the car. They didn't have to talk at all, but Tyce remarked, "You're in one hell of a hurry to get rid of me."

"Ditto," she shortly replied.

"Bella—" He stopped himself as his cell phone vibrated within his pocket. He dragged it out and stared at the screen, brow furrowed.

"Aren't you going to answer it?" she asked. At least his damn phone worked.

"I don't know who it is," he said.

"You should answer it," she said. "Your grandparents might have used someone else's phone."

He sucked in a breath. "I hadn't thought about that…"

"They're getting older." After losing her mom so suddenly, she worried about her dad all the time. But Tyce hadn't ever lost anyone that he'd missed having in his life, so he probably didn't have the same fears she had.

But he did now because he quickly accepted the call. "Tyce Jackson."

His face changed so suddenly, with so many emotions chasing across it, that Bella couldn't keep up. First, it looked like revulsion then anger then fear…

"What is it?" she asked.

He only shook his head in reply.

The elevator stopped and the doors opened. She stepped out before he could do his usual thing of jumping out in front of her.

He cursed. She ignored him, like he'd ignored her inquiry about his call, and hurried down the hall toward her apartment door. Before she could reach for the key above the doorframe, he wound his arms around her and jerked her back against his body. Her feet dangled above the floor.

"What the hell are you doing?" she asked.

"We need to get out of here," Tyce said. "Back to the lobby. And we should clear the building."

She remembered that the last emotion to cross his

face had been fear. Whatever his caller had said had scared him.

"What's going on?" she asked.

"I really don't know," he said as he drew in a shaky breath. "But I think I believe him."

"Who? What the hell's going on?"

Again he didn't answer her, he just carried her back to the elevator. His finger shook when he pressed the button for the lobby. He was definitely scared and now she felt the fear, too, coursing through her.

"Tyce?"

He'd pulled out his phone again. "I'm going to call Parker for the backup I damn well shouldn't have ditched last night. You need to stay in the lobby with the security guard."

"Where are you going?" Was he already quitting as her protection?

The elevator dinged as the doors opened to the lobby. The security guard and doorman looked quizzically at them. "You need to clear the building," he told them. He pointed at the doorman. "Use an intercom, pull the fire alarms—whatever you need to do, you need to get everyone out. Now."

"Tyce—"

But he kept ignoring her. He pointed at the security guard. "This might be a trap to get to her. So I need you to be extra vigilant and make sure nobody gets anywhere near her. But stay close to the lobby exit—in case you need to get out fast."

"What the hell's going on?" Bella shouted the question.

"There's a bomb in your apartment," he said.

The doorman gasped. "Bomb?"

Tyce nodded. "That's what I've been told. I'm going to check to see if it's true. But let's operate under the assumption that it is and take these necessary precautions."

The doorman nodded. "Clear the building…" He pulled an alarm that echoed from the speakers in the lobby. "Should I call the police?"

Tyce held up his phone. "I'm calling for backup."

For Payne Protection backup. But he needed a bomb squad.

Bella clutched at his arm. "You can't go up there."

"It might not be true," he said. "It might only be a trap."

He didn't look as if he believed it. There was dread on his face as he stared down at her. "I need you to stay here with the guard. Don't leave with anyone but Parker." The cell was pressed to his ear and she heard a voice emanating from it. It must have been Parker's.

Tyce tugged his arm free of her grasp and headed for the stairwell. With the alarm blaring, the elevators wouldn't work anymore. If there was a bomb, Tyce would have no quick escape from it. No way of surviving…

Those tears she'd fought won now, pooling in her eyes before brimming over and sliding down her face. No. She didn't want to lose Tyce.

Tyce wished he'd had the doorman wait before pulling that alarm. Because now he had to fight his way up the stairwell through a crowd of people coming down. It could have been worse had it not been a workday; there would have been more residents home who needed to evacuate.

Hopefully no one really needed to evacuate, though. Hopefully there was no bomb. But if there was no bomb, then he'd fallen for a real trap—the one where someone obviously tried to grab Bella.

Parker had assured him that he was close, though. He'd already been in his SUV when Tyce had called. It shouldn't take him long to get there. Like Bella, he'd wanted Tyce to wait before checking the bomb situation.

Tyce had had some training in the Marines, though. He knew what to look for and how to disarm some improvised explosive devices. If that was what this was...

The warning had been vague, but it was the only thing that made sense. The only way someone could kill both him and Bella for certain the minute they walked in the door. Door...

He shuddered as he thought of how close she'd come to opening it. He could have lost her right then.

He couldn't risk trying to open the door, either. So when he got to her floor, he opened the window in the stairwell and stepped out onto the fire escape. It was so close to her balcony that he was able to easily make the leap. His presence was certain to set off an alarm inside, but that wasn't a bad thing.

Damn it!

That was right. There was an alarm. Nobody could get inside without setting it off. No one could have set a trap in the apartment.

He had been tricked.

Damn him!

Why had Tyce been tempted to believe his caller for even a moment? Sure, he'd sounded sincere. He'd sounded concerned. And that should have been his first clue. Why would a man who wanted him dead tip him off to a trap?

He had to be laughing at Tyce now—as he ordered his crew to move in on Bella. The lone security guard and the pudgy doorman would prove no protection for her. He could only hope Parker was as close as he'd claimed—that he got there fast.

Tyce turned from the fire escape to reach for the stairwell window again, and he caught sight of a shadow moving around her apartment. Someone was inside…

Maybe the call hadn't been a trick after all. Tyce moved back toward the balcony windows. He needed to get one open, needed to get in there before the intruder escaped and headed down to find Bella in the lobby. He couldn't see who it was, but since the person had gotten inside without setting off the alarm, it had to be someone she knew.

Someone she must have trusted with a key and the code. She was entirely too trusting, though.

The windows were locked, so Tyce's only recourse was to break the glass. He drew his weapon and started to swing the handle toward the pane. Before he even connected, the glass shattered and the force of the blast knocked him back. He only hoped that he landed on the balcony and not on the street so far below.

That was his last conscious thought…

Parker had been close—but not close enough. He'd just pulled up to Bella Holmes's apartment building when glass and debris rained down on the SUV. Cursing, he left the vehicle in Park in the middle of the street and ran toward the lobby.

Other people were running out of the glass doors, screaming and crying in panic and nearly knocking him down. But he forged through them and got inside the building. Some man was holding on to Bella, trying to push her toward the exit. But she wriggled, fighting to break free of his grasp.

Maybe Tyce had been right and the bomb or whatever had exploded was just a diversion.

Parker drew his gun and pointed it at the man. "Let her go!"

The guy stepped back with his hands in the air. "I was just doing what *he* told me to do."

"Luther?"

Had they finally found someone who would admit that Luther was giving the orders? None of the drug dealer's crew apprehended during the attempts on the lives of the eyewitness or the evidence tech had been willing or brave enough to testify against Mills. Not even to lighten their own prison sentence.

The guy shrugged. "I don't know his name."

Parker cursed.

"Tyce," Bella said. "Tyce told him to keep me down here. But Tyce is up there!" She pointed toward the high ceiling. "The explosion must have come from my apartment. He was going to check it out."

Parker cursed harder. He'd told the damn fool to wait for him—to wait for backup. But of course Tyce hadn't listened.

"It sounded bad," Bella murmured, her voice shaking like her slender frame. "It was so loud."

Alarms were wailing out of the lobby speakers. But

that wasn't all that was roiling out. Smoke billowed, as well. The damn building was on fire.

"We need to get you out of here," Parker said as he reached for her.

She shook her head. "Not without Tyce. We need to check on Tyce." Tears streamed down her face and she pushed against his shoulders, trying to shove him back.

"It's too dangerous," he said. "We need to get you out of here." That was what Tyce would want him to do—to make sure she stayed safe.

"You think it's too late," she accused him. "You think he's dead."

If Tyce had been inside the apartment when the bomb had gone off, Parker wasn't certain his friend could have survived the blast.

Had he lost him?

Chapter 16

Had she lost him?

Was Tyce dead?

It was clear that even his boss thought so. He'd forced her to exit the lobby with him. They were standing on the sidewalk when the firefighters arrived.

"There's at least one person inside," Parker told the man who appeared to be in charge. "Maybe more."

"What the hell happened?" the captain asked as he tipped back his smoke-stained yellow fire helmet and looked up, assessing the building.

"We suspect a bomb," Parker replied.

The older man turned from the building now and studied Parker's face, maybe assessing him as he had the building. "I know you. It wasn't so long ago that a car bomb nearly took you out."

Parker nodded, his face pale. "It took out a couple of our employees instead."

Bella gasped. But she shouldn't have been surprised. Tyce's job was obviously a dangerous one. But he wasn't the one Luther Mills wanted dead.

Whoever had set that bomb had set it in her apartment. She was the one it had been meant to kill.

Tyce could not be gone.

"You need to get inside, to look for him," Bella urged the fire captain.

He shook his head. "Can't. We can't go in until the bomb squad gets here and tells us how to proceed."

"The whole building could be destroyed by then," she said. And Tyce along with it.

If he was up there and hurt, he needed help now. Not later.

"Please," she implored the man. "Don't let him die."

"It might already be too late, ma'am," the captain told her. "And I can't risk my guys' lives, too."

He might not be willing to risk his life or his employees', but Bella was willing to risk hers. She wouldn't be able to carry Tyce out of the building, but maybe she would be able to find him and treat him until help arrived. She had to get inside first, though.

She didn't have to wait long to break away from Parker Payne. As soon as another black SUV pulled up, he headed toward it. And she headed toward the building.

The firefighters were busy gathering their equipment. The police were busy pushing back the crowds. So nobody noticed her heading back into the lobby.

Smoke filled it now and then filled her lungs, making her choke and cough as her eyes watered.

The alarm was still blaring. Either that was making her ears ring or they were ringing from the explosion earlier. It had been just moments ago, but it felt like hours. And she hated that Tyce could be injured with no one coming to help him.

She would.

She blinked and cleared her vision enough to see the lit sign for the stairs. But when she pulled open the door, she found the smoke was even thicker in there. With each step she climbed, it got worse.

And harder and harder for her to breathe. She couldn't see at all. And with that ringing in her ears, she couldn't hear, either. So she jumped when she collided with a body. It was warm and solid.

"Tyce?" Hope burgeoned. It had to be Tyce.

But she had no way of knowing. No way of seeing who she'd bumped into in the smoke-filled stairwell.

A chill chased down her spine despite the heat. Maybe it was someone else.

The person who'd set the bomb…

She started to ease back but her foot slipped off the step. She reached out as she began to fall—into the smoke.

Tyce reached out for Bella, catching her just as she started to fall. The move jarred his shoulder, which was already hurting like hell. The same shoulder with the gunshot wound had slammed against the balcony railing when the blast had propelled him back.

Once he'd regained consciousness, he'd rushed into

her apartment to try to find the person he'd glimpsed inside. The place had already been filling with smoke as a fire burned up the walls from the explosion of the gas fireplace. He'd had to search thoroughly to make sure he hadn't missed a body lying on the ground somewhere, but he'd found no one.

Whoever had been inside must have escaped. Or maybe Tyce had only imagined seeing someone. Maybe it had been his own damn reflection in the glass.

While he might have imagined the intruder, he hadn't imagined the explosion. Someone had set a trap, and it had nearly caught him. He'd hoped Bella was safe—that Parker had made it in time. But then, on his way down the stairwell, he'd bumped into a body in the smoke. And he recognized the body, his instinctive reaction to it.

And she instinctively struggled against him. "Let me go!" Her voice sounded raspy and strained already from smoke inhalation.

"It's me!" he shouted so she would understand him over the blaring of the alarm.

He had to get her the hell out of there. Now. So he swung her up into his arms and carried her the rest of the flights down. Once in the lobby, he veered away from the street exit. He wasn't sure who might be out there, waiting for them. Certainly whoever had set the trap.

They would want to know if it had worked. If not for that call warning him, it might have. It could have killed either one of them or both. He didn't want anyone to know they had survived.

Not yet. Not until he knew who the hell he could trust.

He shoved open a door at the back of the building. It opened onto an alley. The air was only slighter clearer here, but it was clear enough that Bella must have been able to see him.

She stopped struggling. Or maybe she'd just worn herself out. "Tyce…" she murmured. Her fingertips slid gently across his cheek.

He flinched. That shattered glass had struck his cheek. Blood trailed down his face and dripped off his chin.

"You're hurt," she said. "You need medical attention."

"I'm fine," he said. A few scratches weren't going to affect him. But a bullet would. He couldn't trust that the shooter wasn't out there somewhere again, waiting to get off some more rounds. "We need to get out of here—get to someplace safe."

"My car is in the parking garage right there." She pointed to the building on the other side of the alley.

He always drove the SUV, but he knew she had her own car. He remembered some society page photograph of her sitting in a shiny red convertible. He shouldered open the door to the parking garage. "Where is it?"

She wriggled in his arms. "Put me down. I can walk." But after speaking, she started coughing. She hadn't been in the stairwell very long but long enough for the smoke to have affected her. She probably needed oxygen.

But she needed her life more.

He let her slip down his body but winced as she steadied herself with a hand against his wounded shoulder.

"You are hurt," she said. "You need to see a doctor."

"I might need to see a coroner if we don't get out of here soon."

Her head jerked in a quick nod and she started across the concrete floor to the back of the parking structure.

Thank God, he hadn't had to climb any stairs. His lungs burned from all the smoke he'd inhaled, and just that short walk strained them, making him cough and sputter. He bent over to catch his breath and when he straightened, he noticed she'd stopped next to a long SUV.

"Where's the red convertible?"

She tilted her head. "What convertible?"

"There was a picture of you—"

She shook her head. "That wasn't mine. The reporter who did that feature on me didn't think the SUV suited my image." She grimaced. "At least, not the image he wanted to paint of me."

As an empty-headed party girl, if Tyce remembered the article well enough. That was where he'd gotten some of his misinformation about her. Now he wondered what else he'd been wrong about.

And who else.

"Do you have the keys?" he asked.

She shook her head. "You've been driving."

"It's okay." It would take some time, but he'd learned some things growing up where and how he had. His grandparents hadn't been able to keep him away from all the bad influences in the neighborhood. He pulled out his switchblade and used it to open the door. The alarm went off, wailing nearly as loudly as the one inside the apartment.

He cursed. Maybe he'd lost his damn touch. It had been a while since he'd hot-wired anything. He pulled off the bottom of the dash and went to work on the wires and fuses.

The alarm went silent and the lights stopped flashing. Then he slid the knife blade into the ignition and turned it, and the engine started.

Bella gasped. "How do you know—"

"You don't want to know," he told her. "Just hop in. We need to get out of here in case someone heard the alarm."

"Who?"

"Anyone. I'm not sure who the hell set that bomb."

"Luther Mills," she said matter-of-factly.

Tyce shook his head.

"Of course it was him," she insisted.

He shook his head again. "No. It wasn't. He's the one who called to warn me about it."

Bella's eyes widened with shock and her face paled even more than it had been. He led her around the SUV and helped her into the passenger seat. Then he jumped into the driver's seat, sliding behind the wheel, and threw the SUV into Reverse.

He had to start backing up and start over from the beginning. He needed to figure out who wanted him and Bella Holmes dead.

Bradford had seen it on the news—the report of an explosion at an affluent apartment building on the west side of River City. And when the building had flashed across the screen, he'd recognized the Chicago brick structure with all the balconies as the building where Bella lived. Or had lived? Had she survived?

"Where is she?" he shouted as he pushed his way through the police barricade to stand beside Parker Payne.

The younger man stared at the building, shaking his head. "I don't know."

Bradford clutched his heart as a sharp pain stabbed it. "What? Was she inside when it happened?"

Parker shook his head. "No. Tyce had brought her down to the lobby. He had the security guard protecting her."

"What happened?" Bradford asked.

"Someone tipped off Tyce about there being a trap in the apartment."

The judge had been given a tip, too—about another kind of trap entirely. "Where is Tyce?"

Parker grimaced. "He was in the apartment when the explosion happened."

"Are you sure?" Bradford asked.

"He had to be," Parker replied. "Or he would have come down before now."

"What about Bella?" Bradford persisted. "What happened to my daughter? Where did she go?"

Parker stared at the building. Maybe he was waiting for Tyce to magically appear. Or Bella?

"Did she go inside?"

"She wanted to look for Tyce," Parker admitted. "I got her out of there once. But I think that, in all the commotion when the firefighters arrived, she might have slipped back inside."

The lobby doors opened and Bradford drew a deep breath, bracing himself. Parker Payne appeared to do the same. But firefighters stepped out, carrying only their gear.

Parker pushed forward, asking, "Did you find anyone? Was anyone inside?"

One of the firefighters pulled off his mask and replied, "No. Thank God. No casualties."

Bradford wasn't so certain about that. Just because the bodies hadn't been found in the building didn't mean no one had died.

"What happened?" Parker asked. "What caused the explosion?"

"Looks like someone left the gas on in the apartment where the fire started. It was probably a gas fireplace. The place filled up—anything could have ignited it."

Parker's brow furrowed with skepticism. He obviously wasn't buying the accident angle any more than Bradford was. "There are two people missing, though," he said. "Where are they?"

"I heard a car alarm go off briefly near the alley," the fireman replied. "I don't know if that has anything to do with your missing people..." He shrugged and headed toward the fire truck.

Parker was shaking his head as if he was not buying that, either. "It doesn't make sense."

"What doesn't make sense is you assigning Tyce Jackson to protect my daughter!" Bradford bellowed as his rage bubbled up inside him. For years he'd held his temper, holding in his anger over the senseless death of his wife. But now he couldn't contain it anymore—not when it came to Bella.

Parker turned to him, his mouth open in shock. "What are you talking about? You know Tyce. He was a damn good cop, and he's a damn good bodyguard. He protected your daughter from a bullet and now from an explosion."

That was all true. Bradford had known Tyce a long time, and he'd always considered him an honest man. But why would he have kept something so important a secret? Honest men didn't hide something this big.

"You don't know," Bradford said. And he wasn't sure if it made him feel better or worse that Parker had no idea who Tyce Jackson really was.

"I don't know what?" Parker asked. "What are you talking about?"

"Luther Mills and Tyce Jackson," Bradford said. He felt that sickening wave of nausea wash over him again like it had when the assistant district attorney had shared what she'd learned from one of Luther's crew members.

She'd been trying to turn the ones the Payne Protection Agency had caught against Luther. Instead, one of them had turned on the Payne Protection Agency. Not that she probably hadn't prodded them; she'd been suspicious of the bodyguards since the first safe house had come under attack. She'd been certain then that someone on Parker's team had to be conspiring with Luther.

"What about them?" Parker asked.

"Tyce Jackson and Luther Mills are brothers," Bradford replied.

That didn't mean they were close, though, or that Tyce was working for him. But if the bodyguard had nothing to hide, why hadn't Tyce just told everyone that he was related to the person threatening Bella and everyone else associated with the trial? Before coming to Bradford, Ms. Gerber had confirmed, via birth records, that it was true.

Bradford couldn't get over that fact or the fact that he'd entrusted his daughter's life to Luther Mills's brother. And now they were nowhere to be found.

Chapter 17

Bella felt like she was on trial, being badgered on the witness stand. She was actually sitting in the passenger seat of her own SUV, which Tyce had parked just outside his cabin. "I don't know what you're asking me."

"It's simple," he replied. "Who has access to your apartment?"

"I don't know." She shrugged. "The janitor? You. Me. My dad has a key."

Tyce shook his head. That obviously wasn't the answer he wanted. That was why she'd asked him to clarify his question.

"What about your assistant?"

"Camille?" Her head had begun to pound, but she didn't know if that was from his questions or from the alarms and the blast. "Yes, Camille has a key."

Tyce tensed. "She does? Why?"

"She picks up my dry cleaning, handles a lot of my personal errands for me…" She sounded defensive again and hated it. But it wasn't like Camille worked for free. Bella paid her well, and she'd wanted the job.

"I thought she was your friend."

"She is," Bella said.

"But she's your employee, too…"

"Isn't Parker Payne your friend and your boss, too?" she asked. She'd thought their relationship had seemed more than professional. It had actually seemed more personal than hers with Camille—even though she tried to be there for the other woman. It was just that they were always so busy with the charities and the events that they didn't have time to just hang out anymore.

Tyce sighed. "Yes, he is." He glanced at his cell and she saw the missed calls from his boss on his phone.

"But you don't trust him?" she asked.

"I don't know who to trust," he admitted.

She could understand after Luther Mills had tipped him off to the bomb. She wanted to ask about that, but first she had to make something clear to Tyce. "I trust Camille. She would never do anything to hurt me."

"What about that druggie ex of yours?"

She gasped. "What?"

"The guy who recognized me from my undercover job," Tyce said. "Does he have a key?"

Heat rushed to her face and she nodded. "Yes, he does. But I've known Michael all my life. He would never hurt me, either."

"You dumped him," Tyce reminded her.

"Because you told me to."

"You would have stayed with him if not for your needing a bodyguard?" he asked, and his big body had gone rigid with tension.

The question stumped her more than the others had. Would she have continued in the limbo in which she and Michael had dated?

It wasn't as though she'd known then that passion the likes of which she had experienced with Tyce even existed. She'd had no idea what had been missing from her friendly arrangement with Michael until she'd fallen for Tyce.

But love was still missing from her relationship with Tyce. At least love from his side.

"I don't know," she answered honestly. It was all she could do when she had no idea what Tyce was looking for...

Oh, she realized he wanted to know who was responsible for the explosion. She just didn't share his belief that it wasn't Luther Mills. The drug dealer must have had some ulterior motive for tipping off Tyce.

Some other reason.

"And both these people—your assistant and your boyfriend—would they be able to figure out the password you used for the security system?"

Bella's face got hotter yet.

"What did you use?" he asked. "Your birthday?"

"My mother's."

He cursed. "Would either of them know when that was?"

She nodded. "But only because they always spend that day with me, making sure I'm okay and not missing her too much. People who care about me like that wouldn't try to hurt me."

"Any other exes?" he asked.

She wondered now why he was asking. For the investigation or for himself?

"I've dated a few more men than Michael," she said. But just a few.

"Your judgment as bad with them as it was with him?"

It had been—because they'd wanted her money, not her. She glared at him, but admitted, "I can't deny that my judgment isn't the greatest when it comes to men. At least, not lately."

He pressed his hand to his heart. "Direct hit, Princess."

"Glad you didn't miss that," she said.

"You're not exactly subtle," he said then reminded her, "But we're not talking about me. I'm not an ex. I'm not really your boyfriend."

Nope. He was her bodyguard and, for a couple of nights, her lover.

"Tell me about these other guys," he prodded.

"None of them had a key or knew where I stashed the one outside the door," she replied.

"Do you stash it on the casing over the door?"

Her face was burning now with embarrassment over how stupid he was making her sound, but because she was honest, she nodded.

"Anyone could find that," he said. "And pretty much anyone who knows you for five minutes knows your passwords would have something to do with your mother. Either when she came into this world or went out of it…"

She flinched. "I'm sorry I'm so predictable."

"Me, too," he said. "It makes it easier for someone to get to you."

She shivered now. Was he right? Had someone close to her betrayed her?

Who could she trust?

Her father.

"I need to call Daddy," she said as a twinge of guilt struck her heart. She'd been so worried about Tyce that she'd forgotten about her father. "He must have found out about the explosion by now." He would be scared for her—like she was scared for her.

Tyce was right. She had trusted too easily and her judgment wasn't always right. What if she'd made a terrible mistake trusting Tyce?

Tyce saw the fear and doubt cross her face and he felt sick. She needed to trust him. Her life might depend on it, because someone out there—someone probably close to her—wanted her dead.

But that person was close to *her*. Not him. He could trust Parker. Like she'd pointed out, Parker was his friend as well as his boss.

When his phone vibrated again with Parker's call, he pushed the accept button on the screen. "Hey, Parker…"

His friend's voice rattled the phone as he shouted, "Where the hell are you? Or should I ask who the hell you are instead?"

"What are you talking about?"

"Luther Mills. Somebody just told the assistant district attorney what he is to you, and she informed the judge." Parker's voice vibrated with fury. "I should not have been the last to know."

"There's nothing to know," Tyce insisted.

"He's your brother!" Parker shouted so loudly that even though he wasn't on speaker, Bella must have heard him.

She gasped and edged closer to the passenger door. Her hand was on the handle, as if she was thinking about jumping out and running.

So while Tyce spoke into the cell phone, he stared at her as he said, "Don't say that. Don't ever say that again."

"It's not true?"

"I don't know," Tyce admitted. "Rumor has it that we could have the same father." But Tyce had never met him. The man had been a drug dealer, but he'd never gotten to the level Luther had; he hadn't lived long enough. Somebody had killed him many years ago.

"You know how I feel about Luther," Tyce reminded Parker and Bella. "I spent years undercover trying to take him down." But Luther had figured out who he was and had kept him from ever getting enough evidence to bring charges against him. He could have had him killed, though. He'd threatened to do it, but he'd never made good on that threat. Was that why he'd warned him today?

No. It must have been because of Bella—because she was of no use to Luther if she was dead. He needed her alive to threaten the judge.

"Because you kept this a secret, the judge isn't happy with you protecting her now," Parker said.

"Judge Holmes knows me, too," Tyce said. "He knows how badly I wanted to take down Luther Mills."

"Like me, he didn't like being blindsided with this information," Parker said.

"ADA Gerber has been out to get dirt on the Payne Protection Agency since the chief hired us. She's obviously trying to prove the leak isn't in her office, so she threw me under the bus." And put doubts in the minds of people who should have known him better.

The judge must have been there because Tyce could hear the rumble of another voice in the background. "He wants to know that she's okay," Parker said, confirming who'd spoken. "That she wasn't hurt when she went back into the burning building."

"She's fine," Tyce said. "I got her the hell out of there—like you should have. But you lost her."

Parker cursed, but Tyce suspected he was cursing himself—not Tyce. "She slipped away from me."

"And she could have gotten killed," Tyce said. "That trap had to be set by someone close to her—someone with access to her place."

The judge's voice rumbled in the background again and Parker told him, "You need to bring her to the Holmes's estate. I'll have someone else take over now."

"You're firing me?" Tyce asked. He'd thought they were friends. Apparently, Parker no longer did. How could they wonder why he'd never told anyone that Luther could be his brother when their reactions were the very reasons why.

"No," Parker said, but he didn't sound particularly convincing. "I'm just removing you from this assignment."

Tyce had already agreed with Bella that he shouldn't be protecting her anymore, but he'd only agreed because he'd been protecting himself. To make himself stop falling for her…

But he suspected it was already too late for that. He cared too much to just walk away from this assignment—to walk away from her. He moved his finger toward the disconnect button.

As if he knew what Tyce was doing, Parker shouted, "We need to talk, too."

Tyce knew that, but there was someone else he needed to talk to first. He clicked the disconnect button.

Parker had been so loud that Bella must not have missed much of the call. She said, "I want to go. I want to see my father."

The judge was about the only one Tyce trusted to keep her safe. He was the only one who loved her like Tyce did. He realized fighting his feelings had been futile. No matter how different their worlds were, he'd fallen for her. Just like his grandfather had fallen for his grandmother—instantly, deeply and irrevocably.

And because of that, he would do anything to protect her—even if he had to give her up.

Over the past few weeks, Luther's visitor's log had gotten interesting. The eyewitness, Rosie Mendez, had come to see him. A couple bodyguards had and, of course, that sexy damn assistant DA had been there.

But as he settled onto the hard chair and picked up the receiver, he stared through the glass in shock and it wasn't just because the guy looked so damn different with his beard shaved and his hair cut.

"You're the first family member who's come to visit me," he told Tyce Jackson.

The other man flinched. "I'm not your family, Luther."

"We share the same father."

Tyce shook his head. "That's just the rumor."

Some women got so desperate for drugs that they slept with their dealer, so Luther wasn't sure how many damn brothers and sisters he had. Hell, he wasn't even sure how many kids of his own he had.

"We don't know that for certain," Tyce maintained.

"I offered to do a DNA test with you," Luther reminded him. When he'd learned Tyce was undercover in his organization, he'd had him brought to him. He'd intended to kill him—until he'd seen him. Luther hadn't needed the test to know that they were related. He could see it in his brother's face—the sharp features of their father. Tyce had only inherited the old man's looks though—not his ruthlessness.

Luther had gotten all that and then some.

"I don't want your DNA," Tyce told him.

Luther chuckled. "That's too bad, because we both know we share it." Too bad it wasn't enough that Luther could have pinned this damn murder on his brother. But with having different mothers, their DNA wouldn't be that close a match. They didn't even look all that much alike, which was a damn shame since, with his hair cut and his beard shaved, Tyce was a good-looking son of a bitch.

"Is that why you warned me about the trap?" Tyce asked. "Brotherly love?"

Luther laughed harder now. That was funny. They both knew it, too.

Tyce's lips curved into a slight smile. "You're not worried about me staying alive. You want the judge's daughter alive and well, so you can use her to intimidate him into ruling how you want him to."

Everybody was too damn aware of his plan. No wonder it hadn't gone off the way Luther had wanted. "I don't know what you're talking about," he said.

"Who's the spy?" Tyce asked. "You must have someone watching her."

"I just happened to overhear something about something." He shrugged. "None of it has anything to do with me."

"Whoever it is nearly blew up your plan," Tyce reminded him. "You can't trust them. So tell me who it is."

Luther shrugged again. "Could have been anyone…"

"You know who it is, and you know you can't trust them to follow your orders," Tyce said, "or you wouldn't have reached out to me."

Luther loved needling the younger man. Too bad they hadn't grown up together. Luther would have enjoyed tormenting him. And maybe his father wouldn't have hurt him and his mother so much if he'd had someone else as an outlet for his drug-induced rages.

"I warned you because you're my brother," Luther said as if he actually cared.

"Stop saying that," Tyce said.

Luther chuckled some more. "Hey, I'm not proud of it, either, man. You're a cop."

"Was. But because I was, you're not concerned about my life," Tyce said. "That's not why you warned me.

You don't want Bella Holmes dead. She's of no use to you if she is. So you need to tell me who's after her. Then I can make sure she stays alive."

Luther was tempted to tell him. As angry as Tyce seemed, it was clear he'd take care of that little problem of Luther's. Then he wouldn't have to worry about the damn fool himself. He'd already lost so many of his crew—because of the Payne Protection Agency. They were either in jail—with him—awaiting their trials… or they were dead.

Luther wanted this person dead. But he wasn't sure that Tyce would carry out that order for him. He hadn't grown up like Luther had. He wasn't as ruthless.

But there was something different about him now. Something Luther hadn't noticed before. Then it hit him what it was—it was the same thing he'd seen on the face of the eyewitness when Rosie Mendez had tried negotiating with him to save her bodyguard's life.

Love.

Tyce Jackson was in love.

"You fell for her," Luther said. "You fell for the judge's daughter." Then he started laughing again. When he finally stopped, he noticed Tyce had left before he could give him the name of the spy.

He had no doubt now, that despite once being a cop, Tyce would get rid of the person who'd tried killing the woman he loved. And a little frisson of fear chased down his spine. Eventually, Tyce would come after him again then.

Because if the judge didn't rule how he wanted, Luther was going to have to kill the woman his brother loved.

Chapter 18

A week had passed since the fire in her apartment. Or explosion. Or accident.

But if it had been an accident, how had Luther Mills known to call Tyce and warn him?

None of it made sense—least of all how much she missed him. Sure, she loved him. But he obviously hadn't felt the same about her. He'd dropped her at her father's and walked away that day without an argument. He hadn't even spoken to his boss who'd chased him onto the driveway.

Tyce hadn't been able to wait to get away from her. And he had stayed away for the entire week, leaving Bella feeling sick and empty inside. She ached for missing him.

"Are you okay?" Camille asked.

Bella glanced up from her father's desk to focus on her friend. And she was her friend. Her dark eyes were warm with concern. There was no way she would have done anything to hurt Bella.

Emotion rushed up on Bella, making her eyes sting as tears threatened to fill them. She couldn't speak. She knew her voice would crack. So she just shook her head.

"Of course you're not okay," Camille answered for her. "Your apartment was damaged to the point that it's uninhabitable, and so much of your stuff was destroyed." She walked around the judge's desk to put her arm around Bella.

As she did, a man stepped into the doorway of the den and studied them with his almost eerily pale blue eyes. Bella waved off the man. He was as big as Tyce but where Tyce's hair was dark, this guy's was such a pale blond that it was nearly white. "It's okay," Bella told him.

Camille was no threat. He didn't have to save her from her friend.

"Who is he?" Camille asked.

Bella knew she wasn't supposed to tell anyone, but she didn't need to keep secrets from her friend. She shouldn't have to begin with. "He's a bodyguard," Bella said.

Camille gasped. "But why?" Then her face flushed. "The fire at your apartment, that shooting outside the plaza…those were attempts on your life?"

Bella shrugged. "I don't know."

Had the attempts been on her life or on Tyce's life?

Fear gripped her, but she was afraid for him. Not for herself…

"Someone's been threatening my father," she said. "Or using me to threaten him." That was what the photos had been. But she remembered that one had been of Tyce—with that hole through his forehead. Not long after that, he'd wound up with a real hole in his shoulder—from a bullet.

"That other man," Camille said. "The dark-haired one who showed up out of nowhere…"

Bella nodded. "He was a bodyguard, too." She had to blink at the tears stinging her eyes.

"He was more than a bodyguard, though, wasn't he?" her observant friend remarked.

She could only nod.

"Where is he?"

"I don't know."

Camille glanced toward the doorway where the other bodyguard was standing. "Did you ask him?"

She shook her head. She'd already made a fool of herself falling for a man who'd had no respect or appreciation for who she was. She wasn't going to chase after him, too. But she wondered about him…

Had Parker fired him? For what? For being related to a bad man?

That wouldn't have been fair—not after Tyce had risked his life to save hers. Maybe that was why she'd fallen for him—some sort of hero worship for him having been her rescuer.

He was a hero. Surely, Parker hadn't fired him. Maybe he'd quit, though. He had seemed furious with his boss—too furious even to speak to him.

Was he mad at her, too? Like the others, she'd let his secret relationship with Luther Mills cloud her judgment with doubts. For just a moment, she'd mistrusted him. But then she'd remembered how he'd put his life in danger for her over and over again.

"You look miserable," Camille said. "We need to get you out of here."

Bella uttered a wistful sigh. "I wish I could, but *he* would have to go with us."

Camille glanced back at the door. "That might not be a bad thing. He's cute."

"He's either married or engaged…" Bella murmured. "Either way, he's very taken. And I hear his wife or fiancée is quite the badass…"

"You need to be a badass," Camille told her. "You've been so good for so long. Be naughty for once. Sneak out with me. Let your hair down. Have some drinks. You deserve a break."

"But my father…" She shook her head. "He'll be so worried if I disappear." Again. But she'd been safe last time. She'd been with Tyce.

Even though she had a guy equally as big protecting her, she didn't feel as safe as she had felt with Tyce. But as safe as she'd felt physically, she'd been emotionally scared. She'd known he was going to hurt her. And she had not been wrong about that.

"If we're quick, he might not even know," Camille said with a wink.

Bella had gone out with Camille before. She doubted it would be quick once the pretty brunette got to flirting in a bar. And she had no doubt that was where she wanted to go.

"What's your plan?" Bella asked—because she was tempted.

"You go out the window. I pretend I'm talking to you for a while. Then I leave and shut the door, saying you don't want to be disturbed. Easy peasy."

Bella shivered at how easy it did sound. But would it work? If it didn't, her father would reprimand her for trying. If it did, her father would reprimand her for going out without a bodyguard. As much as she loved him, she didn't quite care at the moment. He was the one who'd insisted that Parker remove Tyce from the assignment.

Sure, she'd intended to ask for another bodyguard, and Tyce had agreed. But she doubted that she really would have gone through with it. Her father had given her no choice about having a bodyguard—or even about which bodyguard she would have.

Frustration welled inside her. With him. With Tyce. She was tired of the men she loved making decisions for her. It was about time that she made one of her own.

She nodded. "I'm game."

Camille squeezed her shoulder. "Good for you. We'll have a blast. Now head out the window…"

As she crawled out, Bella felt like a rebellious teenager sneaking off to a party. Or to meet her boyfriend. But she had no boyfriend. She'd dumped Michael for Tyce. And Tyce had only been her undercover boyfriend.

She had no reason to sneak out and no one to meet. But Camille…

At least she had a friend.

Tyce wasn't guarding Bella's body anymore. Her body that he missed so damn much he ached with the need to be buried inside her again. But he was still protecting her. Or at least he was trying.

He was determined to find Luther's spy. The one who'd set the trap in her apartment. And the first place he'd looked was his old customer, Michael Leach. But the man hadn't been easy to find. He'd taken off on some trip right around the time of the explosion. If Michael was the one who'd crossed Luther, he'd been smart to leave.

But he wasn't so smart that he hadn't come back—probably to get more money from his parents. Tyce had been sitting on their estate for almost a week when finally Michael's yellow Maserati pulled up to the wrought-iron gates.

His leaving town after the explosion had confirmed his guilt to Tyce. Michael had to be the one. With fury coursing through him, Tyce barely stopped himself from storming the estate and dragging him out. But then someone would call the police, and he wouldn't have the chance to interrogate Michael. Dragging in a deep breath, he forced himself to wait.

Hours later, the yellow Maserati pulled through the gates again. Where the hell was he heading? Clubs? Dealer?

Tyce followed him closely, knowing that the overgrown frat boy was too stupid to realize he had a tail. The trip was a short one to a parking garage downtown. It was for tenants only, so Tyce had to park on the street.

He followed him into the glass-and-metal apartment building, sticking close so that he caught and passed through all the doors the guy opened with his keycard. Michael's attention was on his phone, though, so he didn't even notice him—until the elevator doors closed and they were alone.

Then Tyce's hand shot out, closed around the guy's neck and lifted him from his feet. "You son of a bitch!"

Michael squirmed and kicked as he struggled against Tyce's hand, pulling at his fingers and scratching his skin. Tyce took his hand away, letting the guy drop hard to the floor of the elevator.

Michael's face was flushed, his eyes wide as he stared up at him. "What the hell are you doing? Who the hell—" Then his eyes widened more. "Jax?"

Tyce didn't care what the hell he called him as long as he told him the truth. The elevator dinged and the doors slid open. Fortunately nobody stood on the floor waiting for it. Tyce was able to grab his arm and pull him out. "What apartment is yours?"

"Down—down here," Michael said and pointed a trembling hand at unit 1231.

Tyce held out his hand. "Keys."

Michael must have been too scared or maybe too stoned to fight. His pupils were dilated. He pulled his keys from his pocket and handed them over.

Tyce opened the door and shoved him through it before quickly following him inside. He didn't want any of Michael's neighbors calling the police—at least not until he had a chance to talk to him.

"I didn't recognize you at first," Michael said as he continued to stare at him. "What do you want, Jax? I don't owe you anything. I haven't bought from you in years."

"I'm not here about drugs," Tyce said. "I'm here about Bella Holmes."

Michael nodded in sudden understanding. "You're the one who's been seeing Bella."

"That piss you off?" Tyce asked. "Is that why you tried to kill us? Jealousy?"

"What?" The guy shook his head but not in denial. He shook it like he couldn't believe what he'd heard. "I don't know what you're talking about. Is Bella okay?"

He actually sounded concerned.

"She's fine." Tyce pulled books off a shelf and flipped through them, looking for hiding places. Michael probably didn't have them to read. Some interior designer had probably included them in the living room for effect. He doubted Michael had decorated the place himself.

"No. She's not fine," Tyce corrected himself. "She's upset over her jewelry being stolen." Where would Michael have hidden it?

Michael just watched as Tyce pulled out drawers and dumped them. His brow was furrowed with confusion. "What are you talking about? What jewelry?"

"You know," Tyce insisted. He had to know. It had to have been Michael. It made the most sense since he was the one person close to Bella who also had a connection to Luther Mills. "Her mother's stuff. You must have taken it to pawn it for money to buy some X or whatever the hell you're into now."

"Just X and marijuana, man. You know I don't do hard drugs," he said. "I'm not a junkie. And I don't need to steal for money. I haven't burned through *my* trust fund."

Tyce tensed and stared down at the smaller man. "You think Bella has?"

"Probably." He chuckled. "But she probably gave all hers away to charity."

"So you do think she stole her own jewelry for an insurance claim?"

"Hell, no," Michael said. "Getting involved with you is the only dangerous thing Bella has ever done. Do *you* think she took it?"

She'd been devastated when she'd discovered it missing. There was no way.

Tyce shook his head. "No. And if her trust fund's gone, it's because, like you said, she probably gave it all to her charities." That was what all her parties were— fund-raisers. She wasn't the party girl he'd tried to believe she was. She was nothing like the women who'd used him for a wild time. She was so much more.

"If anyone stole from Bella, it was probably her back-stabbing sidekick Camille," Michael said with a derisive snort. "She hates her guts."

"What?"

"She's insanely jealous of her. Haven't you noticed? Hasn't she hit on you like she did me?" Michael asked. "She wants whatever Bella has. Hell, she wants her life."

Tyce had found out who Luther's spy was; he only hoped he wasn't too late to save Bella from her.

Parker did not want to tell the judge that he'd lost his daughter again. Well, Lars Ecklund had lost her. But, ultimately, it was Parker's responsibility to make sure she was well protected. The chief had hired Parker's agency for this job. But Parker had had to bring in his brothers' teams for backup because the judge hadn't wanted Tyce anymore.

It had been a mistake taking him off this assignment. Parker didn't care who the hell Tyce was related to—he was a damn good man.

But when his name showed up on Parker's cell, he hesitated to take the call. He didn't want to tell this man that he'd lost Bella Holmes, either. Hell, he wanted to tell Tyce even less than he wanted to tell her father.

Parker drew in a deep breath and hit the accept button. "Yeah?"

"It's Camille," Tyce said.

"What?"

"Bella's assistant—that's who's been spying on her for Luther."

A curse slipped through Parker's lips.

"What?" Tyce asked. "What's going on?"

"The bodyguard on Bella—he lost her." But that wasn't the worst part of it, and Tyce obviously knew it.

"You think she's with Camille."

Parker admitted, "That's the last person the bodyguard saw her with before she disappeared."

Tyce cursed.

"She won't kill her, though—not if she's working for Luther. He needs Bella, to be able to threaten her." Parker flinched as he heard himself, as he heard how hard he was working to convince himself that he hadn't really lost the judge's daughter yet.

"Camille is crazy," Tyce said. "She's not following Luther's orders. That was why he warned me about the trap she'd set for us."

Parker had thought it might have been because they were brothers. But he should have known that family didn't matter to Luther Mills. All that mattered to Luther Mills was Luther Mills.

"Camille hates Bella so much that she's not going to let her live," Tyce said.

"Even if killing her will get her killed? It'd be like suicide for her to cross Luther Mills."

"She's crazy," Tyce repeated.

And that made her unpredictable. "Where the hell do we find her?"

"I'll find her," Tyce said as he disconnected the call.

Parker knew Tyce would do his best to find her. But he couldn't help but think it would be too late.

Bella had been gone for a while.

Chapter 19

Grateful for her friend's efforts to cheer her up, Bella had tried really hard to show Camille a good time. She had pulled some strings to get them a table at the hottest restaurant in town. After their amazing dinner, she'd taken her around to all the clubs Camille had previously mentioned she wished she could get into.

But while Bella concentrated on giving her friend a good time, she wasn't having one herself. She was miserable and edgy, and her mood must have dampened Camille's.

"I'm sorry," she said after Camille let them inside her apartment. "We should have stayed at the club. I know you were having a good time."

Camille shook her head. "Oh, no, we're going to have

a much better time here." She waved Bella toward her couch. It was slipcovered in white, just like Bella's sofa.

Or like Bella's sofa had been.

It had been destroyed in the fire along with so many other things of hers. But they were only things…

Bella wasn't missing them, not even her mother's jewelry anymore. She was missing Tyce.

"I should go," Bella said. "I'm not good company right now."

"That's why you shouldn't be alone," Camille said. She pulled a bottle of wine from a rack in the corner kitchen of the studio apartment.

The place was small but stylishly furnished with so many pieces that resembled things Bella had had. There was even a print on the wall that looked like the one she'd had over the fireplace that had caused the explosion.

She stepped closer to it. Even the frame was the same and the print had been signed by the artist, who'd been a friend of her mother's. It had been signed "To Elizabeth…"

Bella shivered. It wasn't just like her print; it was her print. "I—I thought this was lost in the fire…"

"It would have been," Camille said. "If I hadn't taken it before the explosion. It was worth the risk of going back inside even though your former bodyguard nearly caught me. Don't you think it looks perfect there?"

Bella turned back to find the woman she'd always considered a friend pointing a gun at her with one hand. In the other she held out a wineglass, as if Bella could drink with a barrel pointed at her.

"Why?" she asked. "I don't understand."

"I always admired that picture," Camille said. "I didn't want it to be ruined."

"But why?" Tyce had been right. Someone close to her had been working with Luther. But Bella never would have suspected Camille. "We've been friends for so long."

Camille snorted. "Bullshit. I've been your bitch—the one you boss around to do your bidding. Princess—isn't that what he calls you? He certainly got that right."

"He suspects you," Bella warned her. He actually suspected Michael, too.

Camille laughed. "Yeah, right. If he did, he would be here, wouldn't he? What kind of bodyguard is he?" Her lips curved into a cruel smile. "Oh, that's right. That's not all he was. You seduced him, like you seduce every man, and then you got bored with him."

Bella shook her head. "Seduced him? That wasn't what happened." And she'd certainly not gotten bored with him. She doubted anyone would ever get bored with Tyce Jackson.

"That's always what happens with you," Camille said. "Every man who sees you wants you. It was that way in high school and college…"

But Bella hadn't dated as much as Camille had. She gestured at the gun. "Is this over a guy? Is that why you're mad at me?"

Camille snorted again. "Mad at you?" She laughed. "I despise you. I hate you—detest you…"

Bella shuddered. "But why? What have I done?"

Camille stepped closer. "It's you. It's who you are. What you are…" She acted as if she was gagging on the words before spitting out, "Entitled. Spoiled. Rich."

Tears stung Bella's eyes. She blinked them back. "I—I didn't know you felt that way about me."

Camille shook her head. "You're such an idiot. I told you how I felt about all our classmates. About all those spoiled bitches who treated me like trash because I wasn't paying to go to school with them—because my mom was the hired help."

"She's a teacher," Bella said in defense of the woman she'd always admired. "And a damn good one." Mrs. Thiel had explained chemistry to Bella so well that she'd actually understood it. Camille must have used her mother's lessons to set off that explosion in Bella's apartment.

"Stop it!" Camille shrieked. "Drop the damn act already. It's too much. It's what makes you so much worse than everyone else."

She blinked back the sting of tears. "How—what do you mean? I've always treated you like a friend."

Camille waved the gun at her now, pointing it even closer to her face. "That's what I mean. That's what made it so much worse—your act. We're not friends. I know that. You know that. Why pretend like we're something we're not?"

"I wasn't pretending."

Camille swung the gun at her. Bella stepped back, but the barrel still hit her cheek, the sight nipping into her skin. She cried out at the shock.

And Camille laughed. "That's just the beginning, bitch."

Bella opened her mouth to scream.

But Camille stepped closer and put the barrel nearly

against her teeth. "I'll blow your head off right now if you make a sound."

The door rattled as someone pounded on it.

Camille tensed. "Did you call someone? What did you do?"

Bella shook her head.

"I know you're in there! Let me in!" a deep voice shouted through the door. "Let me in!"

Bella recognized that deep voice. It was Tyce's. But he sounded strange, as if he was slurring his words.

"Did you call him?" Camille asked.

Bella shook her head.

"I wanna talk to you," he said, his words slurring even more. "I wanna see you…"

"No," she whispered. "I don't know how he found me." But she knew—because he was damn good at what he did.

Camille narrowed her eyes as if she didn't believe her. But then that cruel smile spread across her face again. "This might be better yet. This might hurt you even more than putting a bullet in you—when you watch me put another bullet in him. This time I won't miss and hit his shoulder. I'll get his head—just like I promised in that picture."

Bella realized that Tyce must have figured out Camille was the threat. But was he in time to stop Camille from killing her or just in time to die with her?

Tyce's chest ached from the pain that had struck his heart when he'd heard Bella cry out from within the apartment. He had to get inside—without Camille hurting Bella any more. So he'd decided to act like a drunken idiot. Maybe Camille wouldn't consider him a threat then.

He hammered at the door again. "C'mon, lemme in."

"No—" Bella began but then cried out again.

He stepped back, so he had room to kick in the door. But before he could lift his leg, the door opened. He forced himself to stumble and bang his shoulder against the jamb as he entered the apartment. And he pretended like he didn't even notice the gun in Camille's hand.

She slammed the door shut behind him and turned, her back against it, the gun barrel swinging from him to Bella.

Bella stood near an outside wall, a hand pressed over her mouth, as if she was trying to hold back screams of terror. He could see the fear in her eyes. And the knowledge. She knew he wasn't drunk.

But he felt light-headed and disoriented with fury as he noticed blood trickling from the cut on her cheek. Had Camille shot her? Or struck her?

He hadn't heard the gun go off and he hadn't noticed a silencer on the end of the barrel. She must have struck her. Hard. Hard enough to break the skin and make it swell with the beginning of a big bruise.

His heart ached more for Bella's pain. But that was the least she would feel if he couldn't disarm her crazy assistant.

"There she is," Camille said, directing the barrel at Bella again, as if pointing her out to Tyce. "Why do you think she's worth dying over?"

"I don't," he lied. "I'm here to see *you*…"

She turned back toward him, her dark eyes wide with

surprise. And as she turned, she moved the gun barrel with her—away from Bella.

He wanted to shoot Bella a glance, wanted to send her a silent message to get the hell out of the way. Even if she just dropped to the floor...

But he didn't dare look at her for fear he'd draw the crazy girl's attention back to her real target.

"Why me?" Camille asked. And now she was looking at him, really looking at him.

"I talked to old Mikey," he said, forcing himself to keep slurring his words. "We were talking about you. About how you came onto him..."

Camille shook her head. "Is that what he said?"

"I didn't believe him," Tyce said. "I knew you wouldn't waste your time with an overgrown frat boy like him."

Camille's dark eyes narrowed. She probably suspected he was playing her, but she couldn't figure out why or how.

Her jealousy of Bella had obviously driven her crazy, so Tyce wanted to show her she had nothing to be jealous of...

"Any more than I would waste my time with a princess like Bella," he continued.

Unfortunately that made Camille glance at her again. But Bella hadn't moved. She must have been frozen with fear.

"She said she fell for you," Camille said. "She said you were more than her bodyguard."

He felt another twinge in his heart. Had she fallen for him? Did she care about him?

He'd let her down. He'd nearly let her get killed, too.

But hopefully he could make sure that didn't happen. He'd put his weapon in the waistband of his jeans, at the small of his back. But he had to be careful when he made the grab for it—had to make sure he had time to fire before crazy Camille fired hers.

"It was just an act," he told Camille. "It was my cover, pretending to be with her. She wasn't the one I was interested in…" He lurched forward, moving toward her. If he could get close enough, maybe he could get the gun from her without it ever going off.

Camille tilted her head and stared up at him as he approached her. But her dark eyes were narrowed with suspicion. "I saw how you looked at her, like every other damn male with a pulse looks at her…like she's some goddess…" She waved the gun in Bella's direction.

Tyce tried to get closer, but she pointed the gun at him then. "Stop!" she yelled at him. "Don't come any closer to me!"

"Why wouldn't you let me get close to you?" he asked. "Like you let Michael?"

"I had a chance of stealing him from her," she said. "But not you. Michael never looked at her the way you did. And even Michael thought she was too good for him."

She was. Too good for Michael. And much too good for Tyce.

"She's got nothing on you." Tyce tried to convince the girl.

But she laughed bitterly at the blatant lie. "Yeah, right. She's got all that money, the jewelry, the clothes… the looks…"

Bella did have it all. There was no use denying it.

"That's just stuff," Tyce said. "And she didn't work for any of it. She doesn't deserve it—not like you do." He'd noticed the picture hanging near where Bella stood. He'd recognized it from where it had hung over the fireplace at Bella's. Camille must have taken it right before the explosion. She was the shadow he'd seen through the window.

The jewelry was probably around here somewhere, too. She had to be the one who'd taken it.

"I do deserve it," she said. "I worked for it. I work all the time." She pointed the gun in Bella's direction again. "For her. Running her errands. Handling her details."

"I thought you wanted to do it," Bella said. "I thought you wanted the job."

Tyce shot her a glance, trying to silently warn her to stay quiet. The more she talked, the more wound up Camille got. He moved one hand to his back, toward his weapon.

"You wanted to put me in my place," Camille accused her. As she spoke, she waved that gun, but only in Bella's direction now. "You wanted to remind me that I'm just the hired help—like Mama."

"Camille," he said, trying to draw her attention.

But she only glanced at him and the gun barrel remained pointed at Bella.

"Forget about her," he said. "She's not worth your time. I am. We could have a good time together…"

Finally she turned to him, but it was with a weary sigh. "You think I'm an idiot, just like she did when she pretended to be my friend."

"No!" he shouted before she could turn back toward Bella. He stepped forward—getting closer to her. "You're the one I want to be—"

"Stop lying!" she shrieked. "I'll make you stop!" She swung the gun in his direction. As she did, Bella screamed, which drew the weapon toward her as Tyce pulled his from the waistband of his jeans. He squeezed the trigger, but Camille had fired first.

The shots echoed one another and resonated off the walls of the small apartment.

The judge had been pacing his chambers since he'd gotten the call that Bella had gone missing. He couldn't sit—couldn't think of anything or anybody but his precious daughter.

Did Luther Mills have her?

Had he had someone grab her?

The trial was due to start soon. So if Luther intended to manipulate him into ruling for his benefit, he would need to have leverage. He would need to have Bella.

Parker had said that they didn't think her disappearance had anything to do with Luther. But why would anyone want to hurt her—especially the girl to whom his daughter had always been so kind?

How could anyone who knew his amazing, sweet, generous child want to harm her?

His phone rang, and he grabbed for it—not wanting to miss a call that might be about Bella.

"This is Parker Payne," the caller identified himself.

"Did you find her? Do you know where my daughter is?"

"The hospital, sir. She's at the hospital."

His daughter had been hurt. His legs shook and he

dropped onto his chair. "Is she— Is she…?" He couldn't bring himself to ask.

Too many feelings and fears overwhelmed him, reminding him of how his wife had been rushed to the hospital—for no reason. Even before they'd arrived, there was nothing anyone could have done to save her.

Was it too late for Bella, as well?

Chapter 20

These past few weeks had aged her father. He looked so much older and tired. Bella covered his hand, which was wrapped around the railing of her gurney, with hers. "I'm fine, Daddy," she assured him.

He shook his head as if he couldn't believe her.

She touched her cheek where the stitches had pulled the skin back together where the gun barrel sight had cut her. "This is just a scratch."

She had only needed a couple of stitches, which was good since she'd discovered she wasn't any fonder of needles than Tyce was. But he hadn't been with her, hadn't been there to call her a baby like she'd called him.

"You trusted that girl…" His breath shuddered out. "I trusted that girl."

Bella shook her head. How had she never seen it? That hatred? She shivered.

Her father looked around. "Do you need another blanket?"

"No, I'm fine," she said. "I just want to get out of here." She wanted to see Tyce, to make sure that he was really all right. When those shots had rung out in the apartment, she'd fallen to the floor—out of instinct, or fear, or maybe just because her trembling legs had finally given way beneath her. The window, that had been right behind her, had shattered as a bullet hit it.

That bullet could have hit her…

Tyce had seemed to think it had when he'd rushed over to her. He'd looked so concerned, so caring…

Could he return her feelings?

She needed to talk to him.

She struggled to lower the railing on the gurney, so she could swing her legs over it. But her father held it up.

"Wait until the doctor releases you."

"Please, Daddy," she murmured as exhaustion overwhelmed her. "I just want to go home."

"You can't," a deep voice said.

Her heart skipped a beat like it had when he'd stepped into that apartment earlier in the evening, like it had when she'd thought he might have taken a bullet. But he'd been fine.

Fortunately for him, Camille had been a terrible shot.

Unfortunately for her, Tyce was not.

She flinched as she remembered seeing the woman lying on the floor, the woman she'd always considered a friend. There had been no saving Camille.

"It's just a scratch," she told Tyce. "Thanks to you. You saved my life. If you hadn't come in when you had…" She shuddered as she realized that could have been her lying on Camille's apartment floor instead.

She could have been the one dead.

"That's why you can't go home," Tyce said. He turned to the judge. "You need to make her go into a safe house—at least until this trial is over."

At least?

Did he think she would need to be in one longer? That Luther might try for revenge against her father once he was convicted?

He needed to be convicted. She knew that, but she resented that it now involved her. She didn't know this man—had never met him or bought from him like Michael had. He shouldn't affect her life at all. But he had.

Her father must have noticed her resentment because he murmured, "I'm sorry."

But then she realized he wasn't apologizing for his job affecting her life when he added, "Tyce is right. You need to go into protective custody."

She shook her head. "No. Camille was the threat. She was the one who took the pictures. She can't hurt me now." But she knew that was a lie. It hurt just to think of the girl—to think of how much she'd hated Bella.

Did Tyce hate her, too, now? Had she somehow alienated him like she had Camille?

He wouldn't look at her now. He focused on her father instead. And her father ignored her to tell Tyce, "I appreciate that you saved her today, but I am still not comfortable with you being the one protecting her. Not now that I know about your connection to Luther Mills.

I've known you for a long time, and I know that you've done good work. But Luther has a leak in the police department and the district attorney's office, and from what happened with the witness and the evidence tech, Jocelyn Gerber seems to be right that he has one in the Payne Protection Agency, too. I can't take any chances with my daughter's life, Tyce."

Tyce tensed, but he nodded as if he actually agreed with her father.

She didn't agree. "Daddy!" she exclaimed. "That's insulting. Tyce is nothing like that criminal. He saved my life—more than once."

He'd saved her life when he'd made her fall for him—because she hadn't really been living, at least not her life. Like he'd accused her, she'd been trying to live her mother's life—trying to bring back the woman she'd loved and missed so much.

And maybe she hadn't been doing it just for herself but for her father, too. But it was time—past time—that she live her own life again.

She wanted that life to include Tyce. But he didn't seem interested.

"Parker's other bodyguards are good," Tyce said, but again he was speaking to her father. Not her. "And between the chief and Parker, they found good hiding places for the eyewitness and the evidence tech. They'll find a safe spot for your daughter, too."

Your daughter…

Was that all she was to Tyce?

Nothing more than an assignment?

Her father held out his hand to Tyce. "Thank you," he said. "For saving my daughter today. And thank you for understanding that her safety is more important than anything else."

Her safety.

What about her heart?

She felt as if it was breaking when Tyce shook her father's hand and then turned and walked away without so much as a glance in her direction.

Tears rushed to her eyes then brimmed over before she could blink them back. On one side, they ran down her face; on the other, they soaked into the bandage the doctor had put over her stitches. So much for keeping it dry like the doctor had told her...

Her father patted her shoulder. "You're fine now, honey," he said. "This is just shock."

But she wasn't crying because she was in shock. She was in pain. And she was afraid that she wouldn't be fine—not without Tyce.

Tyce had to force himself to keep walking. He couldn't turn around and go back in there. He couldn't push her father aside and lift her from that gurney and carry her out of the hospital. But he wanted to.

He wanted to be the one to protect Bella and not just during the trial but always. That was why he forced himself to keep walking.

He couldn't give her the kind of life that would keep her safe. Not with the kind of life he'd lived, the enemies he'd made during his time with vice and now as a bodyguard. The things he'd had to do...like kill that girl. He'd done it to save Bella. But maybe he could have found another way—a way for Camille to live and get the help she'd obviously needed.

He wasn't the man for Bella. She was too sweet—too innocent—to ever understand a man like him, who'd had to do the things he'd done. No. It was better that he walk away from her, so that nothing and nobody from his past ever hurt her.

And Luther would always be part of his past, even after he was convicted. He remembered hearing the story—the legend—that Luther Mills was the one who'd pulled the trigger that had ended their father's miserable life. And Luther had only been eight years old at the time.

Tyce wasn't sure if it was true. And he really didn't want to know. It didn't matter, though. No matter when or why he'd started, Luther was a killer.

But he wouldn't kill Bella. She was of no use to him then. He only wanted to threaten her because she was the one thing her father loved.

That was another reason Tyce walked away. He'd always respected the judge, but now he understood him in a way he never had before. He understood that the judge wanted to make sure his daughter was safe beyond anything else. That was why he didn't want Tyce protecting her anymore.

And Tyce understood because he loved Bella, too.

Luther owed his brother a favor. Tyce had stopped that crazy bitch from killing Bella Holmes. He'd also taken her out, so Luther hadn't had to worry about her, either. Despite that, though, Luther couldn't repay the favor the way Tyce probably wanted him to; he couldn't leave the judge's daughter alone no matter how his brother felt about her.

Why the hell had Tyce fallen for her? Guys like them didn't wind up with fancy women like Bella Holmes. He was only going to get his heart broken when she left him for some preppy, rich guy. So, really, Luther was doing him a favor.

Sparing him some pain.

But he'd only do that as long as Tyce didn't get in his way.

"What about the bodyguards?" The voice on the other end of the call drew Luther's attention back to the phone in his hand.

Luther glanced around his cell, but nobody was listening as far as he could see. "Same order as before," he said. "Kill as many of Parker Payne's people as you can."

"But what about—"

"About what?" Luther asked, his lips curving into a grin. A lot of people knew about him and Tyce. But they had to know that a man who'd killed his father didn't give a damn about the life of his brother.

"If he gets in your way, kill him, too," Luther ordered. Yet a part of him, a very tiny part of him, kind of hoped that Tyce stayed out of his way. "Just make sure you get the Holmes girl."

He needed her now—the trial was about to start. He needed her where he could hurt her. It was all up to her father just how badly she would be hurt.

If the rumors were true, the old man would do anything for his little girl. So this was Luther's best shot at getting the verdict he needed.

Not guilty.

If the old man refused to cooperate, he'd wind up presiding over his daughter's funeral instead of Luther's trial.

Chapter 21

Bella knew it was for the best, but she hated the thought of running away. She hadn't done it when her mother had died. She could have stayed away at college and pretended it hadn't happened, that her mom would be there when she went home for summer break. But she couldn't have let her father go through that pain and loss on his own. His loss had been so great that she'd tried to fill it by replacing her mother, though she'd told herself she'd only wanted to honor her. Because his loss had been so great, she couldn't make her father go through it again if something happened to her. She'd thought she was safe before, but now that the trial was getting closer and Luther couldn't get to the eyewitness or the evidence tech, he was going to focus on her. That was why she'd agreed to go into hiding. She didn't even know where she was going.

The bodyguards had promised to stop at a department store before boarding the private plane, though. She needed to buy some things since most of her clothes had been damaged in the fire at her apartment.

The last time she'd gone shopping had been with Tyce—for clothes for him. Even though he'd grumbled and complained, she'd had so much fun. She'd always had fun with him even when they'd teased each other. Or maybe because they'd teased each other. She'd never felt the way she had with him with anyone else, and she worried that she would probably never find that kind of connection again.

"The trial shouldn't last too long," the bodyguard sitting next to her remarked. The woman was petite with curly auburn hair and big brown eyes.

Had she been assigned to Bella because of the shopping? They didn't want her to be alone for a moment—even in the dressing room in a busy store?

"With all the evidence and the eyewitness testimony, Luther has no defense," Nikki Payne-Ecklund continued. "It'll be over fast."

Bella hoped so. She wasn't sure what she would do if the trial dragged on for weeks or months. She was used to being busy.

"I should pick up some books, too," she remarked. There were several she'd been hoping to read soon. "Can we stop at a library or bookstore, too?"

Nikki nodded. "We'll have to. The private airport doesn't have a gift shop."

And there must not have been one where she was

going. Maybe having some time away from her life would help Bella figure out how she wanted to live it now. If she wanted to continue her mother's work or find her own place in the world…

It would also give her time to get over Tyce.

In addition to the bodyguard next to her, there were two in the front seat. The pale-haired giant who was married to Nikki Payne and a dark-haired man who would be flying the plane they were taking to who knew where…

They knew.

For some reason they hadn't shared the information with her, though. As if she couldn't be trusted to protect herself. But then, she wasn't always the best judge of character. She'd trusted Camille who'd wanted to kill her. She'd dated Michael without ever really knowing who he was. And she'd fallen for Tyce, who'd so easily walked away from her as if they'd never made love.

Nikki squeezed her hand. "I know," she murmured.

"You know?" Bella asked. "About Tyce?"

Nikki nodded. "You kind of wear your heart on your sleeve."

And her heart belonged to him. "He doesn't want it," Bella grumbled.

"Men are idiots," Nikki said.

"Thanks, dear," Lars said from the front seat.

"Well, you are," Nikki replied. "You run from your feelings."

"I seem to remember someone else doing the running with us," Lars remarked.

Nikki's face flushed. "Yeah, well…"

Lars looked into the rearview mirror at his wife's

face and chuckled, but then he must have noticed some-thing else because he abruptly stopped. His mouth opened, but whatever he'd been about to say was cut off by the crash.

Metal crunched. Airbags exploded from every direc-tion. They'd been hit from every direction, or it felt that way with the impact jerking Bella one way and then an-other and then another. Her body ached and her breath left her lungs. Her last conscious thought was of Tyce.

She was glad that he wasn't her bodyguard right now—because she wasn't certain if any of them would survive the crash.

It should have been him. He should have been with her. Tyce stared at the wreckage. Had she survived it? There was blood on the side airbag near where she'd been sitting. Not much blood…but enough to indicate she'd been hurt.

"What the hell happened?" he shouted at Parker, who was also pacing around the wreckage.

Parker just kept shaking his head. "I don't know. I don't know."

"They came out of nowhere," Lars Ecklund said. "We were all talking and just suddenly they were there—hitting us on all sides."

With armored trucks.

How the hell had Luther's crew gotten their hands on armored trucks? Of course Luther had money. That was how he kept bringing in more manpower despite how many of his crew the Payne Protection Agency had taken out.

And they'd taken out a few more today. Nikki and

Lars had gotten off some shots. Dead men lay on the asphalt around the battered SUV. But Cole Bentler, who'd been on the passenger's side like Bella, had yet to regain consciousness. He'd left in an ambulance before Tyce and Parker had arrived at the scene.

How badly had Bella been hurt?

Luther's crew hadn't cared because they'd moved her anyway—even after some of them had gotten shot. Maybe the blood on the airbag was from one of them.

Tyce hoped like hell it was.

"How did they get her?" He hurled the question at Lars as he stepped forward, standing chest to chest, eye to eye, with the big former Marine.

Small hands pressed against his chest, propelling him back as Nikki stepped between him and her husband. "It wasn't his fault. None of us saw them coming. We had backup—we had other SUVs in the convoy."

Somehow they'd gotten separated from them.

"How did they get her out of the SUV?"

"It all happened so quickly," Nikki murmured. "I think we all lost consciousness for a while. When we came to, they had already gotten her out. They were dragging her toward another vehicle. We tried to stop them." Blood trickled down the side of her face and blood stained the front of Lars's shirt. They were hurt.

It should have been him instead. His heart beat so furiously he thought it was going to explode in his chest. He was such a damn fool. Such a coward.

Tyce ran his hand over his face. "This wouldn't have happened…it wouldn't have happened if I'd been here."

He would have died before he'd let anyone take Bella. But it was too late to do what he should have done. She was gone.

Bradford knew he was right. He'd overheard Tyce Jackson just as he ducked under the crime tape and hurried up to the scene. But it was more what he saw than what he'd heard that made him believe Tyce wouldn't have let anything happen to Bella.

He loved her.

The bodyguard had clearly fallen in love with Bradford's daughter. And because he would have done anything to protect her, he knew that Tyce would have, too.

He'd been such a fool.

Such a damn fool...

He'd told himself he couldn't trust Tyce Jackson because of his connection to a killer. But now he wondered if he'd just been jealous. He'd had all of Bella's attention since her mother died. She'd been so worried about him, about losing him, too, that she'd doted on him. And he hadn't wanted to share her with anyone else.

Now he might have lost her for good. They both might have lost her. He hated himself for his selfishness. He knew Bella—knew that she had more than enough love to share.

Bradford watched as Tyce dropped his hand from his face and focused on his approach. The judge waited for the look of anger or recrimination to cross the bodyguard's face. But there was only concern.

The younger man was worried about him.

"Are you all right?" Tyce asked.

Bradford shook his head. No. He wasn't. He was

ashamed. He could not have misjudged Tyce Jackson any more than he had. And that mistake might have cost him his daughter.

"We'll find her," Parker Payne promised. He seemed to be talking to both of them. He must have known what Bradford had just realized. That Tyce Jackson cared about Bella as much as he did.

Tyce ignored his boss, as if he knew the promise was empty. "Have you heard from him?" Tyce asked. "He'll want you to know that he has her."

Bradford was shaking his head when his phone began to vibrate. He pulled it from his pocket.

"I should get a trace on that," an auburn-haired woman remarked as she stepped closer to the judge. "It has to be the kidnappers."

"Just take it," Tyce directed him. "Find out what they want."

"We both know what that is," Bradford replied. But he pressed both the accept and the speaker buttons. "Hello?"

"Judge Holmes," a strange-sounding voice greeted. It didn't even sound like a person. It must have been mechanically altered so that no one would recognize it. "I believe we might have what you're looking for…"

A big hand wrapped around the phone as Tyce Jackson pulled it toward him. "Prove it," he challenged the caller. "Send us a video showing that she's alive."

"I don't have to prove a damn thing to you."

Following Tyce's lead, Bradford said, "You have to prove it to me. If you want any cooperation on my part, I need to know my daughter is alive."

The call disconnected and Bradford gasped. Had he made a horrible mistake?

Had he already pushed the kidnappers too far?

"They're calling Luther," Tyce deduced. "They're asking him what to do."

Bradford's stomach lurched. He shook his head. "I—we—shouldn't have done that. We shouldn't have pushed Luther Mills." He was too ruthless.

"It was the right thing to do," Parker assured him with a glance of approval at his employee. "We need proof of life."

As Bradford really looked at the wrecked vehicle at the crime scene, he understood why. The big SUV was twisted, bent—every single part of it damaged. The woman standing next to Bradford had obviously been injured in it. She had blood on her, so did the blond man. He knew another bodyguard had been taken to the hospital. So Bella might not have even survived the crash.

"A video was the right thing to ask for," the young woman said. "It'll give us something to analyze for clues to where she's being held."

It made sense. It all made sense. But there was no telling if Luther would agree to their demand. Or if he even could agree...

He couldn't give them proof of life if there was none. Maybe that was why the call had been disconnected so abruptly—because Bella was already dead.

Chapter 22

Pain radiated throughout Bella's skull, but she fought through it, through the blackness. She fought her way back to consciousness. She needed to be awake. She needed to find out what had happened to the others.

Lifting her lids was a physical struggle, a battle to overcome the pain and weakness. But the pain wasn't just in her head. Her body ached, too.

Had the others survived?

Concern for them jerked her awake. But the darkness remained. She blinked, trying to clear it away—until she finally realized she was no longer in the SUV, no longer in the street where all those other vehicles had crashed.

Dampness radiated from the cold concrete beneath her. The air smelled musty, too. Was she in a basement?

She tried to move her hands, but they were bound behind her back. She struggled and the plastic bit into her wrists. She tried to spread her legs to push herself up, but her ankles were bound with something that felt like a plastic zip tie or a twist tie used around a garbage bag.

Had she been thrown out somewhere like the trash?

Metal rattled and hinges creaked as a door opened. Light fell across her face and she flinched at the brightness. But it wasn't that bright. A bare bulb hung from a wire slung over some kind of metal beam.

Was she in a garage? Or a warehouse?

"She's alive," a voice murmured.

Another set of footsteps scraped across the concrete. Two pairs of legs approached her. They were clad in worn, baggy jeans.

Bella peered up into faces that didn't look much older than the kids she'd seen when Tyce had taken her on the tour of his old neighborhood. And, like those kids, these two were armed.

They were also not alone. Someone else remained outside the door, outside the pool of light. She could see only a big shadow falling into the room. And a much more mature-sounding voice told them, "Her *daddy* wants a video for proof of life."

The two boys snickered.

The voice sounded vaguely familiar to her. And she must have been familiar to him since he knew that even though she was a grown woman, she still called her father "Daddy." It was stupid and childish, she knew that. But she also knew that he liked it, which was why she kept doing it. Because she would do anything to make her father happy.

He had to be so worried about her, especially if he'd seen the wreckage from the accident. But it had been no accident. No wonder he wanted proof of life. He probably couldn't believe she'd survived the crash.

Had the others?

She opened her mouth and tried to speak, but her throat was raw, her lips dry. How long had she been unconscious? She coughed and sputtered, and finally she managed to croak, "What about...?"

"What?" the man asked from outside the door. "What the hell do you want to know, Ms. Holmes?"

He sounded like Camille had at the end, like he hated her. Why? Just because she had more money? Maybe that was it—maybe she could use that money to buy her way out of this...

"Everybody else?" she asked. "Did they survive?"

The guy snorted.

And one of the kids cursed. "Damn bodyguards shot up a lot of the crew."

"Most of what was left of the crew," the other added. "And some of the new ones..."

Maybe that was why they were so young. Luther had used a lot of his resources to try to take out the eyewitness and the evidence technician. She'd learned that from Tyce in those weeks he'd been guarding her.

She felt a twinge of regret for more lives being lost. But the bodyguards had to be alive since they'd been able to shoot back.

But had they survived the shooting?

"Get her on her feet and take the damn video," the man ordered.

One of the kids tried to lift her up, but with her ankles together, she fell against him and nearly knocked him down. The second kid grabbed her other arm and steadied her. "Who takes the video?"

"Use one of your damn phones," the man ordered.

Bella realized he didn't want the call traced to him. He didn't want her to be able to identify him, either. So she had to know him or had seen him at least. In her father's chambers? Who the hell was he?

She tried to move toward the door, but with her legs bound, she started to fall over again.

"Untie her damn ankles," the man shouted from the doorway.

She blinked and tried to focus on him but could still only see the silhouette.

One of the kids flipped open a switchblade and cut quickly and neatly through the plastic binding her ankles. Even with her legs free, they were weak and trembling beneath her. She struggled to stand straight.

"I—I think I need medical attention," she murmured as black spots began to swim before her eyes again and her aching head grew light.

"Stop with the tricks," the man advised from outside the door.

"It's not a trick," she said. "And I'm no use to Luther Mills if I'm dead."

If they had to bring in medical help, she would have a chance to get away.

"We'll take our chances that there's nothing mortally wrong with you," the man replied. "Yet."

So they didn't intend to keep her alive. Maybe once the video was made and sent to her father, they would kill her.

"Take the damn video," the man ordered.

Bella felt sick that her suspicions might be right. They might not keep her alive after that.

She needed to give a clue to where she was being held. But she wasn't sure herself. And the kids didn't give her time to think of a plan.

One held up his phone and pointed it at her. "What do you want her to say?" he asked the man.

"That she's alive and if her father wants to keep her that way, he knows what he needs to do."

"What?" the kid asked.

"He wants my dad to rule in Luther Mills's favor," she explained.

"Don't say that!" the guy yelled. "Don't say anything about Luther Mills."

"Why not?" Bella asked. "He's the one who ordered you to abduct me. He's the one behind all of this." She had no doubt this time. She had no other enemies now that Camille was dead.

"Luther can't have his name brought into this at all," the man replied.

"What about yours?" she asked. "Who are you?"

"You better hope you don't figure it out, Ms. Holmes, or there's no way you're going to survive even until the trial."

She silently cursed herself. She'd pushed him too far. "Okay, okay, let me make the video."

She's alive.

The tightness in Tyce's chest eased but not much as he stared at the screen of her father's cell phone. She didn't look good. Her face was pale but for the bruise on the side of her face, which must have been from the airbag. Or the crash itself. Or maybe one of her abductors had struck her like Camille had. This bruise was on the opposite cheek.

Tyce would kill whoever had hurt her.

"Daddy, I'm okay..." She blinked as she said it, as if she was fighting back tears. She wanted to seem brave for her father, to spare him.

She cared more about her dad and her mother's causes than she cared about herself. How had Camille ever thought her spoiled and selfish?

How had Tyce thought that?

No wonder Bella was gone. He hadn't deserved her. But he had to find her now. He had to bring her back—before she was hurt any worse than she already had been.

"They say you know what you have to do to keep me alive," she continued. "Do what you think is best—"

The video switched off and that mechanically altered voice spoke again. "Your daughter is trying to be brave, Judge. But you know what you have to do if you want to see her again."

"He has to see her again," Tyce said into the speaker of the judge's cell. "He has to see her all during Luther Mills's trial or you won't get the outcome Luther wants."

The judge hit the mute button. "I can't say that. I can't say Luther's name, or I need to recuse myself from the trial." If they didn't find her before the trial, he would need to recuse himself. They all knew that. Even the judge. But nobody said it—because they all knew that Luther would have his crew kill Bella for certain. They would have no reason to keep her alive.

He clicked the mute button off. "Mr. Jackson is right. I need to see a video of my daughter every day. I need to know that you're not hurting her."

The caller made no such promise. He just clicked off the phone, probably concerned that the call was being traced. He had to know, because Luther did, that the Payne Protection Agency was involved. And anyone who knew about the Payne Protection Agency knew how damn smart Nikki Payne-Ecklund was about hacking computers and getting information nobody else could find.

The judge's hand was shaking so badly that the cell phone slipped from his grasp. It struck his desk. Then the judge leaned forward in his chair and buried his face in his hands.

Tyce, who'd been standing behind him, put his hand on his shoulder. "Remember. Luther doesn't want her dead. He needs to keep her alive to maintain his leverage over you." But from his years undercover, Tyce knew the worst that could happen to a woman wasn't necessarily death.

Bradford Holmes's voice was muffled in his hands, but it sounded as if he murmured, "Damn Luther Mills." But then he lifted his face and looked over his shoulder at Tyce. His eyes were wet. "She can't be there days or weeks or however the hell long this trial lasts. She won't survive."

"She's tougher than you know," Tyce assured the man. "She's strong and smart. She will survive."

The judge patted Tyce's hand. "You—you…" His voice cracked with emotion.

Tyce nodded. He loved her. That was why he could not lose her. "I will find her."

He'd lived undercover on the meanest streets of River City on and off for years. He'd worked for Luther. He knew Luther. He had to be able to figure out where he would have hidden Bella. She had to be close. Attainable. In an area where no one would hear her scream.

The thought of her screaming made him shake nearly as badly as the judge was. Bella was strong. She would only scream if she was being hurt. She could not be hurt. They had to find her first.

Nikki had cloned the judge's phone with a program on her computer, so everything on it was on her screen, which she stared at intently as she tapped the keyboard.

"Could you trace it?" Parker asked her.

She shook her head. "The signal pings off a tower on the east side of the city. But I can't narrow it down more than that."

"What about the video?" Tyce asked. It had been so short—cut off because Bella had tried to tell her father to do what he needed to do. Not for her. But for justice.

She cared more about that than her own life.

"It's the kind of video that's supposed to disappear once it's viewed," Nikki replied.

"Supposed to?" the judge asked, picking up his phone from the desk. He hit a button and gasped. "It's gone."

"Not on my laptop," Nikki assured him. She hit a key and Bella's voice tremulously stated, "Daddy, I'm okay…"

The judge began to cry, his shoulders shaking.

Nikki closed her eyes as if trying to hold back her own tears.

Tyce exhaled a ragged breath of his own. Bella was okay now. But she wouldn't stay that way. He knew what kind of animals worked for Luther. And Bella was just too beautiful...

He walked around to stare over Nikki's shoulder at the video. She'd muted the sound and had frozen the frame on Bella standing on a concrete floor in front of a rusted metal wall. "She's in a warehouse," he murmured.

On the east side...

She wasn't alone in the frame. His back to the camera, a kid stood next to her. He might have been holding her so she didn't run away or fall over.

The crash had been bad.

Nikki and Lars had survived with only scrapes and bumps. Cole Bentler had a broken arm and was spending the night in the hospital for observation due to a concussion.

Bella couldn't have escaped without any injuries beyond that bruise on her cheek. It was the opposite cheek from the one Camille had struck. That side had healed quickly, the stitches removed.

He forced himself to tear his gaze from her and focus on the kid again. He couldn't see his face, but he could see his clothes, could see his gun tucked into pants that sagged around his skinny waist. He was just a kid. With so many of Luther's crew dead or in jail with him, he would have had to call up younger ones...

East side.

Warehouse.

Young crew...

Tyce had connections over there—where he'd grown

up. He had connections to some of those kids, too. Probably because he'd busted their older brothers or their dads, though. But if he could get them to talk…

He had to get them to talk. Somebody on those streets knew where Bella was being held. And Tyce would do whatever necessary to get that information out of them. He would do whatever necessary to find Bella—before it was too late.

Parker's team was spread thin. Clint Quarters was sequestered with Rosie Mendez only the chief knew where while Hart Fisher was protecting Wendy Thompson, her parents and his daughter in another safe house. That left Parker with Keeli Abbott and Landon Myers. Keeli had come to the judge's house with her principal, the person she was supposed to be protecting. But Spencer Dubridge was not happy about having a bodyguard, especially a female one.

Landon was out with the person he was protecting, the assistant district attorney prosecuting the case. She'd wanted to make another stop before coming to the judge's house.

"I don't want Jocelyn Gerber here," Judge Holmes said.

"You don't trust her, either, Your Honor?" Detective Dubridge asked.

Dubridge had been in the vice unit with Parker and the others. They all had suspicions about why Jocelyn had never been able to make any previous charges against Luther Mills stick. She'd never gotten an indictment despite the evidence they'd brought her.

The judge shook his head. "That's not it. I don't want

any hint of impropriety in this trial, or I'll have to re-cuse myself right now."

And risk his daughter's life. Luther would have no further use for Bella if the judge was no longer presid-ing over his trial. Eventually, though, he would have to recuse himself.

"We want to keep you on this trial, Your Honor," Dubridge said as he drew in a shaky breath. "You're the only damn judge I trust."

And maybe that was why Jocelyn had struggled so hard to make charges stick. Maybe it had had more to do with the judges than the assistant district attorney.

Bradford Holmes's face drained of color. He must have realized what Parker just had. Luther might not be trying to manipulate him with his daughter. He might be trying to get him to recuse himself.

And if the judge did that…

Bella was dead for certain.

"Nikki, do you have anything yet?" Parker asked his sister.

She was hurting from the crash; he could see the pain on her pretty face. But she was one of the stron-gest people he knew, so she was working through it, her gaze intent on her computer screen. She shook her head. "Nothing yet. Still can't pinpoint anything beyond the east side of River City."

"River City East?" Dubridge asked. "That's Tyce's old stomping ground from his days in vice." He glanced around the judge's den. "Where is he?"

Parker's blood chilled as he looked around the room. When the hell had Tyce slipped out? And why hadn't

Parker's new sixth sense alerted him to the danger his friend must have surely put himself in?

The judge released a shaky sigh of relief. "Tyce will find her."

Parker was afraid that he already had and that he would get himself killed trying to rescue her. He pulled his cell from his pocket and punched in Tyce's contact. "Where the hell are you?" he asked.

"On my way to where Bella's being held," the bodyguard answered.

Parker was surprised he'd answered honestly. "Without backup? What the hell are you thinking?"

"I'm thinking I'll have a better chance of getting her back by myself." Tyce once again answered honestly.

"Then you're thinking wrong," Parker told him. "You have a better chance of getting yourself killed that way."

"We can't storm in," Tyce said. "They'll kill her for certain."

"We won't storm in," Parker assured him. "But we need to be there." He waved his arm around, gesturing for the others to follow him out to the Payne Protection Agency SUVs parked in the judge's driveway. "Where the hell are you?"

Tyce gave him an address, which Parker called out to the others as he jumped into his SUV. He knew where it was. He also knew that it was too far away for him to get there in time to help his friend if Tyce decided to go in alone.

And he knew that, with the way Tyce clearly felt about Bella Holmes, he wasn't going to wait for backup. He was going in alone.

And he was probably going to die...

Chapter 23

Pain traveled from Bella's bound wrists, up to her shoulders that were sore from the crash. But she ignored the pain, even though it churned her stomach, and she continued to struggle against her restraints. The plastic nipped deeper into her skin and she felt blood ooze under the plastic.

They hadn't tied her ankles again. So she was able to stand. Her legs were steadier now, too, as she recovered more of her strength. She had to be strong. She had to fight.

Her father would never forgive himself if something happened to her because of his job. She'd nearly lost him when her mother died. He surely wouldn't survive another loss.

But Bella wasn't fighting just for him. She was fighting for herself, too. She wanted to live. Wanted to love…

Tyce.

Thinking of him gave her strength. She would fight for Tyce—like she should have when he'd walked away that day in the hospital. She should have fought for him then. But she would fight for him now.

She was alone in the room again. Alone in the dark. She moved around the space, looking for something that might cut that binding at her wrists. But because she couldn't see, she bumped into a wall. Metal clanked. When the lights were on, she'd seen how old the metal was.

It had corroded into rust, breaking it apart so it had jagged edges.

She spun around and rubbed her wrists against the wall. The rough metal scraped and scratched her skin, like she was rubbing her hands against a particularly sharp cheese grater. She bit her bottom lip and tried to ignore the pain, though, because the metal grated away at the plastic, too, until it was thin enough to snap and free her wrists.

She let out a breath of relief.

She was free.

Sort of.

She just had to find a way out of this damn room and the building beyond it. There had to be a way out.

In the dark, she couldn't even tell where the door was—until she saw a sudden glimmer of light. The bulb dangling outside the door must have been turned back on.

The door rattled and creaked open.

She squinted against the sudden light then focused on the kids walking into the room. She wasn't sure if they were the two from earlier. They looked bigger now. Older.

She didn't like the way they were looking at her. She kept her arms behind her back, acting like her wrists were still bound. She didn't want to be tied back up. But she had a feeling that needed to be the least of her concerns right now.

"Told you she was pretty," one remarked to the other. He nodded, never taking his eyes from her.

She was wearing jeans and a sweater, but she felt naked with the way he was looking at her.

Her heart beat faster with dread and fear. She would have to make a run for it. She wouldn't let them hurt her. But there were two of them. And she could see their guns.

"You're...you're not supposed to touch me," she said.

"Nobody said that..."

"My father—"

"Nobody cares about your daddy!"

"But the man who was here earlier..." She couldn't see his form outside the door.

"The *man* is gone, lady."

There was something about the way he'd said it... Something that made it sound like the man was more than just a man. Like he was a cop or something in law enforcement. But maybe she thought that because his voice had sounded vaguely familiar to her.

"Just us here now..." They started to move closer to her.

Bella shivered at that tone and the way they were looking at her. She was definitely going to get hurt. She needed to run, but she needed room to do that.

Right now they were between her and the door.

But the room was big. She'd known that even in the dark because it had taken her so long to reach the wall. Keeping her hands behind her back, she began to move around them—toward what she thought was an outer wall.

They chuckled, as if she amused them. That, she knew, was what they intended to do—use her for their amusement. And her pain…

A scream burned the back of her throat, but she held it in. She doubted screaming would do her any good…if the man was really gone. But if he wasn't, she doubted the teenagers would have opened the door again.

He'd definitely been the one giving the orders earlier. So why had he left her alone with them? She must have seen or talked to him around her father before. So if he knew her dad, why would he let her be hurt like this?

Because of Luther Mills…

Luther must have been paying or blackmailing him.

"Luther won't want you to hurt me, either," she said.

One of the kids snorted. "Like you and Luther are friends…"

"I know his brother," she said.

"Luther gots lots of brothers."

"Had lots of brothers," the other clarified. "He killed every one that crossed him."

Like Tyce…

Had he already had Tyce killed?

She hadn't seen him since that day in the hospital. But surely if something had happened to him, she would have heard. Nikki would have told her, especially since they'd been talking about him when the crash had happened.

She hoped they were okay—all the bodyguards, but most especially Tyce.

"I don't believe you, lady," the first kid said. "You don't know Luther. You're a fancy lady."

"I'm a rich lady," she said. "I can pay you—whatever you want to let me go. Then you'd be rich, too."

"Rich and dead," the older-looking boy said. "We just said nobody crosses Luther and lives to brag about it."

"Hurting me will cross him," she said. "Luther doesn't want me hurt."

The younger kid snorted. "Luther don't care if you get hurt or dead, lady. Luther don't care about you."

"Nobody but your daddy cares about you," the other added.

Tyce cared. He'd looked so worried when he'd burst into the apartment where Camille had been holding her at gunpoint. But then he'd walked away from her...

He'd thought she would be safe. But he should have known better. Nobody knew Luther better than he did.

Not even these kids...

She kept edging around them, easing closer to the door. But they must have realized what she was doing because they split up—coming at her from each side. Fortunately, only the smaller one stood between her and the door now.

She ran for it.

The boys laughed—like she had no hope of escaping. But when the younger one grabbed her arm, she swung and struck him, hard, with her fist. Either her blow or the surprise of her being untied knocked him back.

She made it through the doorway and into the cavernous space beyond it. But she hadn't made it more than a few steps before one of them reached for her again, grabbed her hair and jerked her head back.

"You ain't getting away, lady. Not till we have some fun with you."

She swung and kicked—fighting them off. And finally that scream she'd been holding back ripped from her throat.

Her scream sent chills racing down Tyce's spine. He'd tried waiting for the rest of his team to arrive, but he'd waited too long.

She was hurt. Or terrified. He heard both in her voice. So he rushed through the door he'd found open at the back of the abandoned warehouse. It could have been a trap. He'd been thinking that since he'd talked one of the street kids he knew—a little too easily—into giving up the location; that was why he'd tried waiting for backup like Parker had ordered him to do.

Sure, the kid who'd given him the tip had owed him a favor from way back—for saving his life and his mama's life. But not everybody believed in honor or repaying old debts, especially in Luther's world.

He knew that when he found the boys standing over Bella. One had ripped her sweater from her shoulder; it dangled down over her black bra. The other kid was reaching for his belt.

"No!" the shout ripped from Tyce's throat. "Get the hell away from her!"

He'd startled the kids, but not enough that they didn't react. One reached for his gun. Tyce shot him, knocking him to the ground. The other reached for Bella, jerking her between him and Tyce.

He had his gun, too, in his hand, the barrel pressed to her head. This kid was bigger than the one Tyce had shot, but not so big that Bella wasn't an effective shield for him.

Tyce didn't have a good shot. If he tried, he would probably hit her, too.

"You a cop?" the kid asked him. "Cuz you ain't putting me in jail."

"I'm not a cop," Tyce said. "You'd be better off if I was—because then you might make it to jail."

"You talk big, big guy," the kid said. "But I got the lady. If you want her alive, you better get the hell out of my way."

Tyce didn't move. Nor did he lower his gun. "You're not going anywhere. And you're not taking her anywhere."

The kid turned his gun toward Tyce and fired.

Tyce moved, ducking behind a metal post holding up the middle of the warehouse. But he hadn't moved quite fast enough. He felt a burning in his side.

And he heard Bella's scream.

"Let her go!" he shouted again. "Let her go and I will let you leave."

"Luther will kill me deader than you could," the kid replied.

"He won't," Tyce said. "I'll tell him not to."

"Why would Luther listen to you?" the kid asked.

"Because I'm his brother."

"You really do know Luther's brother," the kid remarked to Bella.

She must have been using Tyce to try to bargain for her safety. If it hadn't worked for her, it probably wasn't going to work for Tyce. If he wanted to get them all out of there alive, he had to come up with another plan.

Hell, he needed the shot.

But the kid had moved that gun barrel back to Bella's head—probably because she struggled in his grasp. And if she kept struggling like she was, Tyce had the horrible feeling the gun might go off.

He had to do something. Fast.

Luther had finally been about to sleep peacefully. He had the judge's daughter, so he had the upper hand again. His plan was back on track. Even the thin mattress hadn't felt that bad tonight, but then his cell door had buzzed, and he'd been brought down to the visiting area. This wasn't the one where he sat on the other side of the glass and talked through a plastic phone. This was the conference room where he met with his lawyer.

The expensive suit with his slicked-back hair was in the room. But he wasn't alone, which was lucky for him or Luther would have fired his ass.

He couldn't fire the assistant district attorney, though. She didn't work for him despite some people probably thinking that. "It's like my dream come to life," he murmured as he took the seat across from her. "The things you and I were just doing, Jocelyn…"

That should have rattled her. But her blue eyes were as icy as ever as she stared down her perfect little nose at him. "I am not here to discuss your dreams, Mr. Mills," she haughtily told him.

"That's a damn shame," he said. "I think you might

like what I was doing to you…" Or was her body-guard—Landon Myers—doing her now? Seemed like all Parker Payne's bodyguards fell for whoever they were protecting, like Tyce had fallen for the judge's daughter.

"Mr. Mills," his lawyer advised him, "Ms. Gerber called this meeting with concerns that you're behind the abduction of Judge Holmes's daughter." It was clear his damn, chicken-shit lawyer shared those concerns. All the bloodshed was getting to the guy.

How the hell was he a criminal lawyer if he had such a problem with crime?

"The judge has a daughter?" Luther asked. "I didn't even know that…"

Jocelyn glared at him. "Everyone knows how much the judge's daughter means to him."

"More than justice?" Luther scoffed. "I find that hard to believe." That much was true. He'd had a problem from the get-go about his plan. The problem being that the judge still might come down on the side of law and order over love and loyalty.

"Your plan is not going to work," Ms. Gerber advised him.

How did she look so damn good at this hour? Not even a hair was mussed out of place, every black strand hanging like silk around her slender shoulders. There was only a faint trace of dark circles beneath those beautiful eyes of her, as well.

"What do you think my plan is?" he asked her.

What he really wanted to know was who the hell had leaked it. He needed to make that person pay—because once the news had gotten out about his intentions, the chief had hired the Payne Protection Agency. Parker Payne and his damn bodyguards kept messing with Luther's plan.

"You're going to use his daughter to make the judge rule in your favor," Jocelyn accused him.

"You think he would do something like that? That he would compromise the system like that?" He really wanted her answer—to know if his plan would work.

Her brow puckered for a moment before she shook her head. "No. Your scheme won't work," she said. "Judge Holmes will recuse himself and another judge will get assigned to your trial."

Maybe because it was so late, and he was so damn tired, he couldn't keep the grin from curving his lips.

She gasped when she saw it. "That's what you want. Another judge—one who works for you."

"Everybody thinks you work for me, Jocelyn," Luther reminded her. "Because you've conveniently lost every case against me."

"Nothing about that was convenient," she said.

"Hurt your career a bit, huh?" He chuckled. "We both know you wouldn't be trying this case if your boss wasn't on maternity leave."

"In all those other cases against you, I didn't have Judge Holmes."

"Of course, I don't know what you're talking about, but you won't have him now, either. If something happens to his daughter…"

"It won't," she said. "Tyce Jackson has found her."

Luther's heart slammed against his ribs. Damn his brother. He narrowed his eyes and studied the assistant district attorney's face, which was no hardship.

"Really?" Luther asked. "He found her?"

She nodded.

"Alive?" he asked with surprise—because he'd given an order that the judge's daughter was not to be rescued. Her body could be recovered, but she could not be *rescued*. He'd even sent reinforcements to make sure that a rescue was not possible. But had they arrived in time?

His informant hadn't wanted too many people seeing him with the judge's daughter, so he'd limited the number of crew members involved in transporting her to the warehouse. He hadn't wanted anything traced back to him.

Just as nothing could be traced back to Luther. At least, not traced back to where this woman could prove he'd been behind all the attempts on the lives of the eyewitness and the evidence tech and now the judge's daughter...

Jocelyn must had heard the surprise in his voice because she gasped. Now he could tell she was bluffing. She was not a good liar.

He'd hoped to keep the girl alive for the duration of his trial, but he hadn't known if upright and uptight Judge Holmes would be capable of ruling in his favor. He'd figured the guy might recuse himself rather than risk what he would consider a miscarriage of justice.

The judge recusing himself was almost as good as his ruling in Luther's favor. If Tyce had been stupid enough to try to rescue the girl, she was dead, and Luther would get the same outcome. Hopefully, unlike with his wife, this time the judge would be too distraught to work—because he would blame himself and his job for what had happened to his daughter.

Maybe Luther should have just had her killed a while ago. But he didn't know for certain that the new judge assigned to his trial would be one of the ones who had tossed out the charges against him in the past.

He'd heard that the chief and Ms. Gerber were working hard to try to find the leaks within their departments. If they found the judges who'd helped him in the past…

He stared hard at the assistant district attorney. "You were lying, right, Ms. Gerber?" he prodded. "Tyce didn't find her, did he?"

Because if he had, Luther would have lost his brother as well as his leverage against the judge. He'd let it go when Tyce had betrayed him before, when he'd gone undercover to bust his organization. But Luther would not—*could* not—stand for a second betrayal.

That was why he'd told the crew guarding her to kill her if anyone tried to rescue her and to kill whoever tried rescuing her.

When the color left Ms. Gerber's already pale face, he knew she hadn't been bluffing. Tyce had figured out where Bella Holmes was being held. She just didn't know who had made it out alive.

Luther hoped like hell that nobody had.

Chapter 24

The barrel was cold and hard against her temple. Bella knew that she had to get it away from her head—that the gun might go off at any moment. The teenager was quaking so badly. He was scared. So was Bella.

He edged toward his buddy on the ground and kicked at him, probably to see if he was alive. The kid didn't move. Tyce had killed him.

"You're next," Tyce called out. He was partially concealed behind a metal beam in the middle of the warehouse. But the teenage gunman could still see him. Could still shoot him...

Maybe that was what Tyce was trying for—to get that gun away from her head. He'd done the same thing with Camille in her apartment; he'd kept trying to edge between Bella and the gun. But there was no way he could get between Bella and this gun barrel.

"You try to shoot me and she's dead," the kid threatened.

"You hurt her and you're dead." Tyce returned the threat.

The teenager was determined to be tougher than Tyce. Eighteen or nineteen years on the street, some of them spent selling drugs, must have hardened him and his friend. "Maybe you need to be dead first then," he said. And, finally, he pulled the barrel away from Bella's head.

Maybe it was some instinct of self-preservation she hadn't realized she had, or maybe it was Tyce sending her telepathic messages. Either way, she knew what she had to do. With all her strength, she drove her elbow back—into the teenager's skinny stomach. Then she dropped to the concrete as the shots began to ring out.

But it wasn't just Tyce and the kid shooting. There were gunshots ringing outside, as well—echoing off the metal walls of the warehouse.

As the gunfire died down inside, she heard a door creak open and the scraping of shoes against the concrete as people rushed inside. Were they more of Luther's crew? Or Parker Payne's bodyguards?

What the hell...

Where had the other shooters come from? Tyce ducked as bullets whizzed past him. Bella lay on the floor. He wasn't sure...was it because she'd been trying to get out of the way for him to take the shot at the kid who'd been using her as a shield? Or had she been hit?

If she hadn't been hit then, there was a chance that she would be now. Luther must have sent reinforcements to the warehouse to make sure that no one rescued Bella. But since there had been an exchange of gunfire outside, Tyce suspected his reinforcements had arrived, as well.

Ducking low, he rushed to Bella. "Are you okay?" he asked.

She lay in the light of the single bulb swinging from a cord above her. Blood spattered her face and clothes. Was it the teenager's blood?

He was dead. Tyce felt a twinge of regret over that, but he'd had no choice. The kid and his partner had been determined to take out Bella and whoever might try to rescue her. Luther must have given the order— one they hadn't dared to disobey.

Bella stared up at him, her eyes wide with fear. She jerked her head in a nod and said, "Get down!"

Bullets whizzed near them.

More people rushed into the warehouse. Gunfire echoed throughout the metal structure. Flashes of light in the darkness illuminated the shooters.

Tyce recognized Spencer Dubridge, Keeli and Parker. But they weren't alone. Luther had managed to compile another crew and arm them. These guys were older, though. They must have been part of another crew he'd brought in from some other city.

Tyce scooped up Bella from the ground. He had to get her out of there, had to get her to safety. While everyone was converging around the front of the warehouse, he headed for the back. As he made his break for the door, a barrage of bullets followed him—pinging off the metal near his head.

Ignoring the burning pain in his side, he ran as fast as he could. He just wanted to make sure that Bella survived. But her body was limp in his arms and he worried that he'd already failed.

That she was already gone…

Tyce Jackson had found his daughter. But had he gotten to her in time? Had the others?

Bradford should have insisted on going with them when they'd rushed out of his den earlier that evening. But, frozen with fear, he'd moved too slowly.

He hadn't been afraid for himself.

He'd been afraid for his daughter. And for the man she loved.

If anything happened to Tyce while he tried to rescue her, Bella would never forgive herself. She loved him so much. That was why Bradford had wanted to keep them apart. He hadn't wanted his daughter to fall for a man like Tyce. Not because he was related to Luther Mills but because he was a man who regularly risked his life for others.

Eventually she would lose him. And then the judge might lose her—to grief. He'd wallowed in it for years after losing his wife. That hadn't been fair to Bella. As well as dealing with losing her mother, she'd had to deal with losing him, too. How could he have been so selfish?

He needed to apologize to his daughter. He needed to try to make up to her for all the mistakes he'd made. But would he have the chance?

Luther Mills knew him well enough to know that he wouldn't have cared had anyone threatened his life. That it was Bella he cared about…

But he cared about Bella's respect, too. And in her

video, she'd tried telling him to do the right thing—which to her would have meant sending Luther Mills to prison for the rest of his miserable life. If Luther had seen that video, too, he might have ordered her death.

Tyce might have arrived too late.

His cell rang, vibrating across his desk, and the judge jumped, his nerves were so frayed. His hand was shaking so badly, he could barely grab the phone and click the accept button. He had to clear the fear from his throat to speak, and then he only managed to rasp, "Yes?"

He tensed, waiting for that mechanical voice—for another threat.

But in the background of the call, he heard an intercom—someone paging a doctor.

"Who is this?" he shouted.

"Your Honor, it's Parker Payne."

"Are you in the hospital?" He swallowed hard. "Is Bella?"

"Yes, sir—"

Bradford clicked off the phone. He needed to get to her—as soon as possible. He needed to see her—to hold her—even if she was already gone when he got there. He felt a twinge of regret, too, that he hadn't asked Parker about Tyce or about the other bodyguards.

Were they all okay? Or were there several of them being treated?

He grabbed up his keys and hurried out the door. He would find out soon enough—once he got to the hospital. Hell, he didn't even know what hospital they were at…

As he reached for his phone to call Parker Payne, a

text came across the screen. Parker had texted him the name of the hospital. But he hadn't texted anything else.

He hadn't assured him that his daughter was okay.

So she must not have been.

How badly had she been hurt?

Or was it worse than that?

If Luther Mills had hurt Bradford's little girl, he was going to regret ever messing with him. He had tried all this time to form no opinions—to remain as neutral as a judge was supposed to be.

But he knew that if Luther had caused Bella pain—either physically or emotionally—he was going to pay for it. Bradford wouldn't just be the judge.

He would be the jury and the executioner, as well.

Chapter 25

Bella's head pounded, the sounds of gunshots reverberating inside her skull, making her wince and flinch. How many bullets had there been? How many shooters?

But then she realized that the reverberations were just echoes of earlier shots ringing out inside her head. And the darkness…

It wasn't the darkness of that room in which she'd been locked in the warehouse. It was the darkness of oblivion. She'd lost consciousness.

But was that all she'd lost?

What about Tyce?

She fought, trying to drag her lids open. They were so heavy. And the pain…it radiated throughout her. Her body ached everywhere, as did her head.

And her heart…

Her heart ached with love for Tyce and with fear that she'd lost him. She forced herself awake with a jerk, sitting upright in a bed. Something tugged at her arm. For a moment, she thought she was bound again, but then she recognized the tube of an IV.

"You're awake," Tyce said.

"You're alive," she murmured.

He looked rough, though, with dark circles beneath his topaz eyes and a heavy shadow of stubble clinging to his rigidly held jaw. He nodded and a slight grin curved his lips. "So are you…"

His voice was gruff with emotion, as if he'd been worried she wasn't.

"How long was I out?" she asked.

"Too long," he replied.

She tensed. "Days? Hours?"

His grin widened. "Probably just minutes, but it seemed longer."

She pressed a hand to her forehead, which pounded yet. And she noticed the bandages around her wrists. She'd been out long enough to get to the hospital and be treated. "I don't remember what happened."

How the hell had they survived all that gunfire and gotten out of the warehouse alive?

"Did I get shot?"

He shook his head. "No. You have a concussion. It must be from the crash. Your wrists and hands are also cut up pretty good. Did you do that getting yourself loose?"

She nodded, remembering her fear and desperation.

"You didn't need me at all," he said.

That wasn't true. She needed him so damn much.

Tears rushed to her eyes and her throat as she thought of what could have happened to her had he not rescued her. But she was even more upset at what could have happened to him while he was rescuing her. She could have lost him.

Feelings overwhelmed her and she wanted to share them with him. Wanted to tell him how she felt about him…

But before she could say anything, a door opened. They weren't in the ER. She'd been admitted to a room. How bad was her concussion?

"Bella!" her father exclaimed as he rushed to the bed. "Oh, thank God…" He pressed a kiss to her forehead. Then he turned to Tyce, who'd risen from the chair he'd been sitting in next to her bed. "No," he said. "Thank you, Tyce."

Tyce must have taken her father's comment as a dismissal because he headed toward the door. Bella didn't want him to walk out like he had the last time they'd been at the hospital—without so much as a backward glance at her.

She wanted to tell him how much she loved him. "Tyce!" she said.

He stopped but instead of turning back to her, he dropped—his big body falling hard to the floor. And now she screamed his name in dismay. "Tyce!"

Her scream affected Tyce like it had at the warehouse. He wanted to rush to her side. But instead she was the one kneeling next to him.

"Get help!" she yelled. "He's been shot!"

"Wh-what?" her father stammered. "When—what happened?"

"Get a doctor!" she ordered her father.

The judge had to step over him to get to the hall, to push open the door and shout for help.

Bella's fingers skimmed across his neck as she checked for a pulse. "Don't leave me," she implored Tyce. "Don't leave me again!"

He hadn't wanted to leave her before. And he shouldn't have. He'd been such a fool.

He wanted to assure her that he wasn't going anywhere. But he felt strange—almost as if he was floating. The pain he'd felt earlier was gone. There was no burning sensation in his side. He didn't even notice the stickiness of his clothes from where the blood had molded them to his skin.

Maybe he was already dead.

Guilt hanging heavily on his shoulders, Parker paced the waiting room floor. How hadn't he realized that Tyce had been hit? How had he missed the blood?

Sure, it had been dark in the warehouse and outside—where Tyce had carried an unconscious Bella. He'd jumped into an SUV and ordered Parker to drive them to the hospital. But Parker had thought it was for her—because she'd been hurt.

Tyce had been conscious. He'd been talking.

He hadn't acted as if he was in pain. All his attention—all his concern—had been on the woman he'd held. And that blood on her...

Had that been Tyce's?

Parker had thought it was hers.

What kind of boss was he that he hadn't even realized one of his team was hurt? Possibly dying?

A door opened and he glanced up, hoping it was the doctor. But this man didn't wear scrubs. He wore a dark coat, jeans and a mirror image of Parker's face. His twin.

Logan had started the Payne Protection Agency. It had all been his idea and, for years, he'd been the only one in charge. Then he'd offered his brothers—Parker and Cooper—their own franchises and the autonomy to choose their own teams.

Parker shook his head as Logan joined him. "I wasn't ready," he said. "I wasn't ready for this…"

"Nobody is," Logan told him.

Parker realized that Logan thought Tyce was dead, that he'd lost a team member like Logan had lost two not that long ago. Those deaths had been because of Parker, too. The bomb that had killed his former co-workers had been meant for him.

He still carried the guilt of their deaths. He couldn't add Tyce's to that burden.

"I meant that I don't think I was ready to lead a team," Parker admitted. Of all the Paynes, he had always been the playboy—the goof-off.

"You don't think I felt like that when I lost two guys?" Logan asked.

"Stop saying that!" Parker said. "I haven't lost Tyce. I can't have lost Tyce." But he'd been in surgery a long time now. Too long…

How much damage had the bullet done? Or was it all the blood he'd lost because nobody had realized he'd been hit? He'd been more concerned about Bella than he'd been himself.

Just as she was now more concerned about him. She was supposed to be in a hospital bed, supposed to be hooked to her IV. But she'd ripped it out when Tyce had fallen in her room. She'd ripped it out and she'd ripped everyone around them a new one, Parker included, for not realizing that Tyce had needed help.

What kind of team leader was he?

Logan squeezed his shoulder. "I lost two guys," he said. "You haven't lost anyone, Parker. You're doing just fine. You and Cooper have done the Payne Protection Agency proud."

His brother's words would only ease his guilt if Tyce made it. If he didn't…

Parker couldn't even think about it—for his own sake and for Bella Holmes's. She was devastated already, and Tyce was only hurt. If he didn't survive, she might not, either.

Chapter 26

The sun cast glorious hues of orange and red and pink across the water as it sank slowly out of the sky. Bella couldn't remember the last time she'd had the chance to watch the sunset. A wistful sigh escaped her lips.

Strong arms wrapped around her, pulling her back against a long, hard body. "Are you sorry that you came here with me?" a deep voice asked.

She turned in Tyce's arms and pressed her head against his chest. His heart beat fast and strong beneath her ear even though it had just been a couple of weeks since his surgery. Of course the bullet hadn't been close to his heart. It had hit his spleen and his liver instead. But he was healing now.

"I'm only sorry that we didn't come sooner—before you were shot," she said.

"And before you were abducted," he added. "I shouldn't have ever trusted anyone else to protect you." Maybe that was why he'd recovered so quickly. He'd wanted to make sure that he was her bodyguard.

She had refused to leave his side anyway. But Parker Payne had made certain that they'd stayed safe in the hospital. And the minute Tyce had been cleared to travel, they had left for a safe house of their own. They would have stayed at his place, if they hadn't been concerned that Luther would track them down through a property search of deeds. So they'd flown away to an island where nobody would find them.

"We're safe now," she said, and she stared at him just to make certain that he was really all right. "That's all that matters." She didn't want Tyce getting hurt again. But with his job, it might be inevitable.

Tyce shook his head. "That's not all that matters," he said. "You matter. What you do matters…"

"What?" Maybe she hadn't recovered entirely from her concussion yet. "My parties?"

"Your charities," he said.

"My mother's charities," she corrected him. "You were right when you accused me of trying to bring her back."

"She didn't go anywhere," he told her. "She's right here." He reached out and touched her chest, right over her heart.

Her pulse quickened. She'd been careful since he'd been shot. She'd controlled her desire for him, loving him too much to risk hurting him. But now that desire had built inside her so much that she felt as if she might explode with her need for him—to be with him.

"I will always hold my mother in my heart," she said. But he had her heart now. It belonged to him.

"You're not just trying to bring her back by carrying on her work," he said. "You're honoring her. I heard all those patrons at those events. They said you're even better at fund-raising than your mother was. That you're a natural—"

"Party girl," she interrupted him.

"Leader," he corrected her. "You're a natural leader, Bella."

"That's why my assistant wanted to kill me," she said. "Because I'm so good at managing…"

He slid his finger beneath her chin and tipped up her face to his. "Look at me," he said.

As if she could look anywhere else…

Whenever he was near her, she couldn't take her gaze from him. She was just so grateful that he was alive. And she loved him so much. She hadn't told him, though. Even though she knew they were safe, she was still scared—of him.

"I'm looking," she told him.

"It was not your fault how Camille felt," he said. "She had issues that she'd hidden from everyone."

It was true. Camille's mother had reached out. Even in her grief, she'd wanted to make certain that Bella knew she'd done nothing to deserve Camille's resentment.

"She also hid your jewelry," he said. "But I found it."

"You did?" Her heart filled even more with love for him.

He nodded. "After I left you that day at the hospital, I searched her apartment. I found all of it. I had Parker give it to your father."

"Why not to me?" she asked. And she had to know. "Why did you walk away that day without even looking back at me?"

"Because I was scared," he said.

This giant of man who'd taken a bullet and not even reacted…

She snorted. "Yeah, right. You're not afraid of anything."

"I'm afraid of you," he said. "I'm afraid of how much I love you."

She sucked in a breath. She'd hoped he shared her feelings, but hearing him admit it…

She was stunned and humbled. "But why?" she asked.

"Because I don't think I'm good enough for you," he said. "That's why I showed you where I came from—"

"From hardworking people who love you," she said. "You're incredibly lucky."

"I am," he agreed. But he was staring down at her as if she was the reason. Then his topaz eyes darkened for a moment and he murmured, "I also come from a monster. From a man who was a monster who made a monster…" He shuddered.

She slid her arms around him and held him close. But when she remembered his gunshot wound, she jerked back. "I'm sorry. I didn't mean to hurt you."

He pulled her close again. "You didn't. You won't— unless you don't return my feelings…"

She looked up at him in shock. How could he not know how she felt about him?

"I understand if you can't get over that Luther Mills is—"

She pressed her fingers over his lips. "Luther Mills is a criminal and a killer who will be brought to justice. He is nothing to you. You were not raised together. He didn't have the amazing grandparents you have. He doesn't have the heart and the integrity and the—"

He interrupted her by pressing his lips to hers. He kissed her deeply, hungrily. Then he swung her up into his arms.

She pulled back and protested, "Put me down!"

He froze, as if he thought she was rejecting him.

So she explained. "I don't want you to hurt yourself."

He'd carried her from the warehouse. Parker had told her that. With a bullet in his side, he'd saved and protected her and taken her to safety.

He was amazing.

"No," he said. "You're going to hurt me."

She shook her head. "Never. I love you too much."

He grinned, and his eyes glowed with an emotion she recognized all too well because she felt it, too. Love. He carried her through the open sliding doors and into the hotel suite. It had two bedrooms.

He carried her into the one she'd been using. She would have rather slept with him, but she hadn't wanted to inadvertently hurt his healing wound. But he moved with her easily, as if her weight didn't bother him at all.

Then he laid her on the bed and pulled his shirt up and over his head, muscles rippling in his arms, chest and abdomen. The wound on his side was healing. The incisions the surgeon had made to take out the bullet and repair the damage were small, the skin pink where it had been pulled together.

"You're really better?" she asked.

"Do you really love me?" he asked as he stared down at her.

He stared at her as if he couldn't believe that she would—that she could. She reached up and cupped his handsome face in her hands. "How do you not know what an incredible man you are?" she asked him. "You are so strong and brave and protective and honorable. You're my her—"

He used his mouth to interrupt her again, kissing her deeply. But as he kissed her, he untied the straps holding up her sundress and let it slide down her body. It pooled around her knees as she knelt on the mattress, her arms wrapped around him as he leaned over her.

She clutched at his sinewy shoulders, trying to pull him down onto the bed with her. But he pulled back, and she murmured in protest. He chuckled, as if her impatience amused him.

But his hand was shaking slightly as he unbuttoned his jeans and unzipped his fly. Then his jeans dropped to the cool tiled floor. His boxers joined the denim, and he stood before her naked and beautiful.

Her breath escaped on a ragged sigh.

He reached for her, unclasping her strapless bra before he pushed down her panties and threw her dress and underwear off the bed. Now he joined her.

He kissed her again, sliding his lips back and forth across hers as he traced his fingertips across her skin in a soft caress. He touched her throat and her collarbone and the curve of her breasts and waist and hips...

He touched her everywhere. Then he lowered his head and tasted her everywhere.

She shuddered as pleasure flowed through her. But it wasn't enough. She needed him inside her. She needed him to assuage the ache of emptiness she'd felt when he'd walked out of the hospital that day—when he'd left her to other bodyguards to protect.

She wrapped her arms around him and pulled him down on top of her. "Don't leave me," she murmured.

"Never…" Finally he joined their bodies, sliding inside her. He moved in and out, driving the tension tight again.

It became unbearable until he reached between them and touched the most sensitive part of her.

Pleasure overwhelmed her. She cried out his name as she came over and over again.

He tensed and shouted her name as he joined her in ecstasy. He dropped onto his back and curled her against his side, in his arms, so closely it was as if he never intended to let her go.

But still, her heart aching with love for him, she had to implore him again, "Never leave me…"

Tyce finally understood what she wanted. A promise that he would never die and leave her like her mother had left her and her father. He drew in a shaky breath, but he couldn't lie to her. He couldn't make promises he had no way of knowing he could keep.

"I won't ever willingly leave you," he said. "But I don't know what the future holds." He tensed as realization dawned on him. "Do you not want me to be a bodyguard? Is it my job that scares you?"

She shook her head and sighed. "I know that you're good at what you do. And that you're strong. And I know it doesn't matter what we do for a living because we have no control over some things in life. No control over life…"

"All we can do is live it to the fullest," he said. And he wanted to do that with her. "We can treasure every moment and make the most of it."

She smiled and her breath escaped in another wistful-sounding sigh.

"What?" he asked. "Are you okay?"

"Never better," she said. "I miss my dad, but I won't mind if that trial lasts a while. I love being with you."

"That's not going to stop when we go back to River City," he told her. "I meant it when I said I'm not leaving you—not of my own volition."

Her lips curved into a smile.

But the smile slid away when he rolled her off his side and jumped from the bed. "What are you doing?" she protested. "You said you're never leaving me."

"I'm right here," he said. He was on his knees, rummaging in his jeans pockets. When he found what he was looking for, he stayed on his knees—next to the bed.

"What are you doing?" she asked.

"I want you to make the same promise," he told her. "Promise me you'll never leave me of your own volition."

"Of course not," she said. "I was so afraid when I thought I'd lost you…"

"I know. I felt the same way," he said, his voice gruff with emotion. "And that's why I want us to be together. Always."

"Always," she heartily agreed.

"And forever," he continued.

She nodded, but her brow had begun to pucker with confusion.

"I'm asking you to be my wife, Bella," he said.

Her eyes widened and her mouth fell open in shock.

He chuckled. "I know that I'm no prince, but I'm asking you to be my princess."

"You are my prince," she assured him. "And I would love to be your princess."

She no longer took offense at it. She must have known that what had started as teasing her had become a term of endearment to him.

He took her hand and held it in one of his. Then he uncurled his fingers from around the ring in his other hand and slid the ring over her finger.

She gasped. "Tyce! Where did you…? How did you…?" Tears filled her eyes. "That's my mother's ring. Camille didn't have that."

"Your father did," Tyce said. "He gave it to me when we left." With his blessing and his apology.

Tears stung Tyce's eyes as he remembered what her father had told him, how he thought Tyce was the best man he knew, the best man for his daughter, and that the judge would be proud to have him for a son-in-law. He stared down at the beautiful princess-cut diamond in its shiny gold band. "He wanted you to wear your mother's ring because he said he sees in us the same love that he and your mother had for each other."

Bella cried then. And Tyce held her. But they were happy tears, especially the few that slid down his own face—because he had never been as happy as he was now with Bella Holmes as his soul mate and soon-to-be wife.

* * *

Where the hell had everybody gone?

Luther sat alone in the conference room. Even his damn lawyer seemed to have disappeared. Or at least he was late. He'd been getting nervous, worried that he might somehow be implicated in the things Luther had been doing—the things he'd done to try to stop this trial.

He hadn't stopped it.

Yet.

The eyewitness was gone. So was the evidence tech. Even the judge's daughter had disappeared—along with his damn brother.

But Luther still had a few tricks up his sleeve. He wasn't done yet. The door opened and his slick, over-priced attorney walked in, shaking his head.

"What?" Luther asked.

"The assistant district attorney isn't willing to offer a plea deal," he said.

"I didn't tell you to ask," Luther said, fury building up inside him. "I wouldn't have taken one if she offered."

"She's offering them to everybody else," the lawyer said. "To every person she thinks was acting on your orders these past several weeks."

Luther shrugged. "And she didn't get any takers, did she?"

His crew knew better than to cross him. And those he'd figured might be thinking about it had had a few unfortunate accidents. He didn't bother telling the lawyer about those though. The guy kept blathering on about culpable deniability or some such bull crap.

"I am focused only on this trial right now," the lawyer replied. "And Jocelyn Gerber is pretty damn confident she can't lose."

So the black-haired beauty was getting cocky. *This will be fun...*

"She can't if she ain't trying it," Luther said.

The lawyer groaned. "Don't tell me. I don't want to know."

Luther was fine with that. He wanted to make sure Jocelyn Gerber and her damn faithful bodyguard, Landon Myers, never saw it coming. They had no idea who the leak was in the district attorney's office.

And with little Ms. Holmes tucked away somewhere until after the trial, there was no chance of her recognizing his voice like the guy had worried she might have.

Nope. Luther didn't need Jocelyn to offer him a deal—because she was going to be dead soon anyway.

* * * * *

Don't miss other books in the
Bachelor Bodyguards series:

Guarding His Witness
Evidence of Attraction

Available now wherever Harlequin Romantic
Suspense books and ebooks are sold!

And keep an eye out for Lisa Childs's
contribution to the Coltons of Kansas continuity,
coming in November 2020 from
Harlequin Romantic Suspense

commodating. *It must be because I prayed he wouldn't take his anger at me out on Will.* Then she remembered she'd also prayed that *she* wouldn't feel so angry at Josiah, either, and she said, "*Denki.* I'd appreciate that."

"I can help you move it," Will volunteered.

"You probably won't be here—we're going to Sovilla's *haus* today with your *gschwischderkinner.*" After church on Sunday, Arleta had invited a group of mothers with young children to go to her house on Tuesday after lunch. The adults were going to work on sewing projects while the children played outside.

Their neighbor down the road, Martha Ropp, was going to pick them up and take them home, since she and her three children had been invited, too. Anke knew it would be a tight squeeze in the buggy, but she didn't care. Nor did she mind that she'd had an upset stomach. The only thing that mattered was spending as much time away from the *daadi haus* as she could until Josiah was done with the repairs and left for good.

It was nearly four o'clock and Josiah had completed everything he'd agreed to repair inside the *daadi haus* and he'd moved Will's bed into the bedroom, too. If he hurried, he could add an extra step to the porch stairs and leave before Anke and Will returned. Although he still had misgivings about not following through with his commitment to take Will out for pizza, Josiah knew he didn't have any other choice in the matter. But he didn't want to be around when the child realized it was his last day there.

As he was prying the board off the bottom step so he could reconfigure it, he heard a vehicle drive up the

lane. *Someone must have turned down into the driveway by mistake*, he thought. *I hope they're not lost, because I don't want to take the time to give them directions.*

Unfortunately, when he glanced over his shoulder, he noticed an *Englisch* woman with purplish hair get out of the back seat. "Nobody's home," he shouted to her as she began walking toward the main house. "Can I help you with something?"

The woman turned to face him. "I'm looking for Anke Bachman," she called back.

Josiah took a few steps closer so he wouldn't have to keep yelling to be heard. As he approached, he thought, *She looks familiar. Have I seen her in town before?* Just as he reached the driveway, he realized why he seemed to recognize her. *She looks just like Will—that's his mother! That's Clara!* Josiah came to a dead halt.

"Anke's not here," he said. "No one is. They should be back within an hour."

"An hour?" she repeated, biting her thumbnail. "Okay, well, I'll just have to wait, then."

Josiah was so stupefied he couldn't seem to move as he watched her return to the car. She opened the door and got in, but the driver didn't reverse direction. *Are they just going to idle there until Anke returns?* Josiah wondered. He couldn't imagine Velda's reaction to finding an *Englisch* car in the driveway, much less, to seeing Clara with purple hair. But a moment later, Anke's sister got out of the vehicle again. "That's the last time I ever use your service!" she shouted, slamming the door. The car sped away as Clara hurried across the lawn to the main house again.

Josiah shook his head and resumed his work on

the porch step, but his mind could hardly concentrate on what his hands were doing. *Why is Clara here? She couldn't have completed the recovery program already—she's only been there a little over two weeks.* His stomach felt knotted up with dread. *What is Anke going to do when she sees her? And how is Will going to feel?*

"It's locked," Clara announced, jarring him from his thoughts. Josiah hadn't realized she'd crept up right beside him.

"What?" He stopped what he was doing and stood up to speak to her.

"The door to the main house is locked. We never locked the door when I lived here," she explained, biting her pinkie nail this time. Didn't she have any gloves? It was freezing out here. "I'm Clara, Anke's sister. She's been taking care of my son, Will."

"*Jah.* I know," Josiah replied flatly. He begrudgingly told her his name, too.

"It figures. Everyone knows everything about everybody here. You probably know *why* she's been taking care of him, too, don't you?" After Josiah nodded, Clara momentarily glanced down at her feet. Then she looked up and changed the subject. "So, did you buy this place from my family or are you just renting it?"

"Neither. Anke hired me to make repairs so it's livable for her and Will."

Clara's eyes went big and round, just as her son's always did when he was astonished. "They've been staying out here?" After Josiah nodded, she mumbled dolefully, "I should have known Velda wouldn't allow them in the main house with her."

Regardless of how he felt about her sister, Josiah didn't want Clara to worry about her son's living conditions. "It's actually pretty cozy inside," he consoled her.

She immediately perked up. "Good. Then I'll wait in there where it's warm." Bypassing the bottom step, she bounded up the stairs and into the *daadi haus* before Josiah could object.

It's not my haus *anyway, so I can't stop her*, he thought. Besides, now that Clara was there, he had an even more urgent reason to finish his work and leave before Anke and Will returned, so he got back to it. Even though his mind was swirling with concerns about why the boy's mother had returned, Josiah managed to stay focused and he finished installing the step within fifteen minutes. *Now all I need to do is collect my tools from the bedroom and I can get out of here.*

When he pushed open the door, he discovered Clara holding a handful of Will's socks over an open duffel bag. Maybe it was because he noticed she had dropped the pair that Anke had given to the boy—the socks he loved so much because they matched Josiah's—on the floor, but he couldn't stop himself from blurting out, "What do you think you're doing with those?"

"I'm packing. That's why I'm here—I came to get Will. I want to have his things ready so we can leave as soon as he returns." She deposited his clothes into the bag and added defiantly, "Not that it's any of *your* business—or anyone else's. Will is *my* child."

Josiah had been telling himself the same thing for two weeks; he wasn't a member of the Bachman family, so what they did wasn't any of his business. But he no longer cared whether he had any right to voice his opinion

or not. For Will's sake, he was going to speak his mind. "*Jah*, Will *is* your *kind*. But if you take him away from here before you've completed your recovery program, you'll risk losing him for *gut*. Is that what you want?"

Clara turned her back to Josiah and zipped the duffel bag, wordlessly indicating she was going to carry through with her intention to take the boy away from New Hope. Away from Anke.

Softening his tone, Josiah pleaded, "Please don't do this, Clara. It wouldn't be fair to your *suh*. He's been so brave, adjusting to an entirely new home and lifestyle. He's really *kumme* to love it here, even though he's counting down the days until you can be together permanently again. Don't do something rash now that might result in the two of you being separated for a much longer period of time."

Her back still turned, Clara didn't respond for several moments. Just when Josiah decided there was no sense in trying to get through to someone who was ignoring him, she asked, "Do you...do you really think Will's happy here?"

"I *know* he is," Josiah responded without hesitation. Nor did he give it a second thought before saying, "Your *schweschder* has seen to that. You couldn't have trusted him into the care of anyone more capable, loving and devoted than Anke is. I've seen how much she has joyfully sacrificed in order to provide a *hallich* home for Will until you can complete your program. And frankly, it would be selfish of you drop out of it now."

Clara broke out in tears, her shoulders heaving as she sobbed into her hands. "But I miss him so much..." Knowing that her loneliness was at the heart of her ac-

tions, Josiah kept quiet, allowing her time to weep. But meanwhile, he kept peering out the window, anxious that Anke and Will would return any minute.

When Clara's crying subsided, he said, "I can tell how much you love and miss your *suh*. And I can't imagine how difficult it is for the two of you to be separated. But you'll miss him even more if he's put into foster care for the long run."

She finally turned around and looked Josiah in the eye, nodding. "You're right—I know you're right. I shouldn't have *kumme* here. If Will sees me, it's going to make him lonely all over again when I leave. Could you give me a ride to the other side of town so I can meet my sponsor in the diner where none of the other Amish people in New Hope ever go? She'll pick me up and take me back to the center."

Josiah suppressed a groan. *I can just hear the rumors that will crop up if anyone sees me with another* Englisch *alcoholic,* he thought. But Clara was right; if Will saw her, it would be twice as hard for them to part a second time. *"Jah,"* he agreed. "But we'd better hurry."

"Just let me put Will's things back in the drawer." No sooner had she unzipped the duffel bag than a buggy came up the lane. "Oh, no! I can't let him see me! What am I going to do?"

Josiah's stomach lurched, but he said, "Quick—go into that room there and don't make a sound until Anke *kummes* to get you."

"Look! Josiah put in an extra step for me!" Will exclaimed as he and Anke approached the *daadi haus* and

Velda and the other children walked in the opposite direction toward the main house.

"That's *wunderbaar*." Since Martha had dropped everyone off in the driveway, Anke hadn't been able to peek inside the barn to see if Josiah's buggy was there. But since the step was installed, she figured he'd left for the day.

However, just as they reached the porch, he stepped outside, closing the door behind him. "Hello. As you can see, I finished the last of my projects," he said cheerfully.

Anke scowled in response. *Why did he have to announce that? Couldn't he just have said goodbye as if it were any other day?* she silently carped. *Now Will is going want to go to—*

Even before she'd finished her thought, Will asked, "If you're all done, does that mean we get to go out for pizza?"

"We—we can't," Anke faltered. "Not today."

"Oh, that's right, your *bauch* probably still hurts, right?" Apparently, Josiah must have realized his blunder and he was trying to backpedal.

"*Jah*, it does." She pressed a hand against her abdomen.

"That's too bad, because I really had my heart set on pizza. Didn't you, Will?" Josiah asked, causing Anke to wonder if he was being spiteful or if he was really just obtuse. When her nephew agreed that he'd been looking forward to pizza, too, Josiah suggested, "I suppose you and I could go out—if your *ant* didn't mind staying home by herself?"

Will gave Anke a hopeful look. "Can we, *Ant* Anke?"

What in the world is Josiah thinking to suggest something like that in front of Will? Anke wondered. Yet she realized he'd actually come up with a perfect solution for avoiding being together, while also avoiding disappointing her nephew. *He doesn't want to hurt Will's feelings any more than I do...but what if the* bu *has such a great time that he grows even more attached to Josiah?*

As she was internally dithering, Josiah piped up again, "You know what, Will? We should give your *ant* a few minutes to make up her mind. I think I dropped some nails over there in the snow. Let's go see if we can find them while she comes to a decision." As he passed Anke on his way down the steps, he discreetly pressed a piece of paper into her hands.

She unfolded it to read, "Clara is inside the house. She'll explain everything. She doesn't want Will to see her." Anke gasped, her knees almost buckling beneath her.

Several yards away where he'd begun searching the snow for nails, Will jerked his head up. "What's wrong, *Ant* Anke?"

"My—my *bauch* feels really funny. I think you *buwe* should go ahead to the pizzeria without me."

"Denki!" Will cheered, charging forward to hug Anke before racing back to Josiah's side again.

"We won't be back until at least seven thirty. I promise," Josiah said with a pointed look that Anke took to mean he expected Clara would be gone by then.

"Okay. Have *schpass.*" She held on to the porch railing to steady herself as she watched them disappear into the barn. She waited in that position until she saw Josiah's buggy pull out into the driveway and down the

lane. Then she darted up the stairs and into the house. She didn't see her sister in the living room, but when she flung open the bedroom door, Clara dove into her arms.

"Oh, Anke," she cried. "I almost made a huge mistake—*again*."

"*Kumme*, sit with me in the living room and tell me all about it."

So her sister spent the next hour pouring out her heart. She told Anke how much she missed Will, what a struggle it had been to stop drinking and how ashamed she felt for making such poor choices and causing everyone so much pain. In turn, Anke recounted everything she could think of that Will had done since he'd come to live with them, including singing "The *Loblied*" in church. She reminded Clara of Christ's love and forgiveness for everyone who chose to put their faith in Him. And she encouraged her to stick with the recovery program.

"I have no intention of quitting again," Clara assured her. "Although now I'll probably have to stay an extra week or two because I'll have to start over from the beginning. Is it okay if Will stays with you a little longer?"

"Don't be *lappich*. Of course he can!"

Clara checked the time on her cell phone. She had called Yolanda almost forty-five minutes earlier, so she projected if they left now they'd arrive at the diner at about the same time as her sponsor did. "Even if we get there a little early, it's better if I go before Will returns, otherwise, I might not be able to leave at all."

Anke refrained from saying that was her exact wish: for them both to stay in New Hope permanently. The last thing she wanted was for her sister to feel trapped

or pressured. Clara was already extremely emotional. "I'll go tell Ernest I'm taking the buggy. Don't worry— I'll be discreet."

"Can you…can you ask him to *kumme* out for a minute? I'd like to say hello."

So their brother met them in the barn, where he and Clara shared such a sweet embrace that Anke had to turn away, for fear she'd start crying.

Once the sisters arrived at the diner, they chatted in the buggy until they spotted Yolanda's car turning into the parking lot.

"*Denki* for everything you're doing for me and Will," Clara said, giving Anke a goodbye hug. "As Josiah said, I'd never find anyone more loving, capable and devoted to care for my *suh*."

"Josiah said that?"

"Yeah. I can tell he thinks the world of you." Clara pulled back to look her in the eye. "Tell me the truth. He's your suitor, isn't he?"

"*Neh*. He's not."

"That's too bad. He's the kind of man I wish I had chosen. He seems like he'd be a really positive role model for a young boy like Will."

The first thing Anke did after her sister and Yolanda drove away was to bow her head and thank the Lord that Clara had decided to return to the recovery program, and to ask Him to give her strength to start over again. On the way home, Anke's thoughts turned to her sister's observation about Josiah. He really had gone out of his way to protect Will from getting his feelings hurt tonight—both by encouraging Clara to return to her recovery program and by taking Will out for pizza

as he'd promised. Nothing about Josiah's behavior or what he'd said to her sister indicated that he resented Anke's commitment to her family.

Maybe I misjudged him. It's possible that he just reacted poorly in the moment on Sunndaag *because he was disappointed I decided not to go snowshoeing,* she thought. *And Clara herself said she'd like Will to have someone like Josiah for a role model. So maybe we don't have to keep our distance from him after all.*

If her sister had the courage to admit her mistakes and try again in her recovery program, then with God's help, Anke was going to try again with Josiah, too. The question was, did *he* want to start anew with her?

Josiah softly rapped on the door of the *daadi haus* so he wouldn't wake Will, who was asleep in his arms. They had returned later than he'd expected because they'd stopped at the apparel store before going to the pizzeria so Josiah could buy the boy a hat similar to his own. He supposed he should have asked Anke if it was okay first. But he figured she wouldn't be opposed to him giving the boy a traditional Amish piece of clothing as a gift. In any case, they'd gotten to the pizzeria later than he'd intended and it was very crowded, so they'd had to wait for a booth. By the time they'd finished their meal, Will was so full and tired that he'd fallen asleep in the buggy on the way home.

Anke was smiling when she opened the door. "Hello, *buwe—*" she started to stay. But when she saw that her nephew was sleeping, she covered her mouth and whispered, "Oops, sorry."

She gestured for Josiah to follow her into Will's

newly finished bedroom. He laid the boy down on his cot and then helped Anke remove his shoes and coat. After they'd tiptoed into the living room, Anke held up the hat and asked incredulously, "You got this for him?"

"Jah." Josiah stiffened his spine. "I didn't think you'd object."

Anke wrinkled her forehead. "Why would I object? It was very thoughtful…like so many things you've done for us. Especially tonight." She took a step closer and looked him squarely in the eyes. "I can't thank you enough for encouraging Clara to return to the recovery program and for keeping Will from discovering she'd been here."

Josiah brushed off her compliment, saying, "There's no need to thank me. I did it for her *suh.*" He reached for the doorknob, but before turning it, he remarked over his shoulder, "Since you don't want to associate with me anymore, you can put my final paycheck in the mail once you have a chance to write it out. I also left the receipts for the materials I bought on top of the fridge."

"Wait!" Anke placed her hand over his. Her touch was gentle and warm. "I never said I didn't want to associate with you—I said it wasn't a *gut* idea for us to socialize, but I didn't mean forever. I only meant while Will was here. Even so, I made a mistake and I'm very sorry."

Josiah slid his hand out from under hers and dropped it to his side. Facing her, he asked, "You're sorry— what changed your mind? Did the deacon set the record straight with you, too, like he did with Keith Harnish?"

Anke scrunched up her face and tipped her head in what appeared to be genuine bafflement. "Iddo Stoll?

Keith Harnish? What do either of them have to do with my decision about whether to socialize with you?"

Now Josiah was perplexed. "I—I thought I heard Keith telling you about the video of me getting caught with alcohol in the back of my buggy. Isn't that why you wanted to distance yourself from me?"

"*Neh*, of course not. As I told you, I didn't think it was *gut* for Will to get the idea we were a couple. You saw the picture he'd drawn of us holding hands... I was afraid he was beginning to feel like we were replacing his *mamm* and *daed*. Or that he was growing too attached to you, in particular. I didn't want to make it harder for him to leave when the time came."

"But Keith *did* tell you about the video, right?"

"*Jah*. But I assumed that was just a case of mistaken identity."

As relieved as Josiah was that he'd been wrong about Anke's motivation for not wanting to socialize with him, he realized she might change her mind again when he told her what had really happened at the golf course. But it was important to him to know whether she trusted he was telling the truth, so he admitted, "It wasn't a case of mistaken identity. It really was me in the video clip. But the beer in the buggy wasn't mine. I've never had a drop of alcohol in my—"

Anke interrupted. "You don't have to explain. I believe you. I told Keith that, too—I said you'd never break your commitment to abide by the *Ordnung*." She scowled as she added, "I think he was part of the reason I had a *koppweh* that afternoon."

Josiah's legs felt weak when he realized how wrong he'd been about her, so he asked if they could sit down.

Anke perched on the edge of the rocker and he took a seat facing her in Will's armchair. Leaning forward on his knees, he peered into her eyes and confessed, "I'm the one who made a mistake—I wrongly assumed that *you* believed a lie about me. That's why I got so upset after *kurrich* on *Sunndaag*. I'm sorry for how immaturely I behaved. I should have heard you out instead of storming off, but I was defensive because...because of things that happened in my past."

Anke's face blossomed with a smile. "That's okay. I was defensive, too. I assumed you were angry because I was putting my *familye*'s needs above my desire to have *schpass* with you."

"Are you kidding me? Your commitment to your *familye* is one of the qualities I appreciate the most in you." Josiah sat up straighter. "I feel very blessed to have been part of your *familye*'s life. And I'd really like to continue to hang out with you and Will...but aren't you still concerned he'll grow too attached to me?"

"*Neh.* Not since Clara mentioned that she wished Will had a role model like you in his life. That's when I realized that even if he only knows you for a short amount of time, the influence you have on him now could last his entire life. Besides, a *kind* can never have too much love. And the fact of the matter is, he's *already* grown attached to you."

"I've grown attached to him, too." Josiah gazed into her sea-green eyes, adding softly, "And to you, Anke."

Her voice barely a whisper, she replied, "I feel the same way about you, too."

Josiah took her hand in his. "Then will you accept me as your suitor?"

"Jah." She gently squeezed his fingers. "As long as it's okay if Will sometimes comes with us when we go out?"

"Sure. He can be our chaperone—to make sure we don't do too much of this." Josiah leaned forward and gave her a soft, lingering kiss.

"In that case, forget I asked," Anke teased. "He can stay home with his *gschwischderkinner.*"

Epilogue

"I can't believe you're actually moving out," Clara said to Anke as she helped her pack. The sisters and Will had been living in the *daadi haus* together for a little over a year and a half, ever since Clara completed her recovery program and returned to New Hope. But tomorrow was Anke's wedding. After that, she'd live with Josiah in the house he'd built on property he'd bought from his brother. "How will I ever manage without you?"

"You'll do just fine," Anke assured her. In the past year, she had witnessed her sister growing more and more responsible, mature and faithful to the baptismal commitment she'd made to God and her Amish community. "*I'm* the one who's going to feel lost without you and Will."

"*Gott* willing, soon enough you'll have *bobblin* of your own to care for—and you'll have your own *haus*, too. You'll forget all about us. You know what they say—out of sight, out of mind."

"*Neh*, that's not true," Anke insisted somberly, even though she recognized that her sister had only been

teasing. "The entire time you were gone, you were never out of my mind, Clara. You were always in my prayers. And as far as having *bobblin* of my own… I hope I do. But that won't change how much I love Will or any of my nieces and nephews. Or you."

"I know it won't," Clara replied just as seriously. Then she smiled a playful smile. "Do you think your *bobblin* will have hair like Josiah's?"

Before Anke could answer, the two women heard footsteps on the porch. They went into the living room just as Josiah and Will entered from outside. They both wore identical hats, which they swept off their heads and hung on two pegs by the door. Although Will's peg was lower than Josiah's, he no longer had to stand on tiptoe to reach it, the way he did two months ago.

"I'm *hungerich*," the boy announced. "May I have *kuchen,* please?"

After Clara took him into the kitchen to give him warm milk and a cookie, Josiah asked, "Did I hear someone saying my name when I walked in?"

"We were just talking about your hair." Anke stepped closer to him and reached up to finger a curl.

"You mean my rooster's comb?" he asked.

Anke laughed, remembering what Millie had said the first time she'd seen Josiah's vivid red spirals. "I love your hair."

Josiah encircled her waist and pulled her a little nearer. "I love your turtle-blue eyes," he joked, using Will's word for *turquoise*. "But not as much as I love your ears."

"My ears? But they stick out."

"Exactly. It makes them easier to kiss." He demon-

strated several times, which tickled and made Anke giggle so hard that she was afraid Will and Clara would return to the room to see what was so funny.

"*Absatz,*" she whispered.

"Okay, I will," he agreed reluctantly. "But I'm only going to keep my word about that until tomorrow, when we're married..."

* * * * *

If you enjoyed this story by Carrie Lighte,
be sure to pick up the previous books in
The Amish of New Hope miniseries:

Hiding Her Amish Secret
An Unexpected Amish Harvest

Available now from Love Inspired!

And look for more Amish romances every month
from Love Inspired!

Dear Reader,

Although my Amish romance novels are entirely fictitious, lately my imagination has been sparked by reading my favorite Amish newspaper. The publication is composed mostly of letters written by Amish and Mennonite "scribes," across the country, who provide news about the weather, births, deaths and social activities in their areas. Often, these reports contain accounts of accidents, injuries and illnesses, too. They're also highlighted with humorous anecdotes and words of encouragement in the Lord.

In some ways, the publication reminds me of social media but without any of the negative kind of news that can be found online among *Englischers*. For example, no one would ever submit an article about what happened to Josiah at the golf course. This isn't to imply that Amish people don't gossip among themselves, since gossiping is a temptation for all of us. But in general, the newspaper is informative and uplifting, like correspondence from a family member or a good friend.

Speaking of keeping in touch, I love hearing from *you*, too, so please don't hesitate to drop me a line.

Blessings,
Carrie Lighte

he finally had to admit to his body's fierce and instant response to her position. "I've seen him do it. But why…"

Her voice died away, and he had the feeling that only when she had wondered why Cutter would want her on his lap did she realize that's where she was.

"I…" she began, but it trailed off as she stared down at him.

He could feel himself breathing hard, felt his lips dry as his breath rushed over them. But he couldn't stop staring back at her. And because of that he saw the moment when something changed, shifted, when her eyes widened as if in surprise, then, impossibly, warmed.

She kissed him.

In all his imaginings, and he couldn't deny he'd had them, he'd never imagined this. Oh, not her kissing him, because sometimes on sleepless nights long ago he'd imagined exactly that. He'd just never known how it would feel.

Because he'd never in his life felt anything like it.

Don't miss
Operation Second Chance *by Justine Davis,*
available May 2020 wherever
Harlequin Romantic Suspense
books and ebooks are sold.

Harlequin.com

*The only one who blames Adam Kirk more than
Amanda Bonner for her father's death is Adam himself.
And yet the tragedy brings them together to uncover one
last secret. Can the truth of what happened that night
bring forgiveness to them both?*

*Read on for a sneak preview of the next book
in Justine Davis's Cutter's Code miniseries,*
Operation Second Chance.

She ended up on his lap. And the first thing he saw when
he caught his breath was Cutter, standing right there and
looking immensely pleased with himself.

"He bumped me," Amanda said, a little breathlessly. "I
didn't mean to…fall on you, but he came up right behind
me and—"

"Pushed?" Adam suggested.

She looked at him quizzically. "Yes. How—"

"I've been told he…herds people where he wants
them to go."

She laughed. He was afraid to say any more, to explain
any further, because he thought she would get up. And he
didn't want her to. Holding her like this, on his lap, felt
better than anything had in…at least five years.

"I'd buy that," she said, as if she didn't even realize
where she was sitting. Or on what, he added silently as